The GREAT ADVENTURES *of* SHERLOCK HOLMES

The GREAT ADVENTURES *of* SHERLOCK HOLMES

ARTHUR CONAN DOYLE

PUFFIN BOOKS

UK | USA | Canada | Ireland | Australia
India | New Zealand | South Africa

Puffin Books is part of the Penguin Random House group of companies whose addresses can be found at global.penguinrandomhouse.com.

www.penguin.co.uk
www.puffin.co.uk
www.ladybird.co.uk

Penguin Random House UK

This selection published in Puffin Books 1988
Reissued 2011, 2015, 2016
This edition published 2025
001

'The Solitary Cyclist', 'Charles Augustus Milverton', 'Black Peter', 'The Golden Pince-nez' and 'The Priory School' first published in *The Return of Sherlock Holmes*, 1905; 'The Beryl Coronet', 'The Engineer's Thumb' and 'The Red-Headed League' first published in *The Adventures of Sherlock Holmes*, 1982

Set in Minion by Palimpsest Book Production Limited, Falkirk, Stirlingshire
Printed and bound in Great Britain by Clays Ltd, Elcograf S.p.A.

The authorized representative in the EEA is Penguin Random House Ireland, Morrison Chambers, 32 Nassau Street, Dublin D02 YH68

A CIP catalogue record for this book is available from the British Library

ISBN: 978–0–241–72522–1

All correspondence to:
Puffin Books
Penguin Random House Children's
One Embassy Gardens, 8 Viaduct Gardens, London SW11 7BW

MIX
Paper | Supporting responsible forestry
FSC www.fsc.org FSC® C018179

Penguin Random House is committed to a sustainable future for our business, our readers and our planet. This book is made from Forest Stewardship Council® certified paper.

Contents

The Solitary Cyclist

From the years 1894 to 1901 inclusive, Mr Sherlock Holmes was a very busy man. It is safe to say that there was no public case of any difficulty in which he was not consulted during those eight years, and there were hundreds of private cases, some of them of the most intricate and extraordinary character, in which he played a prominent part. Many startling successes and a few unavoidable failures were the outcome of this long period of continuous work. As I have preserved very full notes of all these cases, and was myself personally engaged in many of them, it may be imagined that it is no easy task to know which I should select to lay before the public. I shall, however, preserve my former rule, and give the preference to those cases which derive their interest not so much from the brutality of the crime as from the ingenuity and dramatic quality of the solution. For this reason I will now lay before the reader the facts connected with Miss Violet Smith, the solitary cyclist of Charlington, and the curious sequel of our investigation, which culminated in unexpected tragedy. It is true that the circumstances did not permit of any striking illustration of those powers for which my friend was famous, but there were some points about the case which made it stand out in those long records of crime from which I gather the material for these little narratives.

On referring to my notebook for the year 1895, I find that it was upon Saturday, April 23rd, that we first heard of Miss Violet Smith. Her visit was, I remember, extremely unwelcome to Holmes, for he was immersed at the moment in a very abstruse and complicated problem concerning the peculiar persecution to which John Vincent Harden, the well-known tobacco millionaire, had been subjected. My friend, who loved above all things precision and concentration of thought, resented anything which distracted his attention from the matter in hand. And yet without harshness, which was foreign to his nature, it was impossible to refuse to listen to the story of the young and beautiful woman, tall, graceful and queenly, who presented herself at Baker Street late in the evening and implored his assistance and advice. It was vain to urge that his time was already fully occupied, for the young lady had come with the determination to tell her story, and it was evident that nothing short of force could get her out of the room until she had done so. With a resigned air and a somewhat weary smile, Holmes begged the beautiful intruder to take a seat and to inform us what it was that was troubling her.

‘At least it cannot be your health,’ said he, as his keen eyes darted over her; ‘so ardent a bicyclist must be full of energy.’

She glanced down in surprise at her own feet, and I observed the slight roughening of the side of the sole caused by the friction of the edge of the pedal.

‘Yes, I bicycle a good deal, Mr Holmes, and that has something to do with my visit to you today.’

My friend took the lady’s ungloved hand and examined it with as close an attention and as little sentiment as a scientist would show to a specimen.

‘You will excuse me, I am sure. It is my business,’ said he, as he dropped it. ‘I nearly fell into the error of supposing that you were typewriting. Of course, it is obvious that it is music. You observe the spatulate finger end, Watson, which is common to both professions? There is a spirituality about the face, however’ – he gently turned it towards the light – ‘which the typewriter does not generate. This lady is a musician.’

‘Yes, Mr Holmes, I teach music.’

‘In the country, I presume, from your complexion.’

‘Yes, sir; near Farnham, on the borders of Surrey.’

‘A beautiful neighbourhood, and full of the most interesting associations. You remember, Watson, that it was near there that we took Archie Stamford, the forger. Now, Miss Violet, what has happened to you near Farnham, on the borders of Surrey?’

The young lady, with great clearness and composure, made the following curious statement:

'My father is dead, Mr Holmes. He was James Smith, who conducted the orchestra at the old Imperial Theatre. My mother and I were left without a relation in the world except one uncle, Ralph Smith, who went to Africa twenty-five years ago, and we have never had a word from him since. When Father died we were left very poor, but one day we were told that there was an advertisement in *The Times* inquiring for our whereabouts. You can imagine how excited we were, for we thought that someone had left us a fortune. We went at once to the lawyer whose name was given in the paper. There we met two gentlemen, Mr Carruthers and Mr Woodley, who were home on a visit from South Africa. They said that my uncle was a friend of theirs, that he died some months before in poverty in Johannesburg, and that he had asked them with his last breath to hunt up his relations and see that they were in no want. It seemed strange to us that Uncle Ralph, who took no notice of us when he was alive, should be so careful to look after us when he was dead; but Mr Carruthers explained that the reason was that my uncle had just heard of the death of his brother, and so felt responsible for our fate.'

'Excuse me,' said Holmes; 'when was this interview?'

'Last December – four months ago.'

'Pray proceed.'

'Mr Woodley seemed to me to be a most odious person. He was for ever making eyes at me – a coarse, puffy-faced, red-moustached young man, with his hair plastered down on each side of his forehead. I thought that he was perfectly hateful – and I was sure that Cyril would not wish me to know such a person.'

'Oh, Cyril is his name!' said Holmes, smiling.

The young lady blushed and laughed.

'Yes, Mr Holmes; Cyril Morton, an electrical engineer, and we hope to be married at the end of the Summer. Dear me, how *did* I get talking about him? What I wished to say was that Mr Woodley was perfectly odious, but that Mr Carruthers, who was a much older man, was more agreeable. He was a dark, sallow, clean-shaven, silent person; but he had polite manners and a pleasant smile. He inquired how we were left, and on finding that we were very poor he suggested that I should come and teach music to his only daughter, aged ten. I said that I did not like to leave my mother, on which he suggested that I should go home to her every weekend, and he offered me a hundred a year, which was certainly splendid pay. So it ended by my accepting, and I went down to Chiltern Grange, about six miles from Farnham. Mr Carruthers was a widower, but he had engaged a lady-housekeeper, a very respectable, elderly person, called Mrs Dixon, to look after his establishment. The child was a dear, and everything promised well. Mr Carruthers was very kind and very musical, and we had most pleasant evenings together. Every weekend I went home to my mother in town.

'The first flaw in my happiness was the arrival of the red-moustached Mr Woodley. He came for a visit of a week, and oh, it seemed three months to me! He was a dreadful person, a bully to everyone else, but to me something infinitely worse. He made odious love to me, boasted of his wealth, said that if I married him I would have the finest diamonds in London, and finally, when I would have nothing to do with him, he seized me in his arms one day after dinner – he was hideously strong – and he swore that he would not let me go until I had kissed him. Mr Carruthers came in, and tore him off from me, on which he turned upon his own host, knocking him down and cutting his face open. That was the end of his visit, as you can imagine. Mr Carruthers apologized to me next day, and assured me that I should never be exposed to such an insult again. I have not seen Mr Woodley since.

'And now, Mr Holmes, I come at last to the special thing which has caused me to ask your advice today. You must know that every Saturday forenoon I ride on my bicycle to Farnham Station in order to get the 12.22 to town. The road from Chiltern Grange is a lonely one, and at one spot it is particularly so, for it lies for over a mile between Charlington Heath upon one side and the woods which lie round Charlington Hall upon the other. You could not find a more lonely tract of road anywhere, and it is quite rare to meet so much as a cart, or a peasant, until you reach the high-road near Crooksbury Hill. Two weeks ago I was passing this place when I chanced to look back over my shoulder, and about two hundred yards behind me I saw a man, also on a bicycle. He seemed to be a middle-aged man, with a short, dark beard. I looked back before I reached Farnham, but the man was gone, so I thought no more about it. But you can imagine how surprised I was, Mr Holmes, when on my return on the Monday I saw the same man on the same stretch of road. My astonishment was increased when the incident occurred again, exactly as before, on the following Saturday and Monday. He always kept his distance, and did not molest me in any way, but still it certainly was very odd. I mentioned it to Mr Carruthers, who seemed interested in what I said, and told me that he had ordered a horse and trap, so that in future I should not pass over these lonely roads without some companion.

'The horse and trap were to have come this week, but for some reason they were not delivered, and again I had to cycle to the station. That was this morning. You can think that I looked out when I came to Charlington Heath, and there, sure enough, was the man, exactly as he had been the two weeks before. He always kept so far from me that I could not clearly see his face, but it was certainly someone whom I did not know. He was dressed in a dark suit with a cloth cap. The only thing about his face that I could clearly see was his dark beard. Today I was not alarmed, but I was filled with curiosity, and I determined to find out who he was and what he wanted. I slowed down my machine, but he slowed down his. Then I stopped altogether, but he stopped also. Then I laid a trap for him. There is a sharp turning of the road, and I pedalled very quickly round this, and then I stopped and waited. I expected him to shoot round and pass me before he could stop. But he never appeared. Then I went back and looked round the corner. I could see a mile of road, but he was not on it. To make it the more extraordinary there was no side-road at this point down which he could have gone.'

Holmes chuckled and rubbed his hands.

'This case certainly presents some features of its own,' said he. 'How much time elapsed between your turning the corner and your discovery that the road was clear?'

'Two or three minutes.'

'Then he could not have retreated down the road, and you say that there are no side-roads?'

'None.'

'Then he certainly took a footpath on one side or the other.'

'It could not have been on the side of the heath or I should have seen him.'

'So by the process of exclusion we arrive at the fact that he made his way towards Charlington Hall, which, as I understand, is situated in its own grounds on one side of the road. Anything else?'

'Nothing, Mr Holmes, save that I was so perplexed that I felt I should not be happy until I had seen you and had your advice.'

Holmes sat in silence for some little time.

'Where is the gentleman to whom you are engaged?' he asked at last.

'He is in the Midland Electric Company, at Coventry.'

'He would not pay you a surprise visit?'

'Oh, Mr Holmes! As if I should not know him!'

'Have you had any other admirers?'

'Several before I knew Cyril.'

'And since?'

'There was this dreadful man, Woodley, if you can call him an admirer.'

'No one else?'

Our fair client seemed a little confused.

'Who was he?' asked Holmes.

'Oh, it may be a mere fancy of mine; but it has seemed to me sometimes that my employer, Mr Carruthers, takes a great deal of interest in me. We are thrown rather together. I play his accompaniments in the evening. He has never said anything. He is a perfect gentleman. But a girl always knows.'

'Ha!' Holmes looked grave. 'What does he do for a living?'

'He is a rich man.'

'No carriages or horses?'

'Well, at least he is fairly well-to-do. But he goes into the

City two or three times a week. He is deeply interested in South African gold shares.'

'You will let me know any fresh development, Miss Smith. I am very busy just now, but I will find time to make some inquiries into your case. In the meantime, take no step without letting me know. Goodbye, and I trust that we shall have nothing but good news from you.'

'It is part of the settled order of Nature that such a girl should have followers,' said Holmes, as he pulled at his meditative pipe, 'but for choice not on bicycles in lonely country roads. Some secretive lover, beyond all doubt. But there are curious and suggestive details about the case, Watson.'

'That he should appear only at that point?'

'Exactly. Our first effort must be to find who are the tenants of Charlington Hall. Then, again, how about the connection between Carruthers and Woodley, since they appear to be men of such different types? How came they *both* to be so keen upon looking up Ralph Smith's relations? One more point. What sort of a *ménage* is it which pays double the market price for a governess, but does not keep a horse although six miles from the station? Odd, Watson – very odd.'

'You will go down?'

'No, my dear fellow, *you* will go down. This may be some trifling intrigue, and I cannot break my other important research for the sake of it. On Monday you will arrive early at Farnham; you will conceal yourself near Charlington Heath; you will observe these facts for yourself, and act as your own judgement advises. Then, having inquired as to the occupants of the Hall, you will come back to me and report. And now, Watson, not another word of the matter until we have a few solid stepping stones on which we may hope to get across to our solution.'

We had ascertained from the lady that she went down upon the Monday by the train which leaves Waterloo at 9.50, so I started early and caught the 9.13. At Farnham Station I had no difficulty in being directed to Charlington Heath. It was impossible to mistake the scene of the young lady's adventure, for the road runs between the open heath on one side, and an old yew hedge upon the other, surrounding a park which is studded with magnificent trees. There was a main gateway of lichen studded stone, each side-pillar surmounted by mouldering heraldic emblems; but besides this central carriage drive I observed several points where there were gaps in the hedge and paths leading through them. The house was invisible from the road, but the surroundings all spoke of gloom and decay.

The heath was covered with golden patches of flowering gorse, gleaming magnificently in the light of the bright spring sunshine. Behind one of these clumps I took up my position, so as to command both the gateway of the Hall and a long stretch of the road upon either side. It had been deserted when I left it, but now I saw a cyclist riding down it from the opposite direction to that in which I had come. He was clad in a dark suit, and I saw that he had a black beard. On reaching the end of the Charlington grounds he sprang from his machine and led it through a gap in the hedge, disappearing from my view.

A quarter of an hour passed and then a second cyclist appeared. This time it was the young lady coming from the station. I saw her look about her as she came to the Charlington hedge. An instant later the man emerged from his hiding place, sprang upon his bicycle, and followed her. In all the broad landscape those were the only moving figures, the graceful girl sitting very straight upon her machine and the man behind her bending low over his handle-bar, with a curiously furtive suggestion in every movement. She looked back at him and slowed her pace. He slowed also. She stopped. He at once stopped, too, keeping two hundred yards behind her. Her next movement was as unexpected as it was spirited. She suddenly whisked her wheels round and dashed straight at him! He was as quick as she, however, and darted off in desperate flight. Presently she came back up the road again, her head haughtily in the air, not deigning to take further notice of her silent attendant. He had turned also, and still kept his distance until the curve of the road hid them from my sight.

I remained in my hiding-place, and it was well that I did so, for presently the man reappeared, cycling slowly back. He turned in at the Hall gates and dismounted from his machine. For some minutes I could see him standing among the trees. His hands were raised, and he seemed to be settling his necktie. Then he mounted his bicycle and rode away from me down the drive towards the Hall. I ran across the heath and peered through the trees. Far away I could catch glimpses of the old grey building with its bristling Tudor chimneys, but the drive ran through a dense shrubbery, and I saw no more of my man.

However, it seemed to me that I had done a fairly good morning's work, and I walked back in high spirits to Farnham. The local house agent could tell me nothing about Charlington Hall, and referred me to a well known firm in Pall Mall. There I halted on my way home, and met with courtesy from the representative. No, I could not have Charlington Hall for the Summer. I was just too late. It had been let about a month ago. Mr Williamson was the name of the tenant. He was a respectable elderly gentleman. The polite agent was afraid he could say no more, as the affairs of his clients were not matters which he could discuss.

Mr Sherlock Holmes listened with attention to the long report which I was able to present to him that evening, but it did not elicit that word of curt praise which I had hoped for and should have valued. On the contrary, his austere face was even more severe than usual as he commented upon the things that I had done and the things that I had not.

'Your hiding-place, my dear Watson, was very faulty. You should have been behind the hedge; then you would have had a close view of this interesting person. As it is you were some hundreds of yards away, and can tell me even less than Miss Smith. She thinks she does not know the man; I am convinced she does. Why, otherwise, should he be so desperately anxious that she should not get so near him as to see his features? You describe him as bending over the handle-bar. Concealment again, you see. You really have done remarkably badly. He returns to the house, and you want to find out who he is. You come to a London house agent!'

'What should I have done?' I cried, with some heat.

'Gone to the nearest public-house. That is the centre of country gossip. They would have told you every name, from the master to the scullery-maid. Williamson! It conveys nothing to my mind. If he is an elderly man he is not this active cyclist who springs away from that athletic young lady's pursuit. What have we gained by your expedition? The knowledge that the girl's story is true. I never doubted it. That there is a connection between the cyclist and the Hall. I never doubted that either. That the Hall is tenanted by Williamson. Who's the better for that? Well, well, my dear sir, don't look so depressed. We can do little more until next Saturday, and in the meantime I may make one or two inquiries myself.'

Next morning we had a note from Miss Smith, recounting

shortly and accurately the very incidents which I had seen, but the pith of the letter lay in the postscript:

> I am sure that you will respect my confidence, Mr Holmes, when I tell you that my place here has become difficult owing to the fact that my employer has proposed marriage to me. I am convinced that his feelings are most deep and most honourable. At the same time my promise is, of course, given. He took my refusal very seriously, but also very gently. You can understand, however, that the situation is a little strained.

'Our young friend seems to be getting into deep waters,' said Holmes thoughtfully, as he finished the letter. 'The case certainly presents more features of interest and more possibility of development than I had originally thought. I should be none the worse for a quiet, peaceful day in the country, and I am inclined to run down this afternoon and test one or two theories which I have formed.'

Holmes's quiet day in the country had a singular termination, for he arrived at Baker Street late in the evening with a cut lip and a discoloured lump upon his forehead, besides a general air of dissipation which would have made his own person the fitting object of a Scotland Yard investigation. He was immensely tickled by his own adventures, and laughed heartily as he recounted them.

‘I get so little active exercise that it is always a treat,’ said he. ‘You are aware that I have some proficiency in the good old British sport of boxing. Occasionally it is of service. Today, for example, I should have come to very ignominious grief without it.’

I begged him to tell me what had occurred.

‘I found that country pub which I had already recommended to your notice, and there I made my discreet inquiries. I was in the bar, and a garrulous landlord was giving me all that I wanted. Williamson is a white-bearded man, and he lives alone with a small staff of servants at the Hall. There is some rumour that he is or has been a clergyman; but one or two incidents of his short residence at the Hall struck me as peculiarly unecclesiastical. I have already made some inquiries at a clerical agency, and they tell me that there *was* a man of that name in orders whose career has been a singularly dark one. The landlord further informed me that there are usually weekend visitors – “a warm lot, sir” – at the Hall, and especially one gentleman with a red moustache, Mr Woodley by name, who was always there. We had got as far as this when who should walk in but the gentleman himself, who had been drinking his beer in the taproom, and had heard the whole conversation. Who was I? What did I want? What did I mean by asking questions? He had a fine flow of language, and his adjectives were very vigorous. He ended a string of abuse by a vicious backhander, which I failed to entirely avoid.

The next few minutes were delicious. It was a straight left against a slogging ruffian. I emerged as you see me. Mr Woodley went home in a cart. So ended my country trip, and it must be confessed that, however enjoyable, my day on the Surrey border has not been much more profitable than your own.'

The Thursday brought us another letter from our client:

> You will not be surprised, Mr Holmes (said she), to hear that I am leaving Mr Carruthers' employment. Even the high pay cannot reconcile me to the discomforts of my situation. On Saturday I come up to town, and I do not intend to return. Mr Carruthers has got a trap, and so the dangers of the lonely road, if there ever were any dangers, are now over.
>
> As to the special cause of my leaving, it is not merely the strained situation with Mr Carruthers, but it is the reappearance of that odious man, Mr Woodley. He was always hideous, but he looks more awful than ever now, for he appears to have had an accident and he is much disfigured. I saw him out of the window, but I am glad to say I did not meet him. He had a long talk with Mr Carruthers, who seemed much excited afterwards. Woodley must be staying in the neighbourhood, for he did not sleep here, and yet I caught a glimpse of him again this morning slinking about in the shrubbery. I would sooner have a savage wild animal loose

about the place. I loathe and fear him more than I can say. How *can* Mr Carruthers endure such a creature for a moment? However, all my troubles will be over on Saturday.

'So I trust, Watson, so I trust,' said Holmes gravely. 'There is some deep intrigue going on round that little woman, and it is our duty to see that no one molests her upon that last journey. I think, Watson, that we must spare time to run down together on Saturday morning, and make sure that this curious and inconclusive investigation has no untoward ending.'

I confess that I had not up to now taken a very serious view of the case, which had seemed to me rather grotesque and bizarre than dangerous. That a man should lie in wait for and follow a very handsome woman is no unheard-of thing, and if he had so little audacity that he not only dared not address her, but even fled from her approach, he was not a very formidable assailant. The ruffian Woodley was a very different person, but, except on the one occasion, he had not molested our client, and now he visited the house of Carruthers without intruding upon her presence. The man on the bicycle was doubtless a member of those week-end parties at the Hall of which the publican had spoken; but who he was or what he wanted was as obscure as ever. It was the severity of Holmes's manner and the fact that he slipped a revolver into his pocket before leaving our rooms which impressed me with the feeling that tragedy might prove to lurk behind this curious train of events.

A rainy night had been followed by a glorious morning, and the heath-covered countryside, with the glowing clumps of flowering gorse, seemed all the more beautiful to eyes which were weary of the duns and drabs and slate-greys of London. Holmes and I walked along the broad, sandy road inhaling the fresh morning air, and rejoicing in the music of the birds and the fresh breath of the spring. From a rise of the road on the shoulder of Crooksbury Hill we could see the grim Hall bristling out from amidst the ancient oaks, which, old as they were, were still younger than the building which they surrounded. Holmes pointed down the long tract of road which wound, a reddish-yellow band, between the brown of the heath and the budding green of the woods. Far away, a black dot, we could see a vehicle moving in our direction. Holmes gave an exclamation of impatience.

'I had given a margin of half an hour,' said he. 'If that is her trap she must be making for the earlier train. I fear, Watson, that she will be past Charlington before we can possibly meet her.'

From the instant that we passed the rise we could no longer see the vehicle, but we hastened onwards at such a pace that my sedentary life began to tell upon me, and I was compelled to fall behind. Holmes, however, was always in training, for he had inexhaustible stores of nervous energy upon which to draw. His springy step never slowed, until suddenly, when he was a hundred yards in front of me, he halted, and I saw him throw up his hand with a gesture of grief and despair. At the same instant an empty dog-cart, the horse cantering, the reins trailing, appeared round the curve of the road and rattled swiftly towards us.

'Too late, Watson; too late!' cried Holmes, as I ran panting to his side. 'Fool that I was not to allow for the earlier train! It's abduction, Watson – abduction! Murder! Heaven knows what! Block the road! Stop the horse! That's right. Now jump in, and let us see if I can repair the consequences of my own blunder.'

We had sprung into the dog-cart, and Holmes, after turning the horse, gave it a sharp cut with a whip, and we flew back along the road. As we turned the curve the whole stretch of road between the Hall and the heath was opened up. I grasped Holmes's arm.

'That's the man!' I gasped.

A solitary cyclist was coming towards us. His head was down and his shoulders rounded as he put every ounce of energy that he possessed on to the pedals. He was flying like a racer. Suddenly he raised his bearded face, saw us close to him, and pulled up, springing from his machine. That coal-black beard was in singular contrast to the pallor of his face, and his eyes were as bright as if he had a fever. He stared at us and at the dog-cart. Then a look of amazement came over his face.

'Halloa! Stop there!' he shouted, holding his bicycle to block our road. 'Where did you get that dog-cart? Pull up, man!' he yelled, drawing a pistol from his side pocket. 'Pull up, I say, or, by George, I'll put a bullet into your horse!'

Holmes threw the reins into my lap and sprang down from the cart.

'You're the man we want to see. Where is Miss Violet Smith?' he said in his quick, clear way.

'That's what I am asking you. You're in her dog-cart. You ought to know where she is.'

'We met the dog-cart on the road. There was no one in it. We drove back to help the young lady.'

'Good Lord! Good Lord! What shall I do?' cried the stranger, in an ecstasy of despair. 'They've got her, that hell-hound Woodley and the blackguard parson. Come, man, come, if you really are her friend. Stand by me and we'll save her, if I have to leave my carcass in Charlington Wood.'

He ran distractedly, his pistol in his hand, towards a gap in the hedge. Holmes followed him, and I, leaving the horse grazing beside the road, followed Holmes.

'This is where they came through,' said he, pointing to the marks of several feet upon the muddy path. 'Halloa! Stop a minute! Who's this in the bush?'

It was a young fellow about seventeen, dressed like an ostler, with leather cords and gaiters. He lay upon his back, his knees drawn up, a terrible cut upon his head. He was insensible, but alive. A glance at his wound told me that it had not penetrated the bone.

'That's Peter, the groom,' cried the stranger. 'He drove her. The beasts have pulled him off and clubbed him. Let him lie; we can't do him any good, but we may save her from the worst fate that can befall a woman.'

We ran frantically down the path, which wound among the trees. We had reached the shrubbery which surrounded the house when Holmes pulled up.

'They didn't go to the house. Here are their marks on the left – here, beside the laurel bushes! Ah, I said so!'

As he spoke a woman's shrill scream – a scream which vibrated with a frenzy of horror – burst from the thick green clump of bushes in front of us. It ended suddenly on its highest note with a choke and gurgle.

'This way! This way! They are in the bowling alley,' cried the stranger, darting through the bushes. 'Ah, the cowardly dogs! Follow me, gentlemen! Too late! too late! by the living Jingo!'

We had broken suddenly into a lovely glade of greensward surrounded by ancient trees. On the farther side of it, under the shadow of a mighty oak, there stood a singular group of three people. One was a woman, our client, drooping and faint, a handkerchief round her mouth. Opposite her stood a brutal, heavy-faced, red-moustached young man, his gaitered legs parted wide, one arm akimbo, the other waving a riding-crop, his whole attitude suggestive of a triumphant bravado. Between them an elderly, grey-bearded man, wearing a short surplice over a light tweed suit, had evidently just completed the wedding service, for he pocketed his Prayer Book as we appeared, and slapped the sinister bridegroom upon the back in jovial congratulation.

'They're married!' I gasped.

'Come on!' cried our guide; 'come on!' He rushed across the glade, Holmes and I at his heels. As we approached, the lady staggered against the trunk of the tree for support. Williamson, the ex-clergyman, bowed to us with mock politeness, and the bully Woodley advanced with a shout of brutal and exultant laughter.

'You can take your beard off, Bob,' said he. 'I know you right enough. Well, you and your pals have just come in time for me to be able to introduce you to Mrs Woodley.'

Our guide's answer was a singular one. He snatched off the dark beard which had disguised him and threw it on the ground, disclosing a long, sallow, clean-shaven face below it. Then he raised his revolver and covered the young ruffian, who was advancing upon him with his dangerous riding-crop swinging in his hand.

'Yes,' said our ally, 'I *am* Bob Carruthers, and I'll see this woman righted if I have to swing for it. I told you what I'd do if you molested her, and, by the Lord, I'll be as good as my word!'

'You're too late. She's my wife!'

'No, she's your widow.'

His revolver cracked, and I saw the blood spurt from the front of Woodley's waistcoat. He spun round with a scream and fell upon his back, his hideous red face turning suddenly to a dreadful mottled pallor. The old man, still clad in his surplice, burst into such a string of foul oaths as I have never heard, and pulled out a revolver of his own, but before he could raise it he was looking down the barrel of Holmes's weapon.

'Enough of this,' said my friend coldly. 'Drop that pistol! Watson, pick it up! Hold it to his head! Thank you. You, Carruthers, give me that revolver. We'll have no more violence. Come, hand it over!'

'Who are you, then?'

'My name is Sherlock Holmes.'

'Good Lord!'

'You have heard of me, I see. I will represent the official police until their arrival. Here, you!' he shouted to the frightened groom, who had appeared at the edge of the glade. 'Come here. Take this note as hard as you can ride to Farnham.' He scribbled a few words upon a leaf from his notebook. 'Give it to the superintendent at the police station. Until he comes, I must detain you all under my personal custody.'

The strong, masterful personality of Holmes dominated the tragic scene, and all were equally puppets in his hands. Williamson and Carruthers found themselves carrying the wounded Woodley into the house, and I gave my arm to the frightened girl. The injured man was laid on his bed, and at Holmes's request I examined him. I carried my report to where he sat in the old tapestry-hung dining-room with his two prisoners before him.

'He will live,' said I.

'What!' cried Carruthers, springing out of his chair. 'I'll go upstairs and finish him first. Do you tell me that the girl, that angel, is to be tied to Roaring Jack Woodley for life?'

'You need not concern yourself about that,' said Holmes. 'There are two very good reasons why she should under no circumstances be his wife. In the first place, we are very safe in questioning Mr Williamson's right to solemnize a marriage.'

'I have been ordained,' cried the old rascal.

'And also unfrocked.'

'Once a clergyman, always a clergyman.'

'I think not. How about the licence?'

'We had a licence for the marriage. I have it here in my pocket.'

'Then you got it by a trick. But in any case a forced marriage is no marriage, but it is a very serious felony, as you will discover before you have finished. You'll have time to think the point out during the next ten years or so, unless I am mistaken. As to you, Carruthers, you would have done better to keep your pistol in your pocket.'

'I begin to think so, Mr Holmes; but when I thought of

all the precaution I had taken to shield this girl – for I loved her, Mr Holmes, and it is the only time that ever I knew what love was – it fairly drove me mad to think that she was in the power of the greatest brute and bully in South Africa, a man whose name is a holy terror from Kimberley to Johannesburg. Why, Mr Holmes, you'll hardly believe it, but ever since that girl has been in my employment I never once let her go past this house, where I knew these rascals were lurking, without following her on my bicycle just to see that she came to no harm. I kept my distance from her, and I wore a beard so that she should not recognize me, for she is a good and high-spirited girl, and she wouldn't have stayed in my employment long if she had thought that I was following her about the country roads.'

'Why didn't you tell her of her danger?'

'Because then, again, she would have left me, and I couldn't bear to face that. Even if she couldn't love me it was a great deal to me just to see her dainty form about the house, and to hear the sound of her voice.'

'Well,' said I, 'you call that love, Mr Carruthers, but I should call it selfishness.'

'Maybe the two things go together. Anyhow, I couldn't let her go. Besides, with this crowd about, it was well that she should have someone near to look after her. Then when the cable came I knew they were bound to make a move.'

'What cable?'

Carruthers took a telegram from his pocket.

'That's it!' said he. It was short and concise:

THE OLD MAN IS DEAD

'Hum!' said Holmes. 'I think I see how things worked, and I can understand how this message would, as you say, bring them to a head. But while we wait, you might tell me what you can.'

The old reprobate with the surplice burst into a volley of bad language.

'By Heaven,' said he, 'if you squeal on us, Bob Carruthers, I'll serve you as you served Jack Woodley! You can bleat about the girl to your heart's content, for that's your own affair, but if you round on your pals to this plain-clothes copper it will be the worst day's work that ever you did.'

'Your reverence need not be excited,' said Holmes, lighting a cigarette. 'The case is clear enough against you, and all I ask is a few details for my private curiosity. However, if there's any difficulty in your telling me I'll do the talking, and then you will see how far you have a chance of holding back your secrets. In the first place, three of you came from South Africa on this game – you, Williamson, you, Carruthers, and Woodley.'

'Lie number one,' said the old man; 'I never saw either of them until two months ago, and I have never been in

Africa in my life, so you can put that in your pipe and smoke it, Mr Busybody Holmes!'

'What he says is true,' said Carruthers.

'Well, well, two of you came over. His reverence is our own home-made article. You had known Ralph Smith in South Africa. You had reason to believe he would not live long. You found out that his niece would inherit his fortune. How's that – eh?'

Carruthers nodded, and Williamson swore.

'She was next-of-kin, no doubt, and you were aware that the old fellow would make no will.'

'Couldn't read or write,' said Carruthers.

'So you came over, the two of you, and hunted up the girl. The idea was that one of you was to marry her, and the other have a share of the plunder. For some reason Woodley was chosen as the husband. Why was that?'

'We played cards for her on the voyage. He won.'

'I see. You got the young lady into your service, and there Woodley was to do the courting. She recognized the drunken brute that he was, and would have nothing to do with him. Meanwhile, your arrangement was rather upset by the fact that you had yourself fallen in love with the lady. You could no longer bear the idea of this ruffian owning her.'

'No, by George, I couldn't!'

'There was a quarrel between you. He left you in a rage, and began to make his own plans independently of you.'

'It strikes me, Williamson, there isn't very much that we can tell this gentleman,' cried Carruthers, with a bitter laugh. 'Yes, we quarrelled, and he knocked me down. I am level with him on that, anyhow. Then I lost sight of him. That was when he picked up with this outcast padre here. I found that they had set up housekeeping together at this place on the line that she had to pass for the station. I kept my eye on her after that, for I knew there was some devilry in the wind. I saw them from time to time, for I was anxious to know what they were after. Two days ago Woodley came up to my house with this cable, which showed that Ralph Smith was dead. He asked me if I would stand by the bargain. I said I would not. He asked me if I would marry the girl myself and give him a share. I said I would willingly do so, but that she would not have me. He said, "Let us get her married first, and after a week or two she may see things a bit different." I said I would have nothing to do with violence. So he went off cursing, like the foul-mouthed blackguard that he was, and swearing that he would have her yet. She was leaving me this weekend, and I had got a trap to take her to the station, but I was so uneasy in my mind that I followed her on my bicycle. She had got a start, however, and before I could catch her the mischief was done. The first thing I knew about it was when I saw you two gentlemen driving back in her dog-cart.'

Holmes rose and tossed the end of his cigarette into the grate. 'I have been very obtuse, Watson,' said he. 'When in your report you said that you had seen the cyclist as you thought arrange his necktie in the shrubbery, that alone should have told me all. However, we may congratulate ourselves upon a curious and in some respects a unique case. I perceive three of the county constabulary in the drive, and I am glad to see that the little ostler is able to keep pace with them; so it is likely that neither he nor the interesting bridegroom will be permanently damaged by their morning's adventures. I think, Watson, that in your medical capacity you might wait upon Miss Smith and tell her that if she is sufficiently recovered we shall be happy to escort her to her mother's home. If she is not quite convalescent you will find that a hint that we were about to telegraph to a young electrician in the Midlands would probably complete the cure. As to you, Mr Carruthers, I think that you have done what you could to make amends for your share in an evil plot. There is my card, sir, and if my evidence can be of help to you in your trial it shall be at your disposal.'

In the whirl of our incessant activity it has often been difficult for me, as the reader has probably observed, to round off my narratives, and to give those final details which the curious might expect. Each case has been the prelude to another, and the crisis once over, the actors have passed for ever out of our busy lives. I find, however, a short note at the end of my manuscripts dealing with this case, in which I have put it upon record that Miss Violet Smith did indeed inherit a large fortune, and that she is now the wife of Cyril Morton, the senior partner of Morton and Kennedy, the famous Westminster electricians. Williamson and Woodley were both tried for abduction and assault, the former getting seven years and the latter ten. Of the fate of Carruthers I have no record, but I am sure that his assault was not viewed very gravely by the Court, since Woodley had the reputation of being a most dangerous ruffian, and I think that a few months were sufficient to satisfy the demands of justice.

Charles Augustus Milverton

It is years since the incidents of which I speak took place, and yet it is with diffidence that I allude to them. For a long time, even with the utmost discretion and reticence, it would have been impossible to make the facts public; but now the principal person concerned is beyond the reach of human law, and with due suppression the story may be told in such fashion as to injure no one. It records an absolutely unique experience in the career both of Mr Sherlock Holmes and of myself. The reader will excuse me if I conceal the date or any other fact by which he might trace the actual occurrence.

We had been out for one of our evening rambles, Holmes and I, and had returned about six o'clock on a cold, frosty winter's evening. As Holmes turned up the lamp the light fell upon a card on the table. He glanced at it, and then, with an ejaculation of disgust, threw it on the floor. I picked it up and read:

CHARLES AUGUSTUS MILVERTON
APPLEDORE TOWERS
HAMPSTEAD
Agent

'Who is he?' I asked.

'The worst man in London,' Holmes answered, as he sat down and stretched his legs before the fire. 'Is anything on the back of the card?'

I turned it over.

'Will call at 6.30 – C. A. M.,' I read.

'Hum! He's about due. Do you feel a creeping, shrinking sensation, Watson, when you stand before the serpents in the Zoo and see the slithery, gliding, venomous creatures, with their deadly eyes and wicked, flattened faces? Well, that's how Milverton impresses me. I've had to do with fifty murderers in my career, but the worst of them never gave me the repulsion which I have for this fellow. And yet I can't get out of doing business with him – indeed, he is here at my invitation.'

'But who is he?'

'I'll tell you, Watson. He is the king of all the blackmailers. Heaven help the man, and still more the woman, whose secret and reputation come into the power of Milverton. With a smiling face and a heart of marble he will squeeze and squeeze until he has drained them dry. The fellow is a genius in his way, and would have made his mark in some more savoury trade. His method is as follows: he allows it to be known that he is prepared to pay very high sums for letters which compromise people of wealth or position. He receives these wares not only from treacherous valets or maids, but frequently from genteel ruffians who have gained the confidence and affection of trusting women. He deals with no niggard hand. I happen to know that he paid seven hundred pounds to a footman for a note two lines in length, and that the ruin of a noble family was the result. Everything which is in the market goes to Milverton, and there are hundreds in this great city who turn white at his name. No one knows where his grip may fall, for he is far too rich and far too cunning to work from hand to mouth. He will hold a card back for years in order to play it at the moment when the stake is best worth winning. I have said that he is the worst man in London, and I would ask you how could one compare the ruffian who in hot blood bludgeons his mate with this man, who methodically and at his leisure tortures the soul and wrings the nerves in order to add to his already swollen money-bags?'

I had seldom heard my friend speak with such intensity of feeling.

'But surely,' said I, 'the fellow must be within the grasp of the law?'

'Technically, no doubt, but practically not. What would it profit a woman, for example, to get him a few months' imprisonment if her own ruin must immediately follow? His victims dare not hit back. If ever he blackmailed an innocent person, then, indeed, we should have him; but he is as cunning as the Evil One. No, no; we must find other ways to fight him.'

'And why is he here?'

'Because an illustrious client has placed her piteous case in my hands. It is the Lady Eva Brackwell, the most beautiful *débutante* of last season. She is to be married in a fortnight to the Earl of Dovercourt. This fiend has several imprudent letters – imprudent, Watson, nothing worse – which were written to an impecunious young squire in the country. They would suffice to break off the match. Milverton will send the letters to the earl unless a large sum of money is paid him. I have been commissioned to meet him, and – to make the best terms I can.'

At that instant there was a clatter and a rattle in the street below. Looking down I saw a stately carriage and pair, the brilliant lamps gleaming on the glossy haunches of the noble chestnuts. A footman opened the door, and a small, stout man in a shaggy astrakhan overcoat descended. A minute later he was in the room.

Charles Augustus Milverton was a man of fifty, with a large, intellectual head, a round, plump, hairless face, a perpetual frozen smile, and two keen grey eyes, which gleamed brightly from behind broad, golden-rimmed glasses. There was something of Mr Pickwick's benevolence in his appearance, marred only by the insincerity of the fixed smile and by the hard glitter of those restless and penetrating eyes. His voice was as smooth and suave as his countenance, as he advanced with a plump little hand extended, murmuring his regret for having missed us at his first visit.

Holmes disregarded the outstretched hand and looked at him with a face of granite. Milverton's smile broadened; he shrugged his shoulders, removed his overcoat, folded it with great deliberation over the back of a chair, and then took a seat.

'This gentleman,' said he, with a wave in my direction. 'Is it discreet? Is it right?'

'Dr Watson is my friend and partner.'

'Very good, Mr Holmes. It is only in your client's interests that I protested. The matter is so very delicate –'

'Dr Watson has already heard of it.'

'Then we can proceed to business. You say that you are acting for Lady Eva. Has she empowered you to accept my terms?'

'What are your terms?'

'Seven thousand pounds.'

'And the alternative?'

'My dear sir, it is painful to me to discuss it; but if the money is not paid on the 14th there certainly will be no marriage on the 18th.' His insufferable smile was more complacent than ever. Holmes thought for a little.

'You appear to me,' he said at last, 'to be taking matters too much for granted. I am, of course, familiar with the contents of these letters. My client will certainly do what I may advise. I shall counsel her to tell her future husband the whole story and to trust to his generosity.'

Milverton chuckled.

'You evidently do not know the earl,' said he.

From the baffled look upon Holmes's face I could clearly see that he did.

'What harm is there in the letters?' he asked.

'They are sprightly – very sprightly,' Milverton answered. 'The lady was a charming correspondent. But I can assure you that the Earl of Dovercourt would fail to appreciate them. However, since you think otherwise, we will let it rest at that. It is purely a matter of business. If you think that it is in the best interests of your client that these letters should be placed in the hands of the earl, then you would indeed be foolish to pay so large a sum of money to regain them.' He rose and seized his astrakhan coat.

Holmes was grey with anger and mortification.

'Wait a little,' he said. 'You go too fast. We would certainly make every effort to avoid scandal in so delicate a matter.'

Milverton relapsed into his chair.

'I was sure that you would see it in that light,' he purred.

'At the same time,' Holmes continued, 'Lady Eva is not a wealthy woman. I assure you that two thousand pounds would be a drain upon her resources, and that the sum you name is utterly beyond her power. I beg, therefore, that you will moderate your demands, and that you will return the letters at the price I indicate, which is, I assure you, the highest that you can get.'

Milverton's smile broadened and his eyes twinkled humorously.

'I am aware that what you say is true about the lady's resources,' said he. 'At the same time, you must admit that the occasion of a lady's marriage is a very suitable time for her friends and relatives to make some little effort upon her behalf. They may hesitate as to an acceptable wedding present. Let me assure them that this little bundle of letters would give more joy than all the candelabra and butter-dishes in London.'

'It is impossible,' said Holmes.

'Dear me, dear me, how unfortunate!' cried Milverton, taking out a bulky pocket-book. 'I cannot help thinking that ladies are ill-advised in not making an effort. Look at this!' He held up a little note with a coat-of-arms upon the envelope. 'That belongs to – well, perhaps it is hardly fair to tell the name until tomorrow morning. But at that time it will be in the hands of the lady's husband. And all because she will not find a beggarly sum which she could get in an hour by turning her diamonds into paste. It *is* such a pity. Now, you remember the sudden end of the engagement between the Honourable Miss Miles and Colonel Dorking? Only two days before the wedding there was a paragraph in the *Morning Post* to say that it was all off. And why? It is almost incredible, but the absurd sum of twelve hundred pounds would have settled the whole question. Is it not pitiful? And there I find you, a man of sense, boggling about terms when your client's future and honour are at stake. You surprise me, Mr Holmes.'

'What I say is true,' Mr Holmes answered. 'The money cannot be found. Surely it is better for you to take the substantial sum which I offer than to ruin this woman's career, which can profit you in no way?'

'There you make a mistake, Mr Holmes. An exposure would profit me indirectly to a considerable extent. I have eight or ten similar cases maturing. If it was circulated among them that I had made a severe example of the Lady Eva I should find all of them much more open to reason. You see my point?'

Holmes sprang from his chair.

'Get behind him, Watson. Don't let him out! Now, sir, let us see the contents of that notebook.'

Milverton had glided as quick as a rat to the side of the room, and stood with his back against the wall.

'Mr Holmes, Mr Holmes!' he said, turning the front of his coat and exhibiting the butt of a large revolver, which projected from the inside pocket. 'I have been expecting you to do something original. This has been done so often, and what good has ever come from it? I assure you that I am armed to the teeth, and I am perfectly prepared to use my weapon, knowing that the law will support me. Besides, your supposition that I would bring the letters here in a notebook is entirely mistaken. I would do nothing so foolish. And now, gentlemen, I have one or two little interviews this evening, and it is a long drive to Hampstead.' He stepped forward, took up his coat, laid his hand on his revolver, and turned to the door. I picked up a chair, but Holmes shook his head, and I laid it down again. With a bow, a smile, and a twinkle Milverton was out of the room, and a few moments after we heard the slam of the carriage door and the rattle of the wheels as he drove away.

Holmes sat motionless by the fire, his hands buried deep in his trouser pockets, his chin sunk upon his breast, his eyes fixed upon the glowing embers. For half an hour he was silent and still. Then, with the gesture of a man who has taken his decision, he sprang to his feet and passed into his bedroom. A little later a rakish young workman with a goatee beard and a swagger lit his clay pipe at the lamp before descending into the street. 'I'll be back some time, Watson,' said he, and vanished into the night. I understood that he had opened his campaign against Charles Augustus Milverton; but I little dreamed the strange shape which that campaign was destined to take.

For some days Holmes came and went at all hours in this attire, but beyond a remark that his time was spent at Hampstead, and that it was not wasted, I knew nothing of what he was doing. At last, however, on a wild, tempestuous evening, when the wind screamed and rattled against the windows, he returned from his last expedition, and, having removed his disguise, he sat before the fire and laughed heartily in his silent, inward fashion.

'You would not call me a marrying man, Watson?'

'No, indeed!'

'You will be interested to hear that I am engaged.'

'My dear fellow! I congrat–'

'To Milverton's housemaid.'

'Good heavens, Holmes!'

'I wanted information, Watson.'

'Surely you have gone too far?'

'It was a most necessary step. I am a plumber with a rising business, Escott by name. I have walked out with her each evening, and I have talked with her. Good heavens, those talks! However, I have got all I wanted. I know Milverton's house as I know the palm of my hand.'

'But the girl, Holmes?'

He shrugged his shoulders.

'You can't help it, my dear Watson. You must play your cards as best you can when such a stake is on the table. However, I rejoice to say that I have a hated rival who will certainly cut me out the instant that my back is turned. What a splendid night it is!'

'You like this weather?'

'It suits my purpose. Watson, I mean to burgle Milverton's house tonight.'

I had a catching of the breath, and my skin went cold at the words, which were slowly uttered in a tone of concentrated resolution. As a flash of lightning in the night shows up in an instant every detail of a wide landscape, so at one glance I seemed to see every possible result of such an action – the detection, the capture, the honoured career ending in irreparable failure and disgrace, my friend himself lying at the mercy of the odious Milverton.

'For Heaven's sake, Holmes, think what you are doing!' I cried.

'My dear fellow, I have given it every consideration. I am never precipitate in my actions, nor would I adopt so energetic and indeed so dangerous a course if any other were possible. Let us look at the matter clearly and fairly. I suppose that you will admit that the action is morally justifiable, though technically criminal. To burgle his house is no more than to forcibly take his pocket-book – an action in which you were prepared to aid me.'

I turned it over in my mind.

'Yes,' I said; 'it is morally justifiable so long as our object is to take no articles save those which are used for an illegal purpose.'

'Exactly. Since it is morally justifiable, I have only to consider the question of personal risk. Surely a gentleman should not lay much stress upon this when a lady is in most desperate need of his help?'

'You will be in such a false position.'

'Well, that is part of the risk. There is no other possible way of regaining these letters. The unfortunate lady has not the money, and there are none of her people in whom she could confide. Tomorrow is the last day of grace, and unless we can get the letters tonight this villain will be as good as his word, and will bring about her ruin. I must, therefore, abandon my client to her fate, or I must play this last card. Between ourselves, Watson, it's a Sporting duel between this fellow Milverton and me. He had, as you saw, the best of the first exchanges; but my self-respect and my reputation are concerned to fight it to a finish.'

'Well, I don't like it; but I suppose it must be,' said I. 'When do we start?'

'You are not coming.'

'Then you are not going,' said I. 'I give you my word of honour – and I never broke it in my life – that I will take a cab straight to the police station and give you away unless you let me share this adventure with you.'

'You can't help me.'

'How do you know that? You can't tell what may happen. Anyway, my resolution is taken. Other people besides you have self-respect and even reputations.'

Holmes had looked annoyed, but his brow cleared, and he clapped me on the shoulder.

'Well, well, my dear fellow, be it so. We have shared the same room for some years, and it would be amusing if we ended by sharing the same cell. You know, Watson, I don't mind confessing to you that I have always had an idea that I would have made a highly efficient criminal. This is the chance of my lifetime in that direction. See here!' He took a neat little leather case out of a drawer, and opening it he exhibited a number of shining instruments. 'This is a first-class, up-to-date burgling kit, with nickel-plated jemmy, diamond-tipped glass cutter, adaptable keys, and every modern improvement which the march of civilization demands. Here, too, is my dark lantern. Everything is in order. Have you a pair of silent shoes?'

'I have rubber-soled tennis shoes.'

'Excellent. And a mask?'

'I can make a couple out of black silk.'

'I can see that you have a strong natural turn for this sort of thing. Very good; so you make the masks. We shall have some cold supper before we start. It is now nine-thirty. At eleven we shall drive as far as Church Row. It is a quarter of an hour's walk from there to Appledore Towers. We shall be at work before midnight. Milverton is a heavy sleeper, and retires punctually at ten-thirty. With any luck we should be back here by two, with the Lady Eva's letters in my pocket.'

Holmes and I put on our dress-clothes, so that we might appear to be two theatre-goers homeward bound. In Oxford Street we picked up a hansom and drove to an address in Hampstead. Here we paid off our cab, and with our great-coats buttoned up – for it was bitterly cold, and the wind seemed to blow through us – we walked along the edge of the Heath.

'It's a business that needs delicate treatment,' said Holmes. 'These documents are contained in a safe in the fellow's study, and the study is the ante-room of his bedchamber. On the other hand, like all these stout, little men who do themselves well, he is a plethoric sleeper. Agatha – that's my fiancee – says it is a joke in the servants' hall that it's impossible to wake the master. He has a secretary who is devoted to his interests and never budges from the study all day. That's why we are going at night. Then he has a beast of a dog which roams the garden. I met Agatha late the last two evenings, and she locks the brute up so as to give me a clear run. This is the house, this big one in its own grounds. Through the gate – now to the right among the laurels. We might put on our masks here, I think. You see, there is not a glimmer of light in any of the windows, and everything is working splendidly.'

With our black silk face-coverings, which turned us into two of the most truculent figures in London, we stole up to the silent, gloomy house. A sort of tiled veranda extended along one side of it, lined by several windows and two doors.

'That's his bedroom,' Holmes whispered. 'This door opens straight into the study. It would suit us best, but it is bolted as well as locked, and we should make too much noise getting in. Come round here. There's a greenhouse which opens into the drawing-room.'

The place was locked, but Holmes removed a circle of glass and turned the key from the inside. An instant afterwards he had closed the door behind us, and we had become felons in the eyes of the law. The thick warm air of the conservatory and the rich, choking fragrance of exotic plants took us by the throat. He seized my hand in the darkness and led me swiftly past banks of shrubs which brushed against our faces. Holmes had remarkable powers, carefully cultivated, of seeing in the dark. Still holding my hand in one of his, he opened a door, and I was vaguely conscious that we had entered a large room in which a cigar had been smoked not long before. He felt his way among the furniture, opened another door, and closed it behind us. Putting out my hand I felt several coats hanging from the wall, and I understood that I was in a passage. We passed along it, and Holmes very gently opened a door upon the right-hand side. Something rushed out at us, and my heart sprang into my mouth, but I could have laughed when I realized that it was the cat. A fire was burning in this new room, and again the air was heavy with tobacco smoke. Holmes entered on tiptoe, waited for me to follow, and then very gently closed the door. We were in Milverton's study, and a *portière* at the farther side showed the entrance to his bedroom.

It was a good fire, and the room was illuminated by it. Near the door I saw the gleam of an electric switch, but it was unnecessary, even if it had been safe, to turn it on. At one side of the fireplace was a heavy curtain, which covered the bay window we had seen from outside. On the other side was the door which communicated with the veranda. A desk stood in the centre, with a turning chair of shining red leather. Opposite was a large bookcase, with a marble bust of Athene on the top. In the corner between the bookcase and the wall there stood a tall green safe, the firelight flashing back from the polished brass knobs upon its face. Holmes stole across and looked at it. Then he crept to the door of the bedroom, and stood with slanting head listening intently. No sound came from within. Meanwhile it had struck me that it would be wise to secure our retreat through the outer door, so I examined it. To my amazement it was neither locked nor bolted! I touched Holmes on the arm, and he turned his masked face in that direction. I saw him start, and he was evidently as surprised as I.

'I don't like it,' he whispered, putting his lips to my very ear. 'I can't quite make it out. Anyhow, we have no time to lose.'

'Can I do anything?'

'Yes; stand by the door. If you hear anyone come, bolt it on the inside, and we can get away as we came. If they come the other way, we can get through the door if our job is done, or hide behind these window curtains if it is not. Do you understand?'

I nodded and stood by the door. My first feeling of fear had passed away, and I thrilled now with a keener zest than

I had ever enjoyed when we were the defenders of the law instead of its defiers. The high object of our mission, the consciousness that it was unselfish and chivalrous, the villainous character of our opponent, all added to the sporting interest of the adventure. Far from feeling guilty, I rejoiced and exulted in our dangers. With a glow of admiration I watched Holmes unrolling his case of instruments and choosing his tool with the calm, scientific accuracy of a surgeon who performs a delicate operation. I knew that the opening of safes was a particular hobby with him, and I understood the joy which it gave him to be confronted with this green and gold monster, the dragon which held in its maw the reputations of many fair ladies. Turning up the cuffs of his dress-coat – he had placed his overcoat on a chair – Holmes laid out two drills, a jemmy, and several skeleton keys. I stood at the centre door with my eyes glancing at each of the others, ready for any emergency; though, indeed, my plans were somewhat vague as to what I should do if we were interrupted. For half an hour Holmes worked with concentrated energy, laying down one tool, picking up another, handling each with the strength and delicacy of the trained mechanic. Finally I heard a click, the broad green door swung open, and inside I had a glimpse of a number of paper packets, each tied, sealed, and inscribed. Holmes picked one out, but it was hard to read by the flickering fire, and he drew out his little dark lantern, for it was too dangerous, with Milverton in the next room, to switch on the electric light. Suddenly I saw him halt, listen intently, and then in an instant he had swung the door of the safe to, picked up his coat, stuffed his tools into the pockets, and darted behind the window curtain, motioning me to do the same.

It was only when I had joined him there that I heard what had alarmed his quicker senses. There was a noise somewhere within the house. A door slammed in the distance. Then a confused, dull murmur broke itself into the measured thud of heavy footsteps rapidly approaching. They were in the passage outside the room. They paused at the door. The door opened. There was a sharp snick as the electric light was turned on. The door closed once more, and the pungent reek of a strong cigar was borne to our nostrils. Then the footsteps continued backwards and forwards, backwards and forwards, within a few yards of us. Finally, there was a creak from a chair, and the footsteps ceased. Then a key clicked in a lock, and I heard the rustle of papers. So far I had not dared to look out, but now I gently parted the division of the curtains in front of me and peeped through. From the pressure of Holmes's shoulder against mine I knew that he was sharing my observations. Right in front of us, and almost within our reach, was the broad, rounded back of Milverton. It was evident that we had entirely miscalculated his movements, that he had never been to his bedroom, but that he had been sitting up in some smoking or billiard-room in the farther wing of the house, the windows of which we had not seen. His broad, grizzled head, with its shining patch of baldness, was in the immediate foreground of our vision. He was leaning far back in the red leather chair, his legs outstretched, a long black cigar projecting at an angle from his mouth. He wore a semi-military smoking-jacket, claret-coloured, with a black velvet collar. In his hand he held a long legal document, which he was reading in an indolent fashion, blowing rings of tobacco smoke from his lips as he did so. There was no promise of a speedy departure in his composed bearing and his comfortable attitude.

I felt Holmes's hand steal into mine and give me a reassuring shake, as if to say that the situation was within his powers, and that he was easy in his mind. I was not sure whether he had seen what was only too obvious from my position – that the door of the safe was imperfectly closed, and that Milverton might at any moment observe it. In my own mind I had determined that if I were sure, from the rigidity of his gaze, that it had caught his eye, I would at once spring out, throw my greatcoat over his head, pinion him, and leave the rest to Holmes. But Milverton never looked up. He was languidly interested by the papers in his hand, and page after page was turned as he followed the argument of the lawyer. At least, I thought, when he has finished the document and the cigar he will go to his room; but before he had reached the end of either there came a remarkable development which turned our thoughts into quite another channel.

Several times I had observed that Milverton looked at his watch, and once he had risen and sat down again, with a gesture of impatience. The idea, however, that he might have an appointment at so strange an hour never occurred to me until a faint sound reached my ears from the veranda outside. Milverton dropped his papers and sat rigid in his chair. The sound was repeated, and then there came a gentle tap at the door. Milverton rose and opened it.

'Well,' said he curtly, 'you are nearly half an hour late.'

So this was the explanation of the unlocked door and of the nocturnal vigil of Milverton. There was the gentle rustle of a woman's dress. I had closed the slit between the curtains as Milverton's face turned in our direction, but now I ventured very carefully to open it once more. He had resumed his seat, the cigar still projecting at an insolent angle from the corner of his mouth. In front of him, in the full glare of the electric light, there stood a tall, slim, dark woman, a veil over her face, a mantle drawn round her chin. Her breath came quick and fast and every inch of the lithe figure was quivering with strong emotion.

'Well,' said Milverton, 'you've made me lose a good night's rest, my dear. I hope you'll prove worth it. You couldn't come any other time – eh?'

The woman shook her head.

'Well, if you couldn't you couldn't. If the countess is a hard mistress you have your chance to get level with her now. Bless the girl, what are you shivering about? That's right! Pull yourself together! Now, let us get down to business.' He took a note from the drawer of his desk. 'You say that you have five letters which compromise the Countess d'Albert. You want to sell them. I want to buy them. So far so good. It only remains to fix a price. I should want to inspect the letters, of course. If they are really good specimens – Great heavens, is it you?'

The woman without a word had raised her veil and dropped the mantle from her chin. It was a dark, handsome, clear-cut face which confronted Milverton, a face with a curved nose, strong, dark eyebrows, shading hard, glittering eyes, and a straight, thin-lipped mouth set in a dangerous smile.

'It is I,' she said – 'the woman whose life you have ruined.'

Milverton laughed, but fear vibrated in his voice. 'You were so very obstinate,' said he. 'Why did you drive me to such extremities? I assure you I wouldn't hurt a fly of my own accord, but every man has his business, and what was I to do? I put the price well within your means. You would not pay.'

'So you sent the letters to my husband, and he – the noblest gentleman that ever lived, a man whose boots I was never worthy to lace – he broke his gallant heart and died. You remember that last night when I came through that door I begged and prayed you for mercy, and you laughed in my face as you are trying to laugh now, only your coward heart cannot keep your lips from twitching? Yes; you never thought to see me here again, but it was that night which taught me how I could meet you face to face, and alone. Well, Charles Milverton, what have you to say?'

'Don't imagine that you can bully me,' said he, rising to his feet. 'I have only to raise my voice, and I could call my servants and have you arrested. But I will make allowance for your natural anger. Leave the room at once as you came, and I will say no more.'

The woman stood with her hand buried in her bosom, and the same deadly smile on her thin lips.

'You will ruin no more lives as you have ruined mine. You will wring no more hearts as you wrung mine. I will free the world of a poisonous thing. Take that, you hound, and that! – and that! – and that! – and that!'

She had drawn a little gleaming revolver, and emptied barrel after barrel into Milverton's body, the muzzle within two feet of his shirt-front. He shrank away, and then fell forward upon the table, coughing furiously and clawing among the papers. Then he staggered to his feet, received another shot, and rolled upon the floor. 'You've done me,' he cried, and lay still. The woman looked at him intently and ground her heel into his upturned face. She looked again, but there was no sound or movement. I heard a sharp rustle, the night air blew into the heated room, and the avenger was gone.

No interference upon our part could have saved the man from his fate; but as the woman poured bullet after bullet into Milverton's shrinking body, I was about to spring out, when I felt Holmes's cold, strong grasp upon my wrist. I understood the whole argument of that firm, restraining grip – that it was no affair of ours; that justice had overtaken a villain; that we had our own duties and our own objects which were not to be lost sight of. But hardly had the woman rushed from the room when Holmes, with swift, silent steps, was over at the other door. He turned the key in the lock. At the same instant we heard voices in the house and the sound of hurrying feet. The revolver shots had roused the household. With perfect coolness Holmes slipped across to the safe, filled his two arms with bundles of letters, and poured them all into the fire. Again and again he did it, until the safe was empty. Someone turned the handle and beat upon the outside of the door. Holmes looked swiftly round. The letter which had been the messenger of death for Milverton lay, all mottled with his blood, upon the table. Holmes tossed it in among the blazing papers. Then he drew the key from the outer door, passed through after me, and locked it on the outside. 'This way, Watson,' said he; 'we can scale the garden wall in this direction.'

I could not have believed that an alarm could have spread

so swiftly. Looking back, the huge house was one blaze of light. The front door was open, and figures were rushing down the drive. The whole garden was alive with people, and one fellow raised a view-halloa as we emerged from the veranda and followed hard at our heels. Holmes seemed to know the ground perfectly, and he threaded his way swiftly among a plantation of small trees, I close at his heels, and our foremost pursuer panting behind us. It was a six-foot wall which barred our path, but he sprang to the top and over. As I did the same I felt the hand of the man behind me grab my ankle; but I kicked myself free, and scrambled over a glass-strewn coping. I fell upon my face among some bushes; but Holmes had me on my feet in an instant, and together we dashed away across the huge expanse of Hampstead Heath. We had run two miles, I suppose, before Holmes at last halted and listened intently. All was absolutely silent behind us. We had shaken off our pursuers, and were safe.

We had breakfasted and were smoking our morning pipe, on the day after the remarkable experience which I have recorded, when Mr Lestrade, of Scotland Yard, very solemn and impressive, was ushered into our modest sitting-room.

'Good morning, Mr Holmes,' said he – 'good morning. May I ask if you are very busy just now?'

'Not too busy to listen to you.'

'I thought that, perhaps, if you had nothing particular on hand, you might care to assist us in a most remarkable case which occurred only last night at Hampstead.'

'Dear me!' said Holmes. 'What was that?'

'A murder – a most dramatic and remarkable murder. I know how keen you are upon these things, and I would take it as a great favour if you would step down to Appledore Towers and give us the benefit of your advice. It is no ordinary crime. We have had our eyes upon this Mr Milverton for some time, and, between ourselves, he was a bit of a villain. He is known to have held papers which he used for blackmailing purposes. These papers have all been burned by the murderers. No article of value was taken, as it is probable that the criminals were men of good position, whose sole object was to prevent social exposure.'

'Criminals!' exclaimed Holmes. 'Plural!'

'Yes, there were two of them. They were, as nearly as possible, captured red-handed. We have their footmarks, we have their description; it's ten to one that we trace them. The first fellow was a bit too active, but the second was caught by the under-gardener, and only got away after a struggle. He was a middle-sized, strongly built man – square jaw, thick neck, moustache, a mask over his eyes.'

'That's rather vague,' said Sherlock Holmes. 'Why, it might be a description of Watson!'

'It's true,' said the inspector, with much amusement. 'It might be a description of Watson.'

'Well, I am afraid I can't help you, Lestrade,' said Holmes. 'The fact is that I knew this fellow Milverton, that I considered him one of the most dangerous men in London, and that I think there are certain crimes which the law cannot touch, and which therefore, to some extent, justify private revenge. No, it's no use arguing. I have made up my mind. My sympathies are with the criminals rather than with the victim, and I will not handle this case.'

Holmes had not said one word to me about the tragedy which we had witnessed, but I observed all the morning that he was in the most thoughtful mood, and he gave me the impression, from his vacant eyes and his abstracted manner, of a man who is striving to recall something to his memory. We were in the middle of our lunch, when he suddenly sprang to his feet. 'By Jove, Watson! I've got it!' he cried. 'Take your hat! Come with me!' He hurried at his top speed down Baker Street and along Oxford Street, until we had almost reached Regent Circus. Here on the left hand there stands a shop window filled with photographs of the celebrities and beauties of the day. Holmes's eyes fixed themselves upon one of them, and following his gaze I saw the picture of a regal and stately lady in Court dress, with a high diamond tiara upon her noble head. I looked at that delicately curved nose, at the marked eyebrows, at the straight mouth, and the strong little chin beneath it. Then I caught my breath as I read the time-honoured title of the great nobleman and statesman whose wife she had been. My eyes met those of Holmes, and he put his finger to his lips as we turned away from the window.

Black Peter

I have never known my friend to be in better form, both mental and physical, than in the year '95. His increasing fame had brought with it an immense practice, and I should be guilty of an indiscretion if I were even to hint at the identity of some of the illustrious clients who crossed our humble threshold in Baker Street. Holmes, however, like all great artists, lived for his art's sake, and, save in the case of the Duke of Holdernesse, I have seldom known him claim any large reward for his inestimable services. So unworldly was he – or so capricious – that he frequently refused his help to the powerful and wealthy where the problem made no appeal to his sympathies, while he would devote weeks of most intense application to the affairs of some humble client whose case presented those strange and dramatic qualities which appealed to his imagination and challenged his ingenuity.

In this memorable year '95 a curious and incongruous succession of cases had engaged his attention, ranging from his famous investigation of the sudden death of Cardinal

Tosca – an inquiry which was carried out by him at the express desire of his Holiness the Pope – down to his arrest of Wilson, the notorious canary-trainer, which removed a plague-spot from the East End of London. Close on the heels of these two famous cases came the tragedy of Woodman's Lee, and the very obscure circumstances which surrounded the death of Captain Peter Carey. No record of the doings of Mr Sherlock Holmes would be complete which did not include some account of this very unusual affair.

During the first week of July my friend had been absent so often and so long from our lodgings that I knew he had something on hand. The fact that several rough-looking men called during that time and inquired for Captain Basil made me understand that Holmes was working somewhere under one of the numerous disguises and names with which he concealed his own formidable identity. He had at least five small refuges in different parts of London in which he was able to change his personality. He said nothing of his business to me, and it was not my habit to force a confidence. The first positive sign which he gave me of the direction which his investigation was taking was an extraordinary one. He had gone out before breakfast, and I had sat down to mine, when he strode into the room, his hat upon his head, and a huge barb-headed spear tucked like an umbrella under his arm.

'Good gracious, Holmes!' I cried. 'You don't mean to

say that you have been walking about London with that thing?'

'I drove to the butcher's and back.'

'The butcher's?'

'And I return with an excellent appetite. There can be no question, my dear Watson, of the value of exercise before breakfast. But I am prepared to bet that you will not guess the form that my exercise has taken.'

'I will not attempt it.'

He chuckled as he poured out the coffee.

'If you could have looked into Allardyce's back shop you would have seen a dead pig swung from a hook in the ceiling, and a gentleman in his shirtsleeves furiously stabbing at it with this weapon. I was that energetic person, and I have satisfied myself that by no exertion of my strength can I transfix the pig with a single blow. Perhaps you would care to try?'

'Not for worlds. But why were you doing this?'

'Because it seemed to me to have an indirect bearing upon the mystery of Woodman's Lee. Ah, Hopkins, I got your wire last night, and I have been expecting you. Come and join us.'

Our visitor was an exceedingly alert man, thirty years of age, dressed in a quiet tweed suit, but retaining the erect bearing of one who was accustomed to official uniform. I recognized him at once as Stanley Hopkins, a young police inspector for whose future Holmes had high hopes, while he in turn professed the admiration and respect of a pupil for the scientific methods of the famous amateur. Hopkins's brow was clouded and he sat down with an air of deep dejection.

'No, thank you, sir. I breakfasted before I came round. I spent the night in town, for I came up yesterday to report.'

'And what had you to report?'

'Failure, sir – absolute failure.'

'You have made no progress?'

'None.'

'Dear me! I must have a look at the matter.'

'I wish to heavens that you would, Mr Holmes. It's my first big chance, and I am at my wits' end. For goodness' sake come down and lend me a hand.'

'Well, well, it happens that I have already read all the available evidence, including the report of the inquest, with some care. By the way, what do you make of that tobacco-pouch found on the scene of the crime? Is there no clue there?'

Hopkins looked surprised.

'It was the man's own pouch, sir. His initials were inside it. And it was of sealskin – and he was an old sealer.'

'But he had no pipe.'

'No, sir, we could find no pipe: indeed, he smoked very little. And yet he might have kept some tobacco for his friends.'

'No doubt. I only mention it because if I had been

handling the case I should have been inclined to make that the starting point of my investigation. However, my friend Dr Watson knows nothing of this matter, and I should be none the worse for hearing the sequence of events once more. Just give us some short sketch of the essentials.'

Stanley Hopkins drew a slip of paper from his pocket.

'I have a few dates here which will give you the career of the dead man, Captain Peter Carey. He was born in '45 – fifty years of age. He was a most daring and successful seal and whale fisher. In 1883 he commanded the steam sealer *Sea Unicorn*, of Dundee. He had then had several successful voyages in succession, and in the following year, 1884, he retired. After that he travelled for some years, and finally he bought a small place called Woodman's Lee, near Forest Row, in Sussex. There he has lived for six years, and there he died just a week ago today.

'There were some most singular points about the man. In ordinary life he was a strict Puritan – a silent, gloomy fellow. His household consisted of his wife, his daughter, aged twenty, and two female servants. These last were continually changing, for it was never a very cheery situation, and sometimes it became past all bearing. The man was an intermittent drunkard, and when he had the fit on him he was a perfect fiend. He has been known to drive his wife and his daughter out of doors in the middle of the night, and flog them through the park until the whole village outside the gates was aroused by their screams.

'He was summoned once for a savage assault upon the old vicar, who had called upon him to remonstrate with him upon his conduct. In short, Mr Holmes, you would go far before you found a more dangerous man than Peter Carey, and I have heard that he bore the same character when he commanded his ship. He was known in the trade as Black Peter, and the name was given him, not only on account of his swarthy features and the colour of his huge beard, but for the humours which were the terror of all around him. I need not say that he was loathed and avoided by every one of his neighbours, and that I have not heard one single word of sorrow about his terrible end.

'You must have read in the account of the inquest about the man's cabin, Mr Holmes; but perhaps your friend here has not heard of it. He had built himself a wooden outhouse – he always called it "the cabin" – a few hundred yards from his house, and it was here that he slept every night. It was a little, single-roomed hut, sixteen feet by ten. He kept the key in his pocket, made his own bed, cleaned it himself, and allowed no other foot to cross the threshold. There are small windows on each side, which were covered by curtains, and never opened. One of these windows was turned towards the high-road, and when the light burned in it at night the folk used to point it out to each other, and wonder what Black Peter was doing in there. That's the window, Mr Holmes, which gave us one of the few bits of positive evidence that came out at the inquest.

‘You remember that a stonemason, named Slater, walking from Forest Row about one o’clock in the morning – two days before the murder – stopped as he passed the grounds and looked at the square of light still shining among the trees. He swears that the shadow of a man’s head turned sideways was clearly visible on the blind, and that this shadow was certainly not that of Peter Carey, whom he knew well. It was that of a bearded man, but the beard was short, and bristled forwards in a way very different from that of the captain. So he says, but he had been two hours in the public-house, and it is some distance from the road to the window. Besides, this refers to the Monday, and the crime was done upon the Wednesday.

‘On the Tuesday Peter Carey was in one of his blackest moods, flushed with drink and as savage as a dangerous wild beast. He roamed about the house, and the women ran for it when they heard him coming. Late in the evening he went down to his own hut. About two o’clock the following morning his daughter, who slept with her window open, heard a most fearful yell from that direction, but it was no unusual thing for him to bawl and shout when he was in drink, so no notice was taken. On rising at seven one of the maids noticed that the door of the hut was open, but so great was the terror which the man caused that it was midday before anyone would venture down to see what had become of him. Peeping into the open door, they saw a sight which sent them flying with white faces into the village.

Within an hour I was on the spot, and had taken over the case.

'Well, I have fairly steady nerves, as you know, Mr Holmes, but I give you my word that I got a shake when I put my head into that little house. It was droning like a harmonium with the flies and bluebottles, and the floor and walls were like a slaughterhouse. He had called it a cabin, and a cabin it was, sure enough, for you would have thought that you were in a ship. There was a bunk at one end, a sea-chest, maps and charts, a picture of the *Sea Unicorn*, a line of log-books on a shelf, all exactly as one would expect to find it in a captain's room. And there in the middle of it was the man himself, his face twisted like a lost soul in torment, and his great brindled beard stuck upwards in his agony. Right through his broad breast a steel harpoon had been driven, and it had sunk deep into the wood of the wall behind him. He was pinned like a beetle on a card. Of course, he was quite dead, and had been so from the instant that he uttered that last yell of agony.

'I know your methods, sir, and I applied them. Before I permitted anything to be moved I examined most carefully the ground outside, and also the floor of the room. There were no footmarks.'

'Meaning that you saw none?'

'I assure you, sir, that there were none.'

'My good Hopkins, I have investigated many crimes, but I have never yet seen one which was committed by a flying creature. As long as the criminal remains upon two legs so long must there be some indentation, some abrasion, some trifling displacement which can be detected by the scientific searcher. It is incredible that this blood-bespattered room contained no trace which could have aided us. I understand, however, from the inquest that there were some objects which you failed to overlook?'

The young inspector winced at my companion's ironical comments.

'I was a fool not to call you in at the time, Mr Holmes. However, that's past praying for now. Yes, there were several objects in the room which called for special attention. One was the harpoon with which the deed was committed. It had been snatched down from a rack on the wall. Two others remained there, and there was a vacant place for the third. On the stock was engraved "SS *Sea Unicorn*, Dundee". This seemed to establish that the crime had been done in a moment of fury, and that the murderer had seized the first weapon which came in his way. The fact that the crime was committed at two in the morning, and yet Peter Carey was fully dressed, suggested that he had an appointment with the murderer, which is borne out by the fact that a bottle of rum and two dirty glasses stood upon the table.'

'Yes,' said Holmes; 'I think that both inferences are permissible. Was there any other spirit but rum in the room?'

'Yes; there was a tantalus containing brandy and whisky

on the sea-chest. It is of no importance to us, however, since the decanters were full and it had therefore not been used.'

'For all that its presence has some significance,' said Holmes. 'However, let us hear some more about the objects which do seem to you to bear upon the case.'

'There was this tobacco-pouch upon the table.'

'What part of the table?'

'It lay in the middle. It was of coarse sealskin – the straight-haired skin, with a leather thong to bind it. Inside was "P. C." on the flap. There was half an ounce of strong ship's tobacco in it.'

'Excellent! What more?'

Stanley Hopkins drew from his pocket a drab-covered notebook. The outside was rough and worn; the leaves were discoloured. On the first page were written the initials 'J. H. N.', and the date '1883'. Holmes laid it on the table and examined it in his minute way, while Hopkins and I gazed over each shoulder. On the second page were printed the letters 'C. P. R.', and then came several sheets of numbers. Another heading was Argentine, another Costa Rica, and another São Paulo, each with pages of signs and figures after it.

'What do you make of these?' asked Holmes.

'They appear to be lists of Stock Exchange securities. I thought that "J. H. N." were the initials of a broker, and that "C. P. R." may have been his client.'

'Try Canadian Pacific Railway,' said Holmes.

Stanley Hopkins swore between his teeth, and struck his thigh with his clenched hand.

'What a fool I have been!' he cried. 'Of course it is as you say. Then "J. H. N." are the only initials we have to solve. I have already examined the old Stock Exchange lists, and I can find no one in 1883 either in the House or among the outside brokers whose initials correspond with these. Yet I feel that the clue is the most important one that I hold. You will admit, Mr Holmes, that there is a possibility that these initials are those of the second person who was present – in other words, of the murderer. I would also urge that the introduction into the case of a document relating to large masses of valuable securities gives us for the first time some indication of a motive for the crime.'

Sherlock Holmes's face showed that he was thoroughly taken aback by this new development.

'I must admit both your points,' said he. 'I confess that the notebook, which did not appear at the inquest, modifies any views which I may have formed. I had come to a theory of the crime in which I can find no place for this. Have you endeavoured to trace any of the securities here mentioned?'

'Inquiries are now being made at the offices, but I fear that the complete register of the stockholders of these South American concerns is in South America, and that some weeks must elapse before we can trace the shares.'

Holmes had been examining the cover of the notebook with his magnifying lens.

'Surely there is some discoloration here,' said he.

'Yes, sir, it is a blood-stain. I told you that I picked the book off the floor.'

'Was the blood-stain above or below?'

'On the side next to the boards.'

'Which proves, of course, that the book was dropped after the crime was committed.'

'Exactly, Mr Holmes. I appreciated that point, and I conjectured that it was dropped by the murderer on his hurried flight. It lay near the door.'

'I suppose that none of these securities have been found among the property of the dead man?'

'No, sir.'

'Have you any reason to suspect robbery?'

'No, sir. Nothing seemed to have been touched.'

'Dear me, it is certainly a very interesting case. Then there was a knife, was there not?'

'A sheath-knife, still in its sheath. It lay at the feet of the dead man. Mrs Carey had identified it as being her husband's property.'

Holmes was lost in thought for some time.

'Well,' said he at last, 'I suppose I shall have to come out and have a look at it.'

Stanley Hopkins gave a cry of joy.

'Thank you, sir. That will indeed be a weight off my mind.'

Holmes shook his finger at the inspector.

'It would have been an easier task a week ago,' said he.

'But even now my visit may not be entirely fruitless. Watson, if you can spare the time, I should be very glad of your company. If you will call a four-wheeler, Hopkins, we shall be ready to start for Forest Row in a quarter of an hour.'

Alighting at the small wayside station, we drove for some miles through the remains of widespread woods, which were once part of that great forest which for so long held the Saxon invaders at bay – the impenetrable 'weald', for sixty years the bulwark of Britain. Vast sections of it have been cleared, for this is the seat of the first ironworks of the country, and the trees have been felled to smelt the ore. Now the richer fields of the North have absorbed the trade, and nothing save these ravaged groves and great scars in the earth show the work of the past. Here in a clearing upon the green slope of a hill stood a long, low stone house, approached by a curving drive running through the fields. Nearer the road, and surrounded on three sides by bushes, was a small outhouse, one window and the door facing in our direction. It was the scene of the murder.

Stanley Hopkins led us first to the house, where he introduced us to a haggard, grey-haired woman, the widow of the murdered man, whose gaunt and deep-lined face, with the furtive look of terror in the depths of her red-rimmed eyes, told of the years of hardship and ill-usage which she had endured. With her was her daughter, a pale, fair-haired girl, whose eyes blazed defiantly at us as she told us that she was glad that her father was dead, and that she blessed the hand which had struck him down. It was a terrible household that Black Peter Carey had made for himself, and it was with a sense of relief that we found ourselves in the sunlight again and making our way along the path which had been worn across the fields by the feet of the dead man.

The outhouse was the simplest of dwellings, wooden-walled, single-roofed, one window beside the door, and one on the farther side. Stanley Hopkins drew the key from his pocket, and had stooped to the lock, when he paused with a look of attention and surprise upon his face.

'Someone has been tampering with it,' he said.

There could be no doubt of the fact. The woodwork was cut, and the scratches showed white through the paint, as if they had been that instant done. Holmes had been examining the window.

'Someone has tried to force this also. Whoever it was has failed to make his way in. He must have been a very poor burglar.'

'This is a most extraordinary thing,' said the inspector; 'I could swear that these marks were not here yesterday evening.'

'Some curious person from the village, perhaps,' I suggested.

'Very unlikely. Few of them would dare to set foot in the grounds, far less try to force their way into the cabin. What do you think of it, Mr Holmes?'

'I think that fortune is very kind to us.'

'You mean that the person will come again?'

'It is very probable. He came expecting to find the door open. He tried to get in with the blade of a very small penknife. He could not manage it. What would he do?'

'Come again next night with a more useful tool.'

'So I should say. It will be our fault if we are not there to receive him. Meanwhile, let me see the inside of the cabin.'

The traces of the tragedy had been removed, but the furniture of the little room still stood as it had been on the night of the crime. For two hours, with the most intense concentration, Holmes examined every object in turn, but his face showed that his quest was not a successful one. Once only he paused in his patient investigation.

'Have you taken anything off this shelf, Hopkins?'

'No; I have moved nothing.'

'Something has been taken. There is less dust in this corner of the shelf than elsewhere. It may have been a book lying on its side. It may have been a box. Well, well, I can do nothing more. Let us walk in these beautiful woods, Watson, and give a few hours to the birds and the flowers. We shall meet you here later, Hopkins, and see if we can come to closer quarters with the gentleman who has paid this visit in the night.'

It was past eleven o'clock when we formed our little ambuscade. Hopkins was for leaving the door of the hut open, but Holmes was of the opinion that this would rouse the suspicions of the stranger. The lock was a perfectly simple one, and only a strong blade was needed to push it back. Holmes also suggested that we should wait, not inside the hut, but outside it among the bushes which grew round the farther window. In this way we should be able to watch our man if he struck a light, and see what his object was in this stealthy nocturnal visit.

It was a long and melancholy vigil, and yet it brought with it something of the thrill which the hunter feels when he lies beside the water-pool and waits for the coming of the thirsty beast of prey. What savage creature was it which might steal upon us out of the darkness? Was it a fierce tiger of crime, which could only be taken fighting hard with flashing fang and claw, or would it prove to be some skulking jackal, dangerous only to the weak and unguarded? In absolute silence we crouched among the bushes, waiting for whatever might come. At first the steps of a few belated villagers, or the sound of voices from the village, lightened our vigil; but one by one these interruptions died away, and an absolute stillness fell upon us; save for the chimes of the distant church, which told us of the progress of the night, and for the rustle and whisper of a fine rain falling amid the foliage which roofed us in.

Half-past two had chimed, and it was the darkest hour which precedes the dawn, when we all started as a low but sharp click came from the direction of the gate. Someone had entered the drive. Again there was a long silence, and

I had begun to fear that it was a false alarm, when a stealthy step was heard upon the other side of the hut, and a moment later a metallic scraping and clicking. The man was trying to force the lock! This time his skill was greater or his tool was better, for there was a sudden snap and the creak of the hinges. Then a match was struck, and next instant the steady light from a candle filled the interior of the hut. Through the gauze curtain our eyes were all riveted upon the scene within.

The nocturnal visitor was a young man, frail and thin, with a black moustache which intensified the deadly pallor of his face. He could not have been much above twenty years of age. I have never seen any human being who appeared to be in such a pitiable fright, for his teeth were visibly chattering, and he was shaking in every limb. He was dressed like a gentleman, in Norfolk jacket and knickerbockers, with a cloth cap upon his head. We watched him staring round with frightened eyes. Then he laid the candle-end upon the table and disappeared from our view into one of the corners. He returned with a large book, one of the log-books which formed a line upon the shelves. Leaning on the table, he rapidly turned over the leaves of this volume until he came to the entry which he sought. Then with an angry gesture of his clenched hand, he closed the book, replaced it in the corner, and put out the light. He had hardly turned to leave the hut when Hopkins's hand was on the fellow's collar, and I heard his loud gasp of terror as he understood that he was taken. The candle was relit, and there was our wretched captive shivering and cowering in the grasp of the detective. He sank down upon the sea-chest, and looked helplessly from one of us to the other.

'Now, my fine fellow,' said Stanley Hopkins, 'who are you, and what do you want here?'

The man pulled himself together and faced us with an effort at self-composure.

'You are detectives, I suppose?' said he. 'You imagine I am connected with the death of Captain Peter Carey. I assure you that I am innocent.'

'We'll see about that,' said Hopkins. 'First of all, what is your name?'

'It is John Hopley Neligan.'

I saw Holmes and Hopkins exchange a quick glance.

'What are you doing here?'

'Can I speak confidentially?'

'No, certainly not.'

'Why should I tell you?'

'If you have no answer it may go badly with you at the trial.'

The young man winced.

'Well, I will tell you,' he said. 'Why should I not? And yet I hate to think of this old scandal gaining a new lease of life. Did you ever hear of Dawson & Neligan?'

I could see from Hopkins's face that he never had; but Holmes was keenly interested.

'You mean the West Country bankers,' said he. 'They failed for a million, ruined half the county families of Cornwall, and Neligan disappeared.'

'Exactly. Neligan was my father.'

At last we were getting something positive, and yet it seemed a long gap between an absconding banker and Captain Peter Carey pinned against the wall with one of his own harpoons. We all listened intently to the young man's words.

'It was my father who was really concerned. Dawson had retired. I was only ten years of age at the time, but I was old enough to feel the shame and horror of it all. It has always been said that my father stole all the securities and fled. It is not true. It was his belief that if he were given time in which to realize them all would be well, and every creditor paid in full. He started in his little yacht for Norway just before the warrant was issued for his arrest. I can remember that last night when he bade farewell to my mother. He left us a list of the securities he was taking, and he swore that he would come back with his honour cleared, and that none who had trusted him would suffer. Well, no word was ever heard from him again. Both the yacht and he vanished utterly. We believed, my mother and I, that he and it, with the securities that he had taken with him, were at the bottom of the sea. We had a faithful friend, however, who is a business man, and it was he who discovered some time ago that some of the securities which my father had with him have reappeared on the London market. You can imagine our amazement. I spent months in trying to trace them, and at last, after many doublings and difficulties, I discovered that the original seller had been Captain Peter Carey, the owner of this hut.

'Naturally I made some inquiries about the man. I found that he had been in command of a whaler which was due to return from the Arctic seas at the very same time when my father was crossing to Norway. The autumn of that year was a stormy one and there was a long succession of southerly gales. My father's yacht may well have been blown to the north, and there met by Captain Peter Carey's ship. If that were so, what had become of my father? In any case, if I could prove from Peter Carey's evidence how these securities came in the market, it would be a proof that my father had not sold them, and that he had no view to personal profit when he took them.

'I came down to Sussex with the intention of seeing the captain, but it was at this moment that his terrible death occurred. I read at the inquest a description of his cabin, in which it stated that the old log-books of his vessel were preserved in it. It struck me that if I could see what occurred in the month of August, 1883, on board the *Sea Unicorn*, I might settle the mystery of my father's fate. I tried last night to get at these log-books, but was unable to open the door. Tonight I tried again, and succeeded; but I find that the pages which deal with that month have been torn from the book. It was at that moment I found myself a prisoner in your hands.'

'Is that all?' asked Hopkins.

'Yes, that is all.' His eyes shifted as he said it.

'You have nothing else to tell us?'

He hesitated.

'No, there is nothing.'

'You have not been here before last night?'

'No.'

'Then how do you account for *that*?' cried Hopkins, as he held up the damning notebook, with the initials of our prisoner on the first leaf, and the blood-stain on the cover.

The wretched man collapsed. He sank his face in his hands and trembled all over.

'Where did you get it?' he groaned. 'I did not know. I thought I had lost it at the hotel.'

'That is enough,' said Hopkins sternly. 'Whatever else you have to say you must say in court. You will walk down with me now to the police station. Well, Mr Holmes, I am very much obliged to you and to your friend for coming down to help me. As it turns out your presence was unnecessary, and I would have brought the case to this successful issue without you; but none the less I am very grateful. Rooms have been reserved for you at the Brambletye Hotel, so we can all walk down to the village together.'

'Well, Watson, what do you think of it?' asked Holmes as we travelled back next morning.

'I can see that you are not satisfied.'

'Oh, yes, my dear Watson. I am perfectly satisfied. At the same time Stanley Hopkins's methods do not commend themselves to me. I am disappointed in Stanley Hopkins. I had hoped for better things from him. One should always look for a possible alternative and provide against it. It is the first rule of criminal investigation.'

'What, then, is the alternative?'

'The line of investigation which I have myself been pursuing. It may give nothing. I cannot tell. But at least I shall follow it to the end.'

Several letters were waiting for Holmes at Baker Street. He snatched one of them up, opened it, and burst out into a triumphant chuckle of laughter.

'Excellent, Watson. The alternative develops. Have you telegraph forms? Just write a couple of messages for me: "Sumner, Shipping Agent, Ratcliff Highway. Send three men on, to arrive ten tomorrow morning. – Basil." That's my name in those parts. The other is "Inspector Stanley Hopkins, 46 Lord Street, Brixton. Come breakfast tomorrow at nine-thirty. Important. Wire if unable to come. – Sherlock Holmes." There, Watson, this infernal case has haunted me for ten days. I hereby banish it completely from my presence. Tomorrow I trust that we shall hear the last of it for ever.'

Sharp at the hour named Inspector Stanley Hopkins appeared, and we sat down together to the excellent breakfast which Mrs Hudson had prepared. The young detective was in high spirits at his success.

'You really think that your solution must be correct?' asked Holmes.

'I could not imagine a more complete case.'

'It did not seem to me conclusive.'

'You astonish me, Mr Holmes. What more could one ask for?'

'Does your explanation cover every point?'

'Undoubtedly. I find that young Neligan arrived at the Brambletye Hotel on the very day of the crime. He came on the pretence of playing golf. His room was on the ground floor, and he could get out when he liked. That very night he went down to Woodman's Lee, saw Peter Carey at the hut, quarrelled with him, and killed him with the harpoon. Then, horrified by what he had done, he fled out of the hut, dropping the notebook which he had brought with him in order to question Peter Carey about these different securities. You may have observed that some of them were marked with ticks, and the others – the great majority – were not. Those which are ticked have been traced on the London market; but the others presumably were still in the possession of Carey, and young Neligan, according to his own account, was anxious to recover them in order to do the right thing by his father's creditors. After his flight he did not dare to approach the hut again for some time; but at last he forced himself to do so in order to obtain the information which he needed. Surely that is all simple and obvious?'

Holmes smiled and shook his head.

'It seems to me to have only one drawback, Hopkins, and that is that it is intrinsically impossible. Have you tried to drive a harpoon through a body? No? Tut, tut, my dear sir, you must really pay attention to these details. My friend Watson could tell you that I spent a whole morning in that exercise. It is no easy matter, and requires a strong and practised arm. But this blow was delivered with such violence that the head of the weapon sank deep into the wall. Do you imagine that this anaemic youth was capable of so frightful an assault? Is he the man who hob-nobbed in rum and water with Black Peter in the dead of the night? Was it his profile that was seen on the blind two nights before? No, no, Hopkins; it is another and a more formidable person for whom we must seek.'

The detective's face had grown longer and longer during Holmes's speech. His hopes and his ambitions were all crumbling about him. But he would not abandon his position without a struggle.

'You can't deny that Neligan was present that night, Mr Holmes. The book will prove that. I fancy that I have evidence enough to satisfy a jury, even if you are able to pick a hole in it. Besides, Mr Holmes, I have laid my hand upon *my* man. As to this terrible person of yours, where is he?'

‘I rather fancy that he is on the stair,’ said Holmes serenely. ‘I think, Watson, that you would do well to put that revolver where you can reach it.’ He rose, and laid a written paper upon a side-table. ‘Now we are ready,’ said he.

There had been some talking in gruff voices outside, and now Mrs Hudson opened the door to say that there were three men inquiring for Captain Basil.

‘Show them in one by one,’ said Holmes.

The first who entered was a little ribston-pippin of a man, with ruddy cheeks and fluffy white side-whiskers. Holmes had drawn a letter from his pocket.

‘What name?’ he asked.

‘James Lancaster.’

‘I am sorry, Lancaster, but the berth is full. Here is half a sovereign for your trouble. Just step into this room and wait there for a few minutes.’

The second man was a long, dried-up creature, with lank hair and sallow cheeks. His name was Hugh Pattins. He also received his dismissal, his half-sovereign, and the order to wait.

The third applicant was a man of remarkable appearance. A fierce, bulldog face was framed in a tangle of hair and beard, and two bold dark eyes gleamed behind the cover of thick, tufted, over-hung eyebrows. He saluted and stood sailor-fashion, turning his cap round in his hands.

‘Your name?’ asked Holmes.

‘Patrick Cairns.’

‘Harpooner?’

‘Yes, sir. Twenty-six voyages.’

‘Dundee, I suppose?’

‘Yes, sir.’

‘And ready to start with an exploring ship?’

‘Yes, sir.’

‘What wages?’

‘Eight pounds a month.’

‘Could you start at once?’

‘As soon as I get my kit.’

‘Have you your papers?’

‘Yes, sir.’ He took a sheaf of worn and greasy forms from his pocket. Holmes glanced over them and returned them.

‘You are just the man I want,’ said he. ‘Here’s the agreement on the side-table. If you sign it the whole matter will be settled.’

The seaman lurched across the room and took up the pen.

‘Shall I sign here?’ he asked, stooping over the table.

Holmes leaned over his shoulder and passed both hands over his neck.

‘This will do,’ said he.

I heard a click of steel and a bellow like an enraged bull. The next instant Holmes and the seaman were rolling on the ground together. He was a man of such gigantic strength that, even with the handcuffs which Holmes had so deftly fastened upon his wrist, he would have quickly overpowered my friend had Hopkins and I not rushed to his rescue. Only when I pressed the cold muzzle of the revolver to his temple did he at last understand that resistance was vain. We lashed his ankles with cord and rose breathless from the struggle.

'I must really apologize, Hopkins,' said Sherlock Holmes; 'I fear that the scrambled eggs are cold. However, you will enjoy the rest of your breakfast all the better, will you not, for the thought that you have brought your case to a triumphant conclusion?'

Stanley Hopkins was speechless with amazement.

'I don't know what to say, Mr Holmes,' he blurted out at last, with a very red face. 'It seems to me that I have been making a fool of myself from the beginning. I understand now, what I should never have forgotten, that I am the pupil and you are the master. Even now I see what you have done, but I don't know how you did it, or what it signifies.'

'Well, well,' said Holmes good-humouredly. 'We all learn by experience, and your lesson this time is that you should never lose sight of the alternative. You were so absorbed in young Neligan that you could not spare a thought to Patrick Cairns, the true murderer of Peter Carey.'

The hoarse voice of the seaman broke in on our conversation.

'See here, mister,' said he, 'I make no complaint of being man-handled in this fashion, but I would have you call things by their right names. You say I murdered Peter Carey; I say I *killed* Peter Carey, and there's all the difference.

Maybe you don't believe what I say. Maybe you think I am just slinging you a yarn.'

'Not at all,' said Holmes. 'Let us hear what you have to say.'

'It's soon told, and, by the Lord, every word of it is truth. I knew Black Peter, and when he pulled out his knife I whipped a harpoon through him sharp, for I knew that it was him or me. That's how he died. You can call it murder. Anyhow, I'd as soon died with a rope round my neck as with Black Peter's knife in my heart.'

'How came you there?' asked Holmes.

'I'll tell it you from the beginning. Just sit me up a little so I can speak easy. It was in '83 that it happened – August of that year. Peter Carey was master of the *Sea Unicorn*, and I was spare harpooner. We were coming out of the ice-pack on our way home, with head winds and a week's southerly gale, when we picked up a little craft that had been blown north. There was one man on her – a landsman. The crew had thought she would founder, and had made for the Norwegian coast in the dinghy. I guess they were all drowned. Well, we took him on board, this man, and he and the skipper had some long talks in the cabin. All the baggage we took off with him was one tin box. So far as I know the man's name was never mentioned, and on the second night he disappeared as if he had never been. It was given out that he had either thrown himself overboard or fallen overboard in the heavy weather that we were having.

Only one man knew what had happened to him, and that was me, for with my own eyes I saw the skipper tip up his heels and put him over the rail in the middle watch of a dark night, two days before we sighted the Shetland lights.

'Well, I kept my knowledge to myself and waited to see what would come of it. When we got back to Scotland it was easily hushed up, and nobody asked any questions. A stranger died by an accident, and it was nobody's business to inquire. Shortly after Peter Carey gave up the sea, and it was long years before I could find where he was. I guessed that he had done the deed for the sake of what was in that tin box, and that he could afford now to pay me well for keeping my mouth shut.

'I found out where he was through a sailor man that had met him in London, and down I went to squeeze him. The first night he was reasonable enough, and was ready to give me what would make me free of the sea for life. We were to fix it all two nights later. When I came I found him three-parts drunk and in a vile temper. We sat down and we drank and we yarned about old times, but the more he drank the less I liked the look on his face. I spotted that harpoon upon the wall, and I thought I might need it before I was through. Then at last he broke out at me, spitting and cursing, with murder in his eyes and a great clasp-knife in his hand. He had not time to get it from the sheath before I had the harpoon through him. Heavens! what a yell he gave; and his face gets between me and my sleep! I stood there, with his blood splashing round me, and I waited for a bit; but all was quiet, so I took heart once more. I looked round, and there was the tin box on a shelf. I had as much right to it as Peter Carey, anyhow, so I took it with me and left the hut. Like a fool I left my baccy-pouch upon the table.

'Now I'll tell you the queerest part of the whole story. I had hardly got outside the hut when I heard someone coming, and I hid among the bushes. A man came slinking along, went into the hut, gave a cry as if he had seen a ghost, and legged it as hard as he could run until he was out of sight. Who he was or what he wanted is more than I can tell. For my part, I walked ten miles, got a train at Tunbridge Wells, and so reached London, and no one the wiser.

'Well, when I came to examine the box I found there was no money in it, and nothing but papers that I would not dare to sell. I had lost my hold on Black Peter, and was stranded in London without a shilling. There was only my trade left. I saw these advertisements about harpooners and high wages, so I went to the shipping agents, and they sent me here. That's all I know, and I say again that if I killed Black Peter, the law should give me thanks, for I saved them the price of a hempen rope.'

'A very clear statement,' said Holmes, rising and lighting his pipe. 'I think, Hopkins, that you should lose no time in conveying your prisoner to a place of safety. This room is not well adapted for a cell, and Mr Patrick Cairns occupies too large a portion of our carpet.'

'Mr Holmes,' said Hopkins, 'I do not know how to express my gratitude. Even now I do not understand how you attained this result.'

'Simply by having the good fortune to get the right clue from the beginning. It is very possible that if I had known about this notebook it might have led away my thoughts, as it did yours. But all I heard pointed in the one direction. The amazing strength, the skill in the use of the harpoon, the rum and water, the sealskin tobacco-pouch, with the coarse tobacco – all these pointed to a seaman, and one who had been a whaler. I was convinced that the initials "P. C." upon the pouch were a coincidence, and not those of Peter Carey, since he seldom smoked, and no pipe was found in his cabin. You remember that I asked whether whisky and brandy were in the cabin. You said they were. How many landsmen are there who would drink rum when they could get these other spirits? Yes, I was certain it was a seaman.'

'And how did you find him?'

'My dear sir, the problem had become a very simple one. If it were a seaman, it could only be a seaman who had been with him on the *Sea Unicorn*. So far as I could learn; he had sailed in no other ship. I spent three days in wiring to Dundee, and at the end of that time I had ascertained the names of the crew of the *Sea Unicorn* in 1883. When I found Patrick Cairns among the harpooners my research was nearing its end. I argued that the man was probably in

London, and that he would desire to leave the country for a time. I therefore spent some days in the East End, devised an Arctic expedition, put forward tempting terms for harpooners who would serve under Captain Basil – and behold the result!'

'Wonderful!' cried Hopkins. 'Wonderful!'

'You must obtain the release of young Neligan as soon as possible,' said Holmes. 'I confess that I think you owe him some apology. The tin box must be returned to him, but of course, the securities which Peter Carey has sold are lost for ever. There's the cab, Hopkins, and you can remove your man. If you want me for the trial, my address and that of Watson will be somewhere in Norway – I'll send particulars later.'

The Golden Pince-Nez

When I look at the three massive manuscript volumes which contain our work for the year 1894 I confess that it is very difficult for me, out of such a wealth of material, to select the cases which are most interesting in themselves and at the same time most conducive to a display of those peculiar powers for which my friend was famous. As I turn over the pages I see my notes upon the repulsive story of the red leech and the terrible death of Crosby the banker. Here also I find an account of the Addleton tragedy and the singular contents of the ancient British barrow. The famous Smith-Mortimer succession case comes also within this period, and so does the tracking and arrest of Huret, the Boulevard assassin – an exploit which won for Holmes an autograph letter of thanks from the French President and the Order of the Legion of Honour. Each of these would furnish a narrative, but on the whole I am of opinion that none of them unite so many singular points of interest as the episode of Yoxley Old Place, which includes, not only the lamentable death of young Willoughby Smith, but also those subsequent developments which threw so curious a light upon the causes of the crime.

It was a wild, tempestuous night towards the close of November. Holmes and I sat together in silence all the evening, he engaged with a powerful lens deciphering the remains of the original inscription upon a palimpsest, I deep in a recent treatise upon surgery. Outside the wind howled down Baker Street, while the rain beat fiercely against the windows. It was strange there in the very depths of the town, with ten miles of man's handiwork on every side of us, to feel the iron grip of Nature, and to be conscious that to the huge elemental forces all London was no more than the molehills that dot the fields. I walked to the window and looked out on the deserted street. The occasional lamps gleamed on the expanse of muddy road and shining pavement. A single cab was splashing its way from the Oxford Street end.

'Well, Watson, it's as well we have not to turn out tonight,' said Holmes, laying aside his lens and rolling up the palimpsest. 'I've done enough for one sitting. It is trying work for the eyes. So far as I can make out, it is nothing more exciting than an Abbey's accounts dating from the second half of the fifteenth century. Halloa! halloa! halloa! What's this?'

Amid the droning of the wind there had come the stamping of a horse's hoofs and the long grind of a wheel as it rasped against the kerb. The cab which I had seen had pulled up at our door.

'What can he want?' I ejaculated, as a man stepped out of it.

'Want! He wants us. And we, my poor Watson, want overcoats and cravats and goloshes, and every aid that man ever invented to fight the weather. Wait a bit, though! There's the cab off again! There's hope yet. He'd have kept it if he had wanted us to come. Run down, my dear fellow, and open the door, for all virtuous folk have been long in bed.'

When the light of the hall lamp fell upon our midnight visitor, I had no difficulty in recognizing him. It was young Stanley Hopkins, a promising detective, in whose career Holmes had several times shown a very practical interest.

'Is he in?' he asked eagerly.

'Come up, my dear sir,' said Holmes's voice from above. 'I hope you have no designs upon us on such a night as this.'

The detective mounted the stairs, and our lamp gleamed upon his shining waterproof. I helped him out of it, while Holmes knocked a blaze out of the logs in the grate.

'Now, my dear Hopkins, draw up and warm your toes,' said he. 'Here's a cigar, and the doctor has a prescription containing hot water and a lemon which is good medicine on a night like this. It must be something important which has brought you out in such a gale.'

'It is indeed, Mr Holmes. I've had a bustling afternoon,

I promise you. Did you see anything of the Yoxley case in the latest editions?'

'I've seen nothing later than the fifteenth century today.'

'Well, it was only a paragraph, and all wrong at that, so you have not missed anything. I haven't let the grass grow under my feet. It's down in Kent, seven miles from Chatham and three from the railway line. I was wired for at three-fifteen, reached Yoxley Old Place at five, conducted my investigation, was back at Charing Cross by the last train and straight to you by cab.'

'Which means, I suppose, that you are not quite clear about your case?'

'It means that I can make neither head nor tail of it. So far as I can see, it is just as tangled a business as ever I handled, and yet at first it seemed so simple that one couldn't go wrong. There's no motive, Mr Holmes. That's what bothers me – I can't put my hand on a motive. Here's a man dead – there's no denying that – but, so far as I can see, no reason on earth why anyone should wish him harm.'

Holmes lit his cigar and leaned back in his chair.

'Let us hear about it,' said he.

'I've got my facts pretty clear,' said Stanley Hopkins. 'All I want now is to know what they all mean. The story, so far as I can make it out, is like this. Some years ago this country house, Yoxley Old Place, was taken by an elderly man, who gave the name of Professor Coram. He was an invalid, keeping his bed half the time, and the other half hobbling round the house with a stick, or being pushed about the grounds by the gardener in a bathchair. He was well liked by the few neighbours who called upon him, and he has the reputation down there of being a very learned man. His household used to consist of an elderly housekeeper, Mrs Marker, and of a maid, Susan Tarlton. These have both been with him since his arrival, and they seem to be women of excellent character. The professor is writing a learned book, and he found it necessary about a year ago to engage a secretary. The first two that he tried were not successes; but the third, Mr Willoughby Smith, a very young man straight from the University, seems to have been just what his employer wanted. His work consisted in writing all the morning to the professor's dictation, and he usually spent the evening in hunting up references and passages which bore upon the next day's work. This Willoughby Smith has nothing against him either as a boy at Uppingham or as a young man at Cambridge. I have seen his testimonials, and from the first he was a decent, quiet, hard-working fellow, with no weak spot in him at all. And yet this is the lad who has met his death this morning in the professor's study under circumstances which can point only to murder.'

The wind howled and screamed at the windows. Holmes and I drew closer to the fire while the young inspector slowly and point by point developed his singular narrative.

'If you were to search all England,' said he, 'I don't suppose you could find a household more self-contained or free from outside influences. Whole weeks would pass and not one of them go past the garden gate. The professor was buried in his work and existed for nothing else. Young Smith knew nobody in the neighbourhood, and lived very much as his employer did. The women had nothing to take them from the house. Mortimer, the gardener, who wheels the bathchair, is an Army pensioner – an old Crimean man of excellent character. He does not live in the house, but in a three-roomed cottage at the other end of the garden. Those are the only people that you would find within the grounds of Yoxley Old Place. At the same time, the gate of the garden is a hundred yards from the main London to Chatham road. It opens with a latch, and there is nothing to prevent anyone from walking in.

'Now I will give you the evidence of Susan Tarlton, who is the only person who can say anything positive about the matter. It was in the forenoon, between eleven and twelve. She was engaged at the moment in hanging some curtains in the upstairs front bedroom. Professor Coram was still in bed, for when the weather is bad he seldom rises before midday. The housekeeper was busied with some work in the back of the house. Willoughby Smith had been in his bedroom, which he uses as a sitting-room; but the maid heard him at that moment pass along the passage and descend to the study immediately below her. She did not see him, but she says that she could not be mistaken in his quick, firm tread. She did not hear the study door close, but a minute or so later there was a dreadful cry in the room below. It was a wild, hoarse scream, so strange and unnatural that it might have come either from a man or a woman. At the same instant there was a heavy thud, which shook the whole house, and then all was silence. The maid stood petrified for a moment, and then, recovering her courage, she ran downstairs. The study door was shut, and she opened it. Inside young Mr Willoughby Smith was stretched upon the floor. At first she could see no injury, but as she tried to raise him she saw that blood was pouring from the under side of his neck. It was pierced by a very small but very deep wound, which had divided the carotid artery. The instrument with which the injury had been inflicted lay upon the carpet beside him. It was one of those small sealing-wax knives to be found on old-fashioned writing-tables, with an ivory handle and a stiff blade. It was part of the fittings of the professor's own desk.

'At first the maid thought that young Smith was already dead, but on pouring some water from the carafe over his forehead, he opened his eyes for an instant. "The professor," he murmured – "it was she." The maid is prepared to swear that those were the exact words. He tried desperately to say something else, and he held his right hand up in the air. Then he fell back dead.

'In the meantime the housekeeper had also arrived upon the scene, but she was just too late to catch the young man's dying words. Leaving Susan with the body, she hurried to the professor's room. He was sitting up in bed, horribly agitated, for he had heard enough to convince him that something terrible had occurred. Mrs Marker is prepared to swear that the professor was still in his night clothes, and, indeed, it was impossible for him to dress without the help of Mortimer, whose orders were to come at twelve o'clock. The professor declares that he heard the distant cry, but that he knows nothing more. He can give no explanation of the young man's last words, "The professor – it was she," but imagines that they were the outcome of delirium. He believes that Willoughby Smith had not an enemy in the world, and can give no reason for the crime. His first action was to send Mortimer, the gardener, for the local police. A little later the chief constable sent for me. Nothing was moved before I got there, and strict orders were given that no one should walk upon the paths leading to the house. It was a splendid chance of putting your theories into practice, Mr Sherlock Holmes. There was really nothing wanting.'

'Except Mr Sherlock Holmes!' said my companion, with a somewhat bitter smile. 'Well, let us hear about it. What sort of job did you make of it?'

'I must ask you first, Mr Holmes, to glance at this rough plan, which will give you a general idea of the position of the professor's study and the various points of the case. It will help you in following my investigations.'

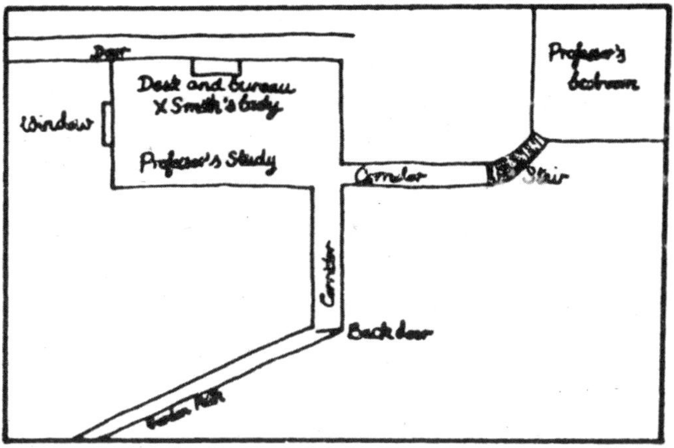

He unfolded the rough chart, which I here reproduce, and he laid it across Holmes's knee. I rose, and, standing behind Holmes, I studied it over his shoulder.

'It is very rough of course, and it only deals with the points which seem to me to be essential. All the rest you will see later for yourself. Now, first of all, presuming that the assassin entered the house, how did he or she come in? Undoubtedly by the garden path and the back door, from which there is direct access to the study. Any other way would have been exceedingly complicated. The escape must also have been made along that line, for of the two other exits from the room one was blocked by Susan as she ran downstairs, and the other leads straight to the professor's bedroom. I therefore directed my attention at once to the garden path, which was saturated with recent rain and would certainly show any footmarks.

'My examination showed me that I was dealing with a cautious and expert criminal. No footmarks were to be found on the path. There could be no question, however, that someone had passed along the grass border which lines the path, and that he had done so in order to avoid leaving a track. I could not find anything in the nature of a distinct impression, but the grass was trodden down and someone had undoubtedly passed. It could only have been the murderer since neither the gardener nor anyone else had been there that morning, and the rain had only begun during the night.'

'One moment,' said Holmes. 'Where does this path lead to?'

'To the road.'

'How long is it?'

'A hundred yards or so.'

'At the point where the path passes through the gate you could surely pick up the tracks?'

'Unfortunately the path was tiled at that point.'

'Well, on the road itself?'

'No; it was all trodden into mire.'

'Tut-tut! Well, then, these tracks upon the grass – were they coming or going?'

'It was impossible to say. There was never any outline.'

'A large foot or a small?'

'You could not distinguish.'

Holmes gave an ejaculation of impatience. 'It has been

pouring rain and blowing a hurricane ever since,' said he. 'It will be harder to read now than the palimpsest. Well, well, it can't be helped. What did you do, Hopkins, after you had made certain that you had made certain of nothing?'

'I think I made certain of a good deal, Mr Holmes. I knew that someone had entered the house cautiously from without. I next examined the corridor. It is lined with coconut matting, and had taken no impression of any kind. This brought me into the study itself. It is a scantily furnished room. The main article is a large writing-table with a fixed bureau. This bureau consists of a double column of drawers with a central small cupboard between them. The drawers were open, the cupboard locked. The drawers, it seems, were always open, and nothing of value was kept in them. There were some papers of importance in the cupboard, but there were no signs that this had been tampered with, and the professor assures me that nothing was missing. It is certain that no robbery had been committed.

'I come now to the body of the young man. It was found near the bureau, and just to the left of it, as marked upon that chart. The stab was on the right side of the neck and from behind forwards, so that it is almost impossible that it could have been self-inflicted.'

'Unless he fell upon the knife,' said Holmes.

'Exactly. The idea crossed my mind. But we found the knife some feet away from the body, so that seems impossible. Then, of course, there are the man's own dying words. And, finally, there was this very important piece of evidence which was found clasped in the dead man's right hand.'

From his pocket Stanley Hopkins drew a small paper packet. He unfolded it, and disclosed a golden pince-nez, with two broken ends of black silk cord dangling from the end of it. 'Willoughby Smith had excellent sight,' he added. 'There can be no question that this was snatched from the face or the person of the assassin.'

Sherlock Holmes took the glasses into his hand and examined them with the utmost attention and interest. He held them on his nose, endeavoured to read through them, went to the window and stared up the street with them, looked at them most minutely in the full light of the lamp, and finally, with a chuckle, seated himself at the table and wrote a few lines upon a sheet of paper, which he tossed across to Stanley Hopkins.

'That's the best I can do for you,' said he. 'It may prove to be of some use.'

The astonished detective read the note aloud. It ran as follows:

> Wanted, a woman of good address, attired like a lady. She has a remarkably thick nose, with eyes which are set close upon either side of it. She has a puckered forehead, a peering expression and probably rounded shoulders. There are indications that she has had

> recourse to an optician at least twice during the last few months. As her glasses are of remarkable strength, and as opticians are not very numerous, there should be no difficulty in tracing her.

Holmes smiled at the astonishment of Hopkins, which must have been reflected upon my features.

'Surely my deductions are simplicity itself,' said he. 'It would be difficult to name any articles which afford a finer field for inference than a pair of glasses, especially so remarkable a pair as these. That they belong to a woman I infer from their delicacy, and also, of course, from the last words of the dying man. As to her being a person of refinement and well dressed, they are, as you perceive, handsomely mounted in solid gold, and it is inconceivable that anyone who wore such glasses could be slatternly in other respects. You will find that the clips are too wide for your nose, showing that the lady's nose was very broad at the base. This sort of nose is usually a short and coarse one, but there are a sufficient number of exceptions to prevent me from being dogmatic or from insisting upon this point in my description. My own face is a narrow one, and yet I find that I cannot get my eyes into the centre, or near the centre, of these glasses. Therefore, the lady's eyes are set very near to the sides of the nose. You will perceive, Watson, that the glasses are concave and of unusual strength. A lady whose vision has been so extremely contracted all her life is sure to have the physical characteristics of such vision, which are seen in the forehead, the eyelids, and the shoulders.'

'Yes,' I said, 'I can follow each of your arguments. I confess, however, that I am unable to understand how you arrive at the double visit to the optician.'

Holmes took the glasses into his hand.

'You will perceive,' he said, 'that the clips are lined with tiny bands of cork to soften the pressure upon the nose. One of these is discoloured and worn to some slight extent, but the other is new. Evidently one has fallen off and been replaced. I should judge that the older of them has not been there more than a few months. They exactly correspond, so I gather that the lady went back to the same establishment for the second.'

'By George, it's marvellous!' cried Hopkins, in an ecstasy of admiration. 'To think that I had all that evidence in my hand and never knew it! I had intended, however, to go the round of the London opticians.'

'Of course you would. Meanwhile, have you anything more to tell us about the case?'

'Nothing, Mr Holmes. I think that you know as much as I do now – probably more. We have had inquiries made as to any stranger seen on the country roads or at the railway station. We have heard of none. What beats me is the utter want of all object in the crime. Not a ghost of a motive can anyone suggest.'

'Ah! there I am not in a position to help you. But I suppose you want us to come out tomorrow?'

'If it is not asking too much, Mr Holmes. There's a train from Charing Cross to Chatham at six in the morning, and we should be at Yoxley Old Place between eight and nine.'

'Then we shall take it. Your case has certainly some features of great interest, and I shall be delighted to look into it. Well, it's nearly one, and we had best get a few hours' sleep. I dare say you can manage all right on the sofa in front of the fire. I'll light my spirit-lamp and give you a cup of coffee before we start.'

The gale had blown itself out next day, but it was a bitter morning when we started upon our journey. We saw the cold winter sun rise over the dreary marshes of the Thames and the long, sullen reaches of the river, which I shall ever associate with our pursuit of the Andaman Islander in the earlier days of our career. After a long and weary journey we alighted at a small station some miles from Chatham. While a horse was being put into a trap at the local inn we snatched a hurried breakfast and so we were all ready for business when we at last arrived at Yoxley Old Place. A constable met us at the garden gate.

'Well, Wilson, any news?'

'No, sir, nothing.'

'No reports of any stranger seen?'

'No, sir. Down at the station they are certain that no stranger either came or went yesterday.'

'Have you had inquiries made at inns and lodgings?'

'Yes, sir; there is no one that we cannot account for.'

'Well, it's only a reasonable walk to Chatham. Anyone might stay there, or take a train without being observed. This is the garden path of which I spoke, Mr Holmes. I'll pledge my word there was no mark on it yesterday.'

'On which side were the marks on the grass?'

'This side, sir. This narrow margin of grass between the path and the flower-bed. I can't see the traces now, but they were clear to me then.'

'Yes, yes; someone has passed along,' said Holmes, stooping over the grass border. 'Our lady must have picked her steps carefully, must she not, since on the one side she would leave a track on the path, and on the other, an even clearer one on the soft bed?'

'Yes, sir, she must have been a cool hand.'

I saw an intent look pass over Holmes's face.

'You say that she must have come back this way?'

'Yes, sir, there is no other.'

'On this strip of grass?'

'Certainly, Mr Holmes.'

'Hum! It was a very remarkable performance – very remarkable. Well, I think we have exhausted the path. Let us go farther. This garden door is usually kept open, I suppose? Then this visitor had nothing to do but to walk in. The idea of murder was not in her mind, or she would have provided herself with some sort of weapon, instead of having to pick this knife off the writing-table. She advanced along this corridor, leaving no traces upon the coconut matting. Then she found herself in this study. How long was she there? We have no means of judging.'

'Not more than a few minutes, sir. I forgot to tell you that Mrs Marker, the housekeeper, had been in there tidying not very long before – about a quarter of an hour she says.'

'Well, that gives us a limit. Our lady enters this room, and what does she do? She goes over to the writing-table. What for? Not for anything in the drawers. If there had been anything worth her taking it would surely have been locked up. No; it was for something in that wooden bureau. Halloa! what is that scratch upon the face of it? Just hold a match, Watson. Why did you not tell me of this, Hopkins?'

The mark which he was examining began upon the brass-work on the right-hand side of the keyhole, and extended for about four inches, where it had scratched the varnish from the surface.

'I noticed it, Mr Holmes. But you'll always find scratches round a keyhole.'

'This is recent – quite recent. See how the brass shines where it is cut. An old scratch would be the same colour as the surface. Look at it through my lens. There's the varnish, too, like earth on each side of a furrow. Is Mrs Marker there?'

A sad-faced, elderly woman came into the room. 'Did you dust this bureau yesterday morning?'

'Yes, sir.'

'Did you notice this scratch?'

'No, sir, I did not.'

'I am sure you did not, for a duster would have swept away these shreds of varnish. Who has the key of this bureau?'

'The professor keeps it on his watch-chain.'

'Is it a simple key?'

'No, sir; it is a Chubb's key.'

'Very good. Mrs Marker, you can go. Now we are making a little progress. Our lady enters the room, advances to the bureau, and either opens it or tries to do so. While she is thus engaged young Willoughby Smith enters the room. In her hurry to withdraw the key she makes this scratch upon the door. He seizes her, and she, snatching up the nearest object, which happens to be this knife, strikes at him in order to make him let go his hold. The blow is a fatal one. He falls and she escapes, either with or without the object for which she has come. Is Susan the maid there? Could anyone have got away through that door after the time that you heard the cry, Susan?'

'No, sir; it is impossible. Before I got down the stair I'd have seen anyone in the passage. Besides, the door never opened, for I would have heard it.'

'That settles this exit. Then no doubt the lady went out

the way she came. I understand that this other passage leads only to the professor's room. There is no exit that way?'

'No, sir.'

'We shall go down it and make the acquaintance of the professor. Halloa, Hopkins! this is very important, very important indeed. The professor's corridor is also lined with coconut matting.'

'Well, sir, what of that?'

'Don't you see any bearing upon the case? Well, well, I don't insist upon it. No doubt I am wrong. And yet it seems to me to be suggestive. Come with me and introduce me.'

We passed down the passage, which was of the same length as that which led to the garden. At the end was a short flight of steps ending in a door. Our guide knocked, and then ushered us into the professor's bedroom. It was a very large chamber, lined with innumerable volumes, which had overflowed from the shelves and lay in piles in the corners, or were stacked all round at the base of the cases. The bed was in the centre of the room, and in it, propped up with pillows, was the owner of the house. I have seldom seen a more remarkable-looking person. It was a gaunt, aquiline face which was turned towards us, with piercing dark eyes, which lurked in deep hollows under overhung and tufted brows. His hair and beard were white, save that the latter was curiously stained with yellow around his mouth. A cigarette glowed amid the tangle of white hair, and the air of the room was fetid with stale tobacco smoke.

As he held out his hand to Holmes I perceived that it also was stained yellow with nicotine.

'A smoker, Mr Holmes?' said he, speaking well-chosen English with a curious little mincing accent. 'Pray take a cigarette. And you, sir? I can recommend them, for I have them especially prepared by Ionides of Alexandria. He sends me a thousand at a time, and I grieve to say that I have to arrange for a fresh supply every fortnight. Bad, sir, very bad; but an old man has few pleasures. Tobacco and my work – that is all that is left to me.'

Holmes had lit a cigarette, and was shooting little darting glances all over the room.

'Tobacco and my work, but now only tobacco,' the old man exclaimed. 'Alas, what a fatal interruption! Who could have foreseen such a terrible catastrophe? So estimable a young man! I assure you that after a few months' training he was an admirable assistant. What do you think of the matter, Mr Holmes?'

'I have not yet made up my mind.'

'I shall indeed be indebted to you if you can throw a light where all is so dark to us. To a poor bookworm and invalid like myself such a blow is paralysing. I seem to have lost the faculty of thought. But you're a man of action – you are a man of affairs. It is part of the everyday routine of your life. You can preserve your balance in every emergency. We are fortunate indeed in having you at our side.'

Holmes was pacing up and down on one side of the room

whilst the old professor was talking. I observed that he was smoking with extraordinary rapidity. It was evident that he shared our host's liking for the fresh Alexandrian cigarettes.

'Yes, sir, it is a crushing blow,' said the old man. 'That is my *magnum opus* – the pile of papers on the side-table yonder. It is my analysis of the documents found in the Coptic monasteries of Syria and Egypt, a work which will cut deep at the very foundation of revealed religion. With my enfeebled health I do not know whether I shall ever be able to complete it now that my assistant has been taken from me. Dear me, Mr Holmes, why, you are even a quicker smoker than I am myself.'

Holmes smiled.

'I am a connoisseur,' said he, taking another cigarette from the box – his fourth – and lighting it from the stub of that which he had finished. 'I will not trouble you with any lengthy cross-examination, Professor Coram, since I gather that you were in bed at the time of the crime and could know nothing about it. I would only ask this – What do you imagine that this poor fellow meant by his last words; "The professor – it was she?"'

The professor shook his head.

'Susan is a country girl,' said he, 'and you know the incredible stupidity of that class. I fancy that the poor fellow murmured some incoherent, delirious words, and that she twisted them into this meaningless message.'

'I see. You have no explanation yourself of the tragedy?'

'Possibly an accident; possibly – I only breathe it among ourselves – a suicide. Young men have their hidden troubles – some affair of the heart, perhaps, which we have never known. It is a more probable supposition than murder.'

'But the eyeglasses?'

'Ah! I am only a student – a man of dreams. I cannot explain the practical things of life. But still, we are aware, my friend, that love-gages may take strange shapes. By all means take another cigarette. It is a pleasure to see anyone appreciate them so. A fan, a glove, glasses – who knows what article may be carried as a token or treasured when a man puts an end to his life? This gentleman speaks of footsteps on the grass; but, after all, it is easy to be mistaken on such a point. As to the knife, it might well be thrown far from the unfortunate man as he fell. It is possible that I speak as a child, but to me it seems that Willoughby Smith has met his fate by his own hand.'

Holmes seemed struck by the theory thus put forward, and he continued to walk up and down for some time, lost in thought and consuming cigarette after cigarette.

'Tell me, Professor Coram,' he said at last, 'what is in that cupboard in the bureau?'

'Nothing that would help a thief. Family papers, letters from my poor wife, diplomas of Universities which have done me honour. Here is the key. You can look for yourself.'

Holmes picked up the key and looked at it for an instant; then he handed it back.

‘No; I hardly think that it would help me,’ said he. ‘I should prefer to go quietly down to your garden and turn the whole matter over in my head. There is something to be said for the theory of suicide which you have put forward. We must apologize for having intruded upon you, Professor Coram, and I promise that we won’t disturb you until after lunch. At two o’clock we will come again and report to you anything which may have happened in the interval.’

Holmes was curiously distrait, and we walked up and down the garden path for some time in silence.

‘Have you a clue?’ I asked at last.

‘It depends upon those cigarettes that I smoked,’ said he. ‘It is possible that I am utterly mistaken. The cigarettes will show me.’

‘My dear Holmes,’ I exclaimed, ‘how on earth –’

‘Well, well, you may see for yourself. If not, there’s no harm done. Of course, we always have the optician clue to fall back upon, but I take a short cut when I can get it. Ah, here is the good Mrs Marker! Let us enjoy five minutes of instructive conversation with her.’

I may have remarked before that Holmes had, when he liked, a peculiarly ingratiating way with women, and that he very readily established terms of confidence with them. In half the time which he had named he had captured the housekeeper’s goodwill, and was chatting with her as if he had known her for years.

‘Yes, Mr Holmes, it is as you say, sir. He does smoke

something terrible. All day and sometimes all night, sir. I've seen that room of a morning – well, sir, you'd have thought it was a London fog. Poor young Mr Smith, he was a smoker also, but not as bad as the professor. His health – well, I don't know that it's better nor worse for the smoking.'

'Ah,' said Holmes, 'but it kills the appetite.'

'Well, I don't know about that, sir.'

'I suppose the professor eats hardly anything?'

'Well, he is variable. I'll say that for him.'

'I'll wager he took no breakfast this morning, and won't face his lunch after all the cigarettes I saw him consume.'

'Well, you're out there, sir, as it happens, for he ate a remarkably big breakfast this morning. I don't know when I've known him make a better one, and he's ordered a good dish of cutlets for his lunch. I'm surprised myself, for since I came into that room yesterday and saw young Mr Smith lying there on the floor I couldn't bear to look at food. Well, it takes all sorts to make a world, and the professor hasn't let it take his appetite away.'

We loitered the morning away in the garden. Stanley Hopkins had gone down to the village to look into some rumours of a strange woman who had been seen by some children on the Chatham road the previous morning. As to my friend, all his usual energy seemed to have deserted him. I had never known him handle a case in such a half-hearted fashion. Even the news brought back by Hopkins that he had found the children and that they had undoubtedly seen a woman exactly corresponding with Holmes's description, and wearing either spectacles or eye-glasses, failed to rouse any sign of keen interest. He was more attentive when Susan, who waited upon us at lunch, volunteered the information that she believed Mr Smith had been out for a walk yesterday morning, and that he had only returned half an hour before the tragedy occurred. I could not myself see the bearing of this incident, but I clearly perceived that Holmes was weaving it into the general scheme which he had formed in his brain. Suddenly he sprang from his chair, and glanced at his watch. 'Two o'clock, gentlemen,' said he. 'We must go up and have it out with our friend the professor.'

The old man had just finished his lunch, and certainly his empty dish bore evidence to the good appetite with which his housekeeper had credited him. He was, indeed, a weird figure as he turned his white mane and his glowing eyes towards us. The eternal cigarette smouldered in his mouth. He had been dressed and was seated in an armchair by the fire.

'Well, Mr Holmes, have you solved this mystery yet?' He shoved the large tin of cigarettes which stood on a table beside him towards my companion. Holmes stretched out his hand at the same moment, and between them they tipped the box over the edge. For a minute or two we were all on our knees retrieving stray cigarettes from impossible places. When we rose again I observed that Holmes's eyes were shining and his cheeks tinged with colour. Only at a crisis have I seen those battle-signals flying.

'Yes,' said he, 'I have solved it.'

Stanley Hopkins and I stared in amazement. Something like a sneer quivered over the gaunt features of the old professor.

'Indeed! In the garden?'

'No, here.'

'Here! When?'

'This instant.'

'You are surely joking, Mr Sherlock Holmes. You compel me to tell you that this is too serious a matter to be treated in such a fashion.'

'I have forged and tested every link of my chain, Professor Coram, and I am sure that it is sound. What your motives are or what exact part you play in this strange business, I am not yet able to say. In a few minutes I shall probably hear it from your own lips. Meanwhile, I will reconstruct what is past for your benefit, so that you may know the information which I still require.

'A lady yesterday entered your study. She came with the intention of possessing herself of certain documents which were in your bureau. She had a key of her own. I have had an opportunity of examining yours, and I do not find that slight discoloration which the scratch made upon the varnish would have produced. You were not an accessory, therefore, and she came, so far as I can read the evidence, without your knowledge to rob you.'

The professor blew a cloud from his lips.

'This is most interesting and instructive,' said he. 'Have you no more to add? Surely, having traced this lady so far, you can also say what has become of her.'

'I will endeavour to do so. In the first place, she was seized by your Secretary, and stabbed him in order to escape. This catastrophe I am inclined to regard as an unhappy accident, for I am convinced that the lady had no intention of inflicting so grievous an injury. An assassin does not come unarmed. Horrified by what she had done, she rushed wildly away from the scene of the tragedy. Unfortunately for her she had lost her glasses in the scuffle, and as she was extremely short-sighted she was really helpless without them. She ran down a corridor, which she imagined to be that by which she had come – both were lined with coconut matting – and it was only when it was too late that she understood that she had taken the wrong passage and that her retreat was cut off behind her. What was she to do? She could not go back. She could not remain where she was. She must go on. She went on. She mounted a stair, pushed open a door, and found herself in your room.'

The old man sat with his mouth open staring wildly at Holmes. Amazement and fear were stamped upon his expressive features. Now, with an effort, he shrugged his shoulders and burst into insincere laughter.

'All very fine, Mr Holmes,' said he. 'But there is one little flaw in a splendid theory. I was myself in my room, and I never left it during the day.'

'I am aware of that, Professor Coram.'

'And you mean to say that I could lie upon that bed and not be aware that a woman had entered my room?'

'I never said so. You *were* aware of it. You spoke with her. You recognized her. You aided her to escape.'

Again the professor burst into high-keyed laughter. He had risen to his feet, and his eyes glowed like embers.

'You are mad!' he cried. 'You are talking insanely. I helped her to escape? Where is she now?'

'She is there,' said Holmes, and he pointed to a high bookcase in the corner of the room.

I saw the old man throw up his arms, a terrible convulsion passed over his grim face, and he fell back in his chair. At the same instant the bookcase at which Holmes pointed swung round upon a hinge, and a woman rushed out into the room.

'You are right,' she cried, in a strange foreign voice. 'You are right! I am here.'

She was brown with the dust and draped with the cobwebs which had come from the walls of her hiding-place. Her face, too, was streaked with grime, and at the best she could never have been handsome, for she had the exact physical characteristics which Holmes had divined, with, in addition, a long and obstinate chin. What with her natural blindness, and what with the change from dark to light, she stood as one dazed, blinking about her to see where and who we were. And yet, in spite of all these disadvantages, there was a certain nobility in the woman's bearing, a gallantry in the defiant chin and in the upraised head, which compelled something of respect and admiration. Stanley Hopkins had laid his hand upon her arm and claimed her as his prisoner, but she waved him aside gently, and yet with an over-mastering dignity which compelled obedience. The old man lay back in his chair, with a twitching face, and stared at her with brooding eyes.

'Yes, sir, I am your prisoner,' she said. 'From where I stood I could hear everything, and I know that you have learned the truth. I confess it all. It was I who killed the young man. But you are right, you who say that it was an accident. I did not even know that it was a knife which I held in my hand, for in my despair I snatched anything from the table and struck at him to make him let me go. It is the truth that I tell.'

'Madame,' said Holmes, 'I am sure that it is the truth. I fear that you are far from well.'

She had turned a dreadful colour, the more ghastly under the dark dust-streaks upon her face. She seated herself on the side of the bed; then she resumed.

'I have only a little time here,' she said, 'but I would have you to know the whole truth. I am this man's wife. He is not an Englishman. He is a Russian. His name I will not tell.'

For the first time the old man stirred. 'God bless you, Anna!' he cried. 'God bless you!'

She cast a look of the deepest disdain in his direction. 'Why should you cling so hard to that wretched life of yours, Sergius?' said she. 'It has done harm to many and good to none – not even to yourself. However, it is not for me to cause the frail thread to be snapped before God's time. I have enough already upon my soul since I crossed the threshold of this cursed house. But I must speak, or I shall be too late.

'I have said, gentlemen, that I am this man's wife. He was fifty and I a foolish girl of twenty when we married. It was in a city of Russia, a University – I will not name the place.'

'God bless you, Anna!' murmured the old man again.

'We were reformers – revolutionists – Nihilists, you understand. He and I and many more. Then there came a time of trouble, a police officer was killed, many were arrested, evidence was wanted, and in order to save his own life and to earn a great reward my husband betrayed his own wife and his companions. Yes; we were all arrested upon his confession. Some of us found our way to the gallows and some to Siberia. I was among these last, but my term was not for life. My husband came to England with his ill-gotten gains, and has lived in quiet ever since, knowing well that if the Brotherhood knew where he was not a week would pass before justice would be done.'

The old man reached out a trembling hand and helped himself to a cigarette. 'I am in your hands, Anna,' said he. 'You were always good to me.'

'I have not yet told you the height of his villainy!' said she. 'Among our comrades of the Order there was one who was the friend of my heart. He was noble, unselfish, loving – all that my husband was not. He hated violence. We were all guilty – if that is guilt – but he was not. He wrote for ever dissuading me from such a course. These letters would have saved him. So would my diary, in which from day to day I had entered both my feelings towards him and the view which each of us had taken. My husband found and kept both diary and letters. He hid them, and he tried hard to swear away the young man's life. In this he failed, but Alexis was sent a convict to Siberia, where now, at this moment, he works in a salt mine. Think of that, you villain, you villain; now, now, at this very moment, Alexis, a man whose name you are not worthy to speak, works and lives like a slave, and yet I have your life in my hands and I let you go!'

'You were always a noble woman, Anna,' said the old man, puffing at his cigarette.

She had risen, but she fell back again with a little cry of pain.

'I must finish,' she said. 'When my term was over I set myself to get the diary and letters, which if sent to the

Russian Government, would procure my friend's release. I knew that my husband had come to England. After months of searching I discovered where he was. I knew that he still had the diary, for when I was in Siberia I had a letter from him once reproaching me and quoting some passages from its pages. Yet I was sure that with his revengeful nature he would never give it to me of his own free will. I must get it for myself. With this object I engaged an agent from a private detective firm, who entered my husband's house as secretary – it was your second secretary, Sergius, the one who left you so hurriedly. He found that papers were kept in the cupboard, and he got an impression of the key. He would not go farther. He furnished me with a plan of the house, and he told me that in the forenoon the study was always empty, as the secretary was employed up here. So at last I took my courage in both hands and I came down to get the papers for myself. I succeeded, but at what a cost!

'I had just taken the papers and was locking the cupboard when the young man seized me. I had seen him already that morning. He had met me in the road, and I had asked him to tell me where Professor Coram lived, not knowing that he was in his employ.'

'Exactly! Exactly!' said Holmes. 'The secretary came back and told his employer of the woman he had met. Then in his last breath he tried to send a message that it was she – the she whom he had just discussed with him.'

'You must let me speak,' said the woman, in an imperative

voice, and her face contracted as if in pain. 'When he had fallen I rushed from the room, chose the wrong door, and found myself in my husband's room. He spoke of giving me up. I showed him that if he did so his life was in my hands. If he gave me to the law I could give him to the Brotherhood. It was not that I wished to lie for my own sake, but it was that I desired to accomplish my purpose. He knew that I would do what I said – that his own fate was involved in mine. For that reason, and for no other, he shielded me. He thrust me into that dark hiding-place, a relic of old days, known only to himself. He took his meals in his own room, and so was able to give me part of his food. It was agreed that when the police left the house I should slip away by night and come back no more. But in some way you have read our plans.' She tore from the bosom of her dress a small packet. 'These are my last words,' said she; 'here is the packet which will save Alexis. I confide it to your honour and to your love of justice. Take it! You will deliver it at the Russian Embassy. Now I have done my duty, and –'

'Stop her!' cried Holmes. He had bounded across the room and had wrenched a small phial from her hand.

'Too late!' she said, sinking back on the bed. 'Too late! I took the poison before I left my hiding-place. My head swims! I am going! I charge you, sir, to remember the packet.'

*

'A simple case, and yet in some ways an instructive one,' Holmes remarked as we travelled back to town. 'It hinged from the outset upon the pince-nez. But for the fortunate chance of the dying man having seized these I am not sure that we could ever have reached our solution. It was clear to me from the strength of the glasses that the wearer must have been very blind and helpless when deprived of them. When you asked me to believe that she walked along a narrow strip of grass without once making a false step I remarked, as you may remember, that it was a noteworthy performance. In my mind, I set it down as an impossible performance, save in the unlikely case that she had a second pair of glasses. I was forced, therefore, to seriously consider the hypothesis that she had remained within the house. On perceiving the similarity of the two corridors, it became clear that she might very easily have made such a mistake, and in that case it was evident that she must have entered the professor's room. I was keenly on the alert, therefore, for whatever would bear out this supposition, and I examined the room narrowly for anything in the shape of a hiding-place. The carpet seemed continuous and firmly nailed, so I dismissed the idea of a trap-door. There might well be a recess behind the books. As you are aware, such devices are common in old libraries. I observed that books were piled on the floor at all other points, but that one bookcase was left clear. This, then, might be the door. I could see no marks to guide me, but the carpet was of a dun colour, which lends itself very well to examination. I therefore smoked a great number of those excellent cigarettes, and I dropped the ash all over the space in front of the suspected bookcase. It was a simple trick, but exceedingly effective. I then went downstairs, and I ascertained in your presence, Watson, without your quite perceiving the drift of my remarks, that Professor Coram's consumption of food had increased – as one would expect when he is supplying a second person. We then ascended to the room again, when, by upsetting the cigarette-box, I obtained a very excellent view of the floor, and was able to see quite clearly, from the traces upon the cigarette ash, that the prisoner had, in our absence, come out from her retreat. Well, Hopkins, here we are at Charing Cross, and I congratulate you on having brought your case to a successful conclusion. You are going to headquarters, no doubt. I think, Watson, you and I will drive together to the Russian Embassy.'

The Priory School

We have had some dramatic entrances and exits upon our small stage at Baker Street, but I cannot recollect anything more sudden and startling than the first appearance of Dr Thorneycroft Huxtable, MA, PH.D., etc. His card, which seemed too small to carry the weight of his academic distinctions, preceded him by a few seconds, and then he entered himself – so large, so pompous, and so dignified that he was the very embodiment of self-possession and solidity. And yet his first action when the door had closed behind him was to stagger against the table, whence he slipped down upon the floor, and there was that majestic figure prostrate and insensible upon our bearskin hearthrug.

We had sprung to our feet, and for a few moments we stared in silent amazement at this ponderous piece of wreckage, which told of some sudden and fatal storm far out on the ocean of life. Then Holmes hurried with a cushion for his head, and I with brandy for his lips. The heavy white face was seamed with lines of trouble, the hanging pouches under the closed eyes were leaden in colour, the loose mouth drooped dolorously at the corners, the rolling chins were unshaven. Collar and shirt bore the grime of a long journey, and the hair bristled unkempt from the well-shaped head. It was a sorely stricken man who lay before us.

'What is it, Watson?' asked Holmes.

'Absolute exhaustion – possibly mere hunger and fatigue,' said I, with my finger on the thready pulse, where the stream of life trickled thin and small.

'Return ticket from Mackleton, in the North of England,' said Holmes, drawing it from the watch-pocket. 'It is not twelve o'clock yet. He has certainly been an early starter.'

The puckered eyelids had begun to quiver, and now a pair of vacant grey eyes looked up at us. An instant later the man had scrambled on to his feet, his face crimson with shame.

'Forgive this weakness, Mr Holmes; I have been a little overwrought. Thank you, if I might have a glass of milk and a biscuit I have no doubt that I should be better. I came personally, Mr Holmes, in order to ensure that you would return with me. I feared that no telegram would convince you of the absolute urgency of the case.'

'When you are quite restored –'

'I am quite well again. I cannot imagine how I came to be so weak. I wish you, Mr Holmes, to come to Mackleton with me by the next train.'

My friend shook his head.

'My colleague, Dr Watson, could tell you that we are very busy at present. I am retained in this case of the Ferrers Documents, and the Abergavenny murder is coming up for trial. Only a very important issue could call me from London at present.'

'Important!' Our visitor threw up his hands. 'Have you heard nothing of the abduction of the only son of the Duke of Holdernesse?'

'What! the late Cabinet Minister?'

'Exactly. We had tried to keep it out of the papers, but there was some rumour in the *Globe* last night. I thought it might have reached your ears.'

Holmes shot out his long, thin arm and picked out Volume 'H' in his encyclopaedia of reference.

'"Holdernesse, sixth Duke, KG, PC" – half the alphabet! "Baron Beverley, Earl of Carston" – dear me, what a list! "Lord-Lieutenant of Hallamshire since 1900. Married Edith, daughter of Sir Charles Appledore, 1888. Heir and only child, Lord Saltire. Owns about two hundred and fifty thousand acres. Minerals in Lancashire and Wales. Address: Carston House Terrace; Holdernesse Hall, Hallamshire; Carston Castle, Bangor, Wales. Lord of the Admiralty, 1872. Chief Secretary of State for –" Well, well, this man is certainly one of the greatest subjects of the Crown!'

'The greatest and perhaps the wealthiest. I am aware, Mr Holmes, that you take a very high line in professional matters, and that you are prepared to work for the work's sake. I may tell you, however, that his Grace has already intimated that a cheque for five thousand pounds will be handed over to the person who can tell him where his son is, and another thousand to him who can name the man, or men, who have taken him.'

'It is a princely offer,' said Holmes. 'Watson, I think that we shall accompany Dr Huxtable back to the North of England. And now, Dr Huxtable, when you have consumed that milk you will kindly tell me what has happened, when it happened, how it happened, and, finally, what Dr Thorneycroft Huxtable, of the Priory School, near Mackleton, has to do with the matter, and why he comes three days after an event – the state of your chin gives the date – to ask for my humble services.'

Our visitor had consumed his milk and biscuits. The light had come back to his eyes and the colour to his cheeks as he set himself with great vigour and lucidity to explain the situation.

'I must inform you, gentlemen, that the Priory is a preparatory school, of which I am the founder and principal. *Huxtable's Sidelights on Horace* may possibly recall my name to your memories. The Priory is, without exception, the best and most select preparatory school in England. Lord Leverstoke, the Earl of Blackwater, Sir Cathcart Soames – they all have entrusted their sons to me. But I felt that my school had reached its zenith when, three weeks ago, the Duke of Holdernesse sent Mr James Wilder, his secretary, with the intimation that young Lord Saltire, ten years old, his only son and heir, was about to be committed to my charge. Little did I think that this would be the prelude to the most crushing misfortune of my life.

'On May 1st the boy arrived, that being the beginning of the summer term. He was a charming youth, and he soon fell into our ways. I may tell you – I trust that I am not indiscreet; half-confidences are absurd in such a case – that he was not entirely happy at home. It is an open secret that the duke's married life had not been a peaceful one, and the matter had ended in a separation by mutual consent, the duchess taking up her residence in the South of France. This had occurred very shortly before, and the boy's sympathies are known to have been strongly with his mother. He moped after her departure from Holdernesse Hall, and it was for this reason that the duke desired to send him to my establishment. In a fortnight the boy was quite at home with us, and was apparently absolutely happy.

'He was last seen on the night of May 13th – that is, the night of last Monday. His room was on the second floor, and was approached through another larger room in which two boys were sleeping. These boys saw and heard nothing, so that it is certain that young Saltire did not pass out that way. His window was open, and there is a stout ivy plant leading to the ground. We could trace no footmarks below, but it is sure that this is the only possible exit.

'His absence was discovered at seven o'clock on Tuesday morning. His bed had been slept in. He had dressed himself fully before going off in his usual school suit of black Eton jacket and dark grey trousers. There were no signs that anyone had entered the room, and it is quite certain that anything in the nature of cries or a struggle would have been heard, since Caunter, the elder boy in the inner room, is a very light sleeper.

'When Lord Saltire's disappearance was discovered I at once called a roll of the whole establishment – boys, masters, and servants. It was then that we ascertained that Lord Saltire had not been alone in his flight. Heidegger, the German master, was missing. His room was on the second floor, at the farther end of the building, facing the same way as Lord Saltire's. His bed had also been slept in; but he had apparently gone away partly dressed, since his shirt and socks were lying on the floor. He had undoubtedly let himself down by the ivy, for we could see the marks of his feet where he had landed on the lawn. His bicycle was kept in a small shed beside this lawn, and it also was gone.

'He had been with me for two years, and came with the best references; but he was a silent, morose man, not very popular with either masters or boys. No trace could be found of the fugitives, and now on Thursday morning we are as ignorant as we were on Tuesday. Inquiry was, of course, made at once at Holdernesse Hall. It is only a few miles away, and we imagined that in some sudden attack of homesickness he had gone back to his father; but nothing had been heard of him. The duke is greatly agitated – and as to me, you have seen yourselves the state of nervous prostration to which the suspense and the responsibility have reduced me. Mr Holmes, if ever you put forward your full powers, I implore you to do so now, for never in your life could you have a case which is more worthy of them.'

Sherlock Holmes had listened with the utmost intentness to the statement of the unhappy schoolmaster. His drawn brows and the deep furrow between them showed that he needed no exhortation to concentrate all his attention upon a problem which, apart from the tremendous interests involved, must appeal so directly to his love of the complex and the unusual. He now drew out his notebook and jotted down one or two memoranda.

'You have been very remiss in not coming to me sooner,' said he severely. 'You start me on my investigation with a very serious handicap. It is inconceivable, for example, that this ivy and this lawn would have yielded nothing to an expert observer.'

'I am not to blame, Mr Holmes. His Grace was extremely desirous to avoid all public scandal. He was afraid of his family unhappiness being dragged before the world. He has a deep horror of anything of the kind.'

'But there has been some official investigation?'

'Yes, sir, and it has proved most disappointing. An

apparent clue was at once obtained, since a boy and a young man were reported to have been seen leaving a neighbouring station by an early train. Only last night we had news that the couple had been hunted down in Liverpool, and they prove to have no connection whatever with the matter in hand. Then it was that in my despair and disappointment, after a sleepless night, I came straight to you by the early train.'

'I suppose the local investigation was relaxed while this false clue was being followed up?'

'It was entirely dropped.'

'So that three days have been wasted. The affair has been most deplorably handled.'

'I feel it, and admit it.'

'And yet the problem should be capable of ultimate solution. I shall be very happy to look into it. Have you been able to trace any connection between the missing boy and this German master?'

'None at all.'

'Was he in the master's class?'

'No; he never exchanged a word with him, so far as I know.'

'That is certainly very singular. Had the boy a bicycle?'

'No.'

'Was any other bicycle missing?'

'No.'

'Is that certain?'

'Quite.'

'Well, now, you do not mean to seriously suggest that this German rode off upon a bicycle in the dead of the night bearing the boy in his arms?'

'Certainly not.'

'Then what is the theory in your mind?'

'The bicycle may have been a blind. It may have been hidden somewhere, and the pair gone off on foot.'

'Quite so; but it seems rather an absurd blind, does it not? Were there other bicycles in this shed?'

'Several.'

'Would he not have hidden a *couple* had he desired to give the idea that they had gone off upon them?'

'I suppose he would.'

'Of course he would. The blind theory won't do. But the incident is an admirable starting-point for an investigation. After all, a bicycle is not an easy thing to conceal or to destroy. One other question. Did anyone call to see the boy on the day before he disappeared?'

'No.'

'Did he get any letters?'

'Yes; one letter.'

'From whom?'

'From his father.'

'Do you open the boys' letters?'

'No.'

'How do you know it was from the father?'

'The coat-of-arms was on the envelope, and it was addressed in the duke's peculiar stiff hand. Besides, the duke remembers having written.'

'When had he a letter before that?'

'Not for several days.'

'Had he ever had one from France?'

'No; never.'

'You see the point of my questions, of course. Either the boy was carried off by force or he went of his own free will. In the latter case you would expect that some prompting from outside would be needed to make so young a lad do such a thing. If he has had no visitors, that prompting must have come in letters. Hence I try to find out who were his correspondents.'

'I fear I cannot help much. His only correspondent, so far as I know, was his own father.'

'Who wrote to him on the very day of his disappearance. Were the relations between father and son very friendly?'

'His Grace is never very friendly with anyone. He is completely immersed in large public questions, and is rather inaccessible to all ordinary emotions. But he was always kind to the boy in his own way.'

'But the sympathies of the latter were with the mother?'

'Yes.'

'Did he say so?'

'No.'

'The duke, then?'

'Good heavens, no!'

'Then how could you know?'

'I have had some confidential talk with Mr James Wilder, his Grace's secretary. It was he who gave me the information about Lord Saltire's feelings.'

'I see. By the way, that last letter of the duke's – was it found in the boy's room after he was gone?'

'No; he had taken it with him. I think, Mr Holmes, it is time that we were leaving for Euston.'

'I will order a four-wheeler. In a quarter of an hour we shall be at your service. If you are telegraphing home, Mr Huxtable, it would be well to allow the people in your neighbourhood to imagine that the inquiry is still going on in Liverpool, or wherever else that red herring led your pack. In the meantime, I will do a little quiet work at your own doors, and perhaps the scent is not so cold but that two old hounds like Watson and myself may get a sniff of it.'

That evening found us in the cold, bracing atmosphere of the Peak country, in which Dr Huxtable's famous school is situated. It was already dark when we reached it. A card was lying on the hall table, and the butler whispered something to his master, who turned to us with agitation in every heavy feature.

'The duke is here,' said he. 'The duke and Mr Wilder are in the study. Come, gentlemen, and I will introduce you.'

I was, of course, familiar with the pictures of the famous

statesman, but the man himself was very different from his representation. He was a tall and stately person, scrupulously dressed, with a drawn, thin face, and a nose which was grotesquely curved and long. His complexion was of a dead pallor, which was more startling by contrast with a long, dwindling beard of vivid red, which flowed down over his white waistcoat, with his watch-chain gleaming through its fringe. Such was the stately presence who looked stonily at us from the centre of Dr Huxtable's hearthrug. Beside him stood a very young man, whom I understood to be Wilder, the private secretary. He was small, nervous, alert, with intelligent, light blue eyes and mobile features. It was he who at once, in an incisive and positive tone, opened the conversation.

'I called this morning, Dr Huxtable, too late to prevent you from starting for London. I learned that your object was to invite Mr Sherlock Holmes to undertake the conduct of this case. His Grace is surprised, Dr Huxtable, that you should have taken such a step without consulting him.'

'When I learned the police had failed –'

'His Grace is by no means convinced that the police have failed.'

'But surely, Mr Wilder –'

'You are well aware, Dr Huxtable, that his Grace is particularly anxious to avoid all public scandal. He prefers to take as few people as possible into his confidence.'

'The matter can be easily remedied,' said the brow-beaten

doctor. 'Mr Sherlock Holmes can return to London by the morning train.'

'Hardly that, Doctor, hardly that,' said Holmes, in his blandest voice. 'This northern air is invigorating and pleasant, so I propose to spend a few days upon your moors, and to occupy my mind as best I may. Whether I have the shelter of your roof or of the village inn is, of course, for you to decide.'

I could see that the unfortunate doctor was in the last stage of indecision, from which he was rescued by the deep, sonorous voice of the red-bearded duke, which boomed out like a dinner-gong.

'I agree with Mr Wilder, Dr Huxtable, that you would have done wisely to consult me. But since Mr Holmes has already been taken into your confidence, it would indeed be absurd that we should not avail ourselves of his services. Far from going to the inn, Mr Holmes, I should be pleased if you would come and stay with me at Holdernesse Hall.'

'I thank your Grace. For the purposes of my investigation I think that it would be wiser for me to remain at the scene of the mystery.'

'Just as you like, Mr Holmes. Any information which Mr Wilder or I can give you is, of course, at your disposal.'

'It will probably be necessary for me to see you at the Hall,' said Holmes. 'I would only ask you now, sir, whether you have formed any explanation in your own mind as to the mysterious disappearance of your son?'

'No, sir, I have not.'

'Excuse me if I allude to that which is painful to you, but I have no alternative. Do you think that the duchess had anything to do with the matter?'

The great minister showed perceptible hesitation.

'I do not think so,' he said at last.

'The other most obvious explanation is that the child has been kidnapped for the purpose of levying ransom. You have not had any demand of the sort?'

'No, sir.'

'One more question, your Grace. I understand that you wrote to your son upon the day when this incident occurred.'

'No! I wrote upon the day before.'

'Exactly. But he received it on that day?'

'Yes.'

'Was there anything in your letter which might have unbalanced him or induced him to take such a step?'

'No, sir, certainly not.'

'Did you post that letter yourself?'

The nobleman's reply was interrupted by his secretary, who broke in with some heat.

'His Grace is not in the habit of posting letters himself,' said he. 'The letter was laid with others upon the study table, and I myself put them in the post-bag.'

'You are sure this one was among them?'

'Yes; I observed it.'

'How many letters did your Grace write that day?'

‘Twenty or thirty. I have a large correspondence. But surely this is somewhat irrelevant?’

‘Not entirely,’ said Holmes.

‘For my own part,’ the duke continued, ‘I have advised the police to turn their attention to the South of France. I have already said that I do not believe that the duchess would encourage so monstrous an action, but the lad had the most wrong-headed opinions, and it is possible that he may have fled to her, aided and abetted by this German. I think, Dr Huxtable, that we will now return to the Hall.’

I could see that there were other questions which Holmes would have wished to put; but the nobleman’s abrupt manner showed that the interview was at end. It was evident that to his intensely aristocratic nature this discussion of his intimate family affairs with a stranger was most abhorrent, and that he feared lest every fresh question would throw a fiercer light into the discreetly shadowed corners of his ducal history.

When the nobleman and his secretary had left, my friend flung himself at once with characteristic eagerness into the investigation.

The boy’s chamber was carefully examined, and yielded nothing save the absolute conviction that it was only through the window that he could have escaped. The German master’s room and effects gave no further clue. In his case a trailer of ivy had given way under his weight, and we saw by the light of a lantern the mark on the lawn where his heels had come down. That one dent in the short green grass was the only material witness left of this inexplicable nocturnal flight.

Sherlock Holmes left the house alone, and only returned after eleven. He had obtained a large ordnance map of the neighbourhood, and this he brought into my room, where he laid it out on the bed, and, having balanced the lamp in the middle of it, he began to smoke over it, and occasionally to point out objects of interest with the reeking amber of his pipe.

'This case grows upon me, Watson,' said he. 'There are decidedly some points of interest in connection with it. In this early stage I want you to realize these geographical features, which may have a good deal to do with our investigation.

'Look at this map. This dark square is the Priory School. I'll put a pin in it. Now, this line is the main road. You see that it runs east and west past the school, and you see also there is no side-road for a mile either way. If these two folk passed away by road it was *this* road.'

'Exactly.'

'By a singular and happy chance we are able to some extent to check what passed along this road during the night in question. At this point, where my pipe is now resting, a country constable was on duty from twelve to six. It is, as you perceive, the first crossroad on the east side. This man declares that he was not absent from his post for an instant,

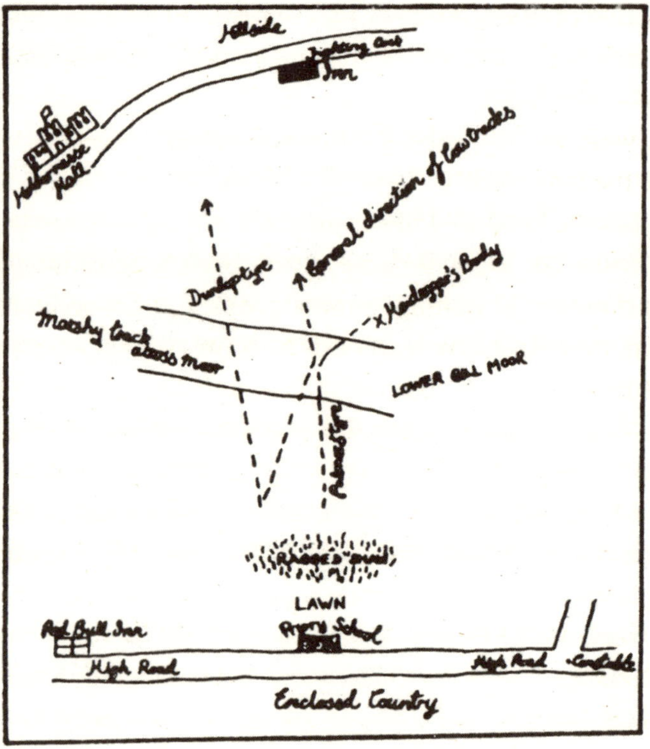

and he is positive that neither boy nor man could have gone that way unseen. I have spoken with this policeman tonight, and he appears to me to be a perfectly reliable person. That blocks this end. We have now to deal with the other. There is an inn here, the Red Bull, the landlady of which was ill. She had sent to Mackleton for a doctor, but he did not arrive until morning, being absent at another case. The people at the inn were alert all night, awaiting his coming, and one or other of them seems to have continually had an eye upon the road. They declare that no one passed. If their evidence is good, then we are fortunate enough to be able to block the west, and also to be able to say that the fugitives did *not* use the road at all.'

'But the bicycle?' I objected.

'Quite so. We will come to the bicycle presently. To continue our reasoning: if these people did not go by the road, they must have traversed the country to the north of the house or to the south of the house. That is certain. Let us weigh the one against the other. On the south of the house is, as you perceive, a large district of arable land, cut up into small fields, with stone walls between them. There, I admit that a bicycle is impossible. We can dismiss the idea. We turn to the country on the north. Here there lies a grove of trees, marked as the "Ragged Shaw", and on the farther side stretches a great rolling moor, Lower Gill Moor, extending for ten miles, and sloping gradually upwards. Here, at one side of this wilderness, is Holdernesse Hall, ten miles by road, but only six across the moor. It is a peculiarly desolate plain. A few moor farmers have small holdings, where they rear sheep and cattle. Except these, the plover and the curlew are the only inhabitants until you come to the Chesterfield high-road. There is a church there, you see, a few cottages, and an inn. Beyond that the hills become precipitous. Surely it is here to the north that our quest must lie.'

'But the bicycle?' I persisted.

'Well, well!' said Holmes impatiently. 'A good cyclist does not need a high-road. The moor is intersected with paths, and the moon was at the full. Halloa! What is this?'

There was an agitated knock at the door, and an instant afterwards Dr Huxtable was in the room. In his hand he held a blue cricket-cap, with a white chevron on the peak.

'At last we have a clue!' he cried. 'Thank Heaven, at last we are on the dear boy's track! It is his cap.'

'Where was it found?'

'In the van of the gypsies who camped on the moor. They left on Tuesday. Today the police traced them down and examined their caravan. This was found.'

'How do they account for it?'

'They shuffled and lied – said that they found it on the moor on Tuesday morning. They know where he is, the rascals! Thank goodness, they are all safe under lock and key. Either the fear of the law or the duke's purse will certainly get out of them all that they know.'

'So far, so good,' said Holmes, when the doctor had at last left the room. 'It at least bears out the theory that it is on the side of the Lower Gill Moor that we must hope for results. The police have really done nothing locally, save the arrest of these gypsies. Look here, Watson! There is a water-course across the moor. You see it marked here in the map. In some parts it widens into a morass. This is particularly so in the region between Holdernesse Hall and the school. It is vain to look elsewhere for tracks in this dry weather;

but at *that* point there is certainly a chance of some record being left. I will call you early tomorrow morning, and you and I will try if we can to throw some light upon the mystery.'

The day was just breaking when I woke to find the long, thin form of Holmes by my bedside. He was fully dressed, and had apparently already been out.

'I have done the lawn and the bicycle shed,' said he. 'I have also had a ramble through the Ragged Shaw. Now, Watson, there is cocoa ready in the next room. I must beg you to hurry, for we have a great day before us.'

His eyes shone, and his cheek was flushed with the exhilaration of the master workman who sees his work lies ready before him. A very different Holmes, this active, alert man, from the introspective and pallid dreamer of Baker Street. I felt, as I looked upon that supple figure, alive with nervous energy, that it was indeed a strenuous day that awaited us.

And yet it opened in the blackest disappointment. With high hopes we struck across the peaty, russet moor, intersected with a thousand sheep-paths, until we came to the broad light-green belt which marked the morass between us and Holdernesse. Certainly, if the lad had gone homewards, he must have passed this, and he would not pass it without leaving his trace. But no sign of him or the German could be seen. With a darkening face my friend strode along the margin, eagerly observant of every muddy stain upon the mossy surface. Sheep-marks there were in profusion, and at one place, some miles down, cows had left their tracks. Nothing more.

'Check number one,' said Holmes, looking gloomily over the rolling expanse of the moor. 'There is another morass down yonder, and a narrow neck between. Halloa! halloa! halloa! What have we here?'

We had come on a small black ribbon of pathway. In the middle of it, clearly marked on the sodden soil, was the track of a bicycle.

'Hurrah!' I cried. 'We have it.'

But Holmes was shaking his head, and his face was puzzled and expectant rather than joyous.

'A bicycle certainly, but not *the* bicycle,' said he. 'I am familiar with forty-two different impressions left by tyres. This, as you perceive, is a Dunlop, with a patch upon the outer cover. Heidegger's tyres were Palmers', leaving longitudinal stripes. Aveling, the mathematical master, was sure upon the point. Therefore it is not Heidegger's track.'

'The boy's, then?'

'Possibly, if we could prove a bicycle to have been in his possession. But this we have utterly failed to do. This track, as you perceive, was made by a rider who was going from the direction of the school.'

'Or towards it?'

'No, no, my dear Watson. The more deeply sunk impression is, of course, the hind wheel, upon which the weight rests. You perceive several places where it has passed across and obliterated the more shallow mark of the front one. It was undoubtedly heading away from the school. It may or may not be connected with our inquiry, but we will follow it backwards before we go any farther.'

We did so, and at the end of a few hundred yards lost the tracks as we emerged from the boggy portion of the moor. Following the path backwards, we picked out another spot, where a spring trickled across it. Here, once again, was the mark of the bicycle, though nearly obliterated by the hoofs of cows. After that there was no sign, but the path ran right on into Ragged Shaw, the wood which backed on to the school. From this wood the cycle must have emerged. Holmes sat down on a boulder and rested his chin in his hands. I had smoked two cigarettes before he moved.

'Well, well,' said he at last. 'It is, of course, possible that a cunning man might change the tyre of his bicycle in order to leave unfamiliar tracks. A criminal who was capable of such a thought is a man whom I should be proud to do business with. We will leave this question undecided and hark back to our morass again, for we have left a good deal unexplored.'

We continued our systematic survey of the edge of the sodden portion of the moor, and soon our perseverance was gloriously rewarded.

Right across the lower part of the bog lay a miry path. Holmes gave a cry of delight as he approached it. An impression like a fine bundle of telegraph wires ran down the centre of it. It was the Palmer tyre.

'Here is Herr Heidegger, sure enough!' cried Holmes exultantly. 'My reasoning seems to have been pretty sound, Watson.'

'I congratulate you.'

'But we have a long way still to go. Kindly walk clear of the path. Now let us follow the trail. I fear that it will not lead very far.'

We found, however, as we advanced, that this portion of the moor was intersected with soft patches, and, though we frequently lost sight of the track, we always succeeded in picking it up once more.

'Do you observe,' said Holmes, 'that the rider is now undoubtedly forcing the pace? There can be no doubt of it. Look at this impression, where you get both tyres clear. The one is as deep as the other. That can only mean that the rider is throwing his weight on to the handle-bar as a man does when he is sprinting. By Jove! he has had a fall.'

There was a broad irregular smudge covering some yards of the track. Then there were a few footmarks, and the tyre reappeared once more.

'A side-slip,' I suggested.

Holmes held up a crumpled branch of flowering gorse. To my horror I perceived that the yellow blossoms were all dabbled with crimson. On the path, too, and among the heather were dark stains of clotted blood.

'Bad!' said Holmes. 'Bad! Stand clear, Watson! Not an unnecessary footstep! What do I read here? He fell wounded, he stood up, he remounted, he proceeded. But there is no other track. Cattle on this side-path. He was surely not gored by a bull? Impossible! But I see no traces of anyone else. We must push on, Watson. Surely, with stains as well as the track to guide us, he cannot escape us now.'

Our search was not a very long one. The tracks of the tyre began to curve fantastically upon the wet and shining path. Suddenly, as I looked ahead, the gleam of metal caught my eye from amid the thick gorse bushes. Out of them we dragged a bicycle, Palmer-tyred, one pedal bent, and the whole front of it horribly smeared and slobbered with blood. On the other side of the bushes a shoe was projecting. We ran round, and there lay the unfortunate rider. He was a tall man, full bearded, with spectacles, one glass of which had been knocked out. The cause of his death was a frightful blow upon the head, which had crushed in part of his skull. That he could have gone on after receiving such an injury said much for the vitality and courage of the man. He wore shoes, but no socks, and his open coat disclosed a night-shirt beneath it. It was undoubtedly the German master.

Holmes turned the body over reverently, and examined it with great attention. He then sat in deep thought for a time, and I could see by his ruffled brow that this grim discovery had not, in his opinion, advanced us much in our inquiry.

'It is a little difficult to know what to do, Watson,' said he, at last. 'My own inclinations are to push this inquiry on, for we have already lost so much time that we cannot afford to waste another hour. On the other hand, we are bound to inform the police of this discovery, and to see that this poor fellow's body is looked after.'

'I could take a note back.'

'But I need your company and assistance. Wait a bit! There is a fellow cutting peat up yonder. Bring him over here, and he will guide the police.'

I brought the peasant across, and Holmes dispatched the frightened man with a note to Dr Huxtable.

'Now, Watson,' said he, 'we have picked up two clues this morning. One is the bicycle with the Palmer tyre, and we see what that has led to. The other is the bicycle with the patched Dunlop. Before we start to investigate that, let us try to realize what we *do* know, so as to make the most of it, and to separate the essential from the accidental.

'First of all, I wish to impress upon you that the boy certainly left of his own free will. He got down from his window and he went off, either alone or with someone. That is sure.'

I assented.

'Well, now, let us turn to this unfortunate German master. The boy was fully dressed when he fled. Therefore he foresaw what he would do. But the German went without his socks. He certainly acted on very short notice.'

'Undoubtedly.'

'Why did he go? Because, from his bedroom window, he saw the flight of the boy. Because he wished to overtake him and bring him back. He seized his bicycle, pursued the lad, and in pursuing him met his death.'

'So it would seem.'

'Now I come to the critical part of my argument. The natural action of a man in pursuing a little boy would be to run after him. He would know that he could overtake him. But the German does not do so. He turns to his bicycle. I am told that he was an excellent cyclist. He would not do this if he did not see that the boy had some swift means of escape.'

'The other bicycle.'

'Let us continue our reconstruction. He meets his death five miles from the school – not by a bullet, mark you, which even a lad might conceivably discharge, but by a savage blow dealt by a vigorous arm. The lad, then, *had* a companion in his flight. And the flight was a swift one, since it took five miles before an expert cyclist could overtake them. Yet we survey the ground round the scene of the tragedy. What do we find? A few cattle tracks, nothing more. I took a wide sweep round, and there is no path within fifty yards. Another cyclist could have had nothing to do with the actual murder. Nor were there any human footmarks.'

'Holmes,' I cried, 'this is impossible.'

'Admirable!' he said. 'A most illuminating remark. It *is* impossible as I state it, and therefore I must in some respect have stated it wrong. Yet you saw for yourself. Can you suggest any fallacy?'

'He could not have fractured his skull in a fall?'

'In a morass, Watson?'

'I am at my wits' end.'

'Tut, tut; we have solved some worse problems. At least we have plenty of material, if we can only use it. Come, then, and, having exhausted the Palmer, let us see what the Dunlop with the patched cover has to offer us.'

We picked up the track and followed it onwards for some distance; but soon the moor rose into a long, heather-tufted curve, and we left the watercourse behind us. No further help from tracks could be hoped for. At the spot where we saw the last of the Dunlop tyre it might equally have led to Holdernesse Hall, the stately towers of which rose some miles to our left, or to a low, grey village which lay in front of us, and marked the position of the Chesterfield high-road.

As we approached the forbidding and squalid inn, with the sign of a game-cock above the door, Holmes gave a sudden groan and clutched me by the shoulder to save himself from falling. He had had one of those violent strains of the ankle which leave a man helpless. With difficulty he limped up to the door, where a squat, dark, elderly man was smoking a black clay pipe.

‘How are you, Mr Reuben Hayes?’ said Holmes.

‘Who are you, and how do you get my name so pat?’ the countryman answered, with a suspicious flash of a pair of cunning eyes.

‘Well, it’s printed on the board above your head. It’s easy to see a man who is master of his own house. I suppose you haven’t such a thing as a carriage in your stables?’

‘No; I have not.’

‘I can hardly put my foot to the ground.’

‘Don’t put it to the ground.’

‘But I can’t walk.’

‘Well, then, hop.’

Mr Reuben Hayes’s manner was far from gracious, but Holmes took it with admirable good humour.

‘Look here, my man,’ said he. ‘This is really rather an awkward fix for me. I don’t mind how I get on.’

‘Neither do I,’ said the morose landlord.

‘The matter is very important. I would offer you a sovereign for the use of a bicycle.’

The landlord pricked up his ears.

‘Where do you want to go?’

‘To Holdernesse Hall.’

‘Pals of the dook, I suppose?’ said the landlord, surveying our mud-stained garments with ironical eyes.

Holmes laughed good-naturedly.

‘He’ll be glad to see us, anyhow.’

‘Why?’

'Because we bring him news of his lost son.'

The landlord gave a very visible start.

'What, you're on his track?'

'He has been heard of in Liverpool. They expect to get him every hour.'

Again a swift change passed over the heavy, unshaven face. His manner was suddenly genial.

'I've less reason to wish the dook well than most men,' said he, 'for I was his headcoachman once, and cruel bad he treated me. It was him that sacked me without a character on the word of a lying corn-chandler. But I'm glad to hear that the young lord was heard of in Liverpool, and I'll help you to take the news to the Hall.'

'Thank you,' said Holmes. 'We'll have some food first. Then you can bring round the bicycle.'

'I haven't got a bicycle.'

Holmes held up a sovereign.

'I tell you, man, that I haven't got one. I'll let you have two horses as far as the Hall.'

'Well, well,' said Holmes, 'we'll talk about it when we've had something to eat.'

When we were left alone in the stone-flagged kitchen it was astonishing how rapidly that sprained ankle recovered. It was nearly nightfall, and we had eaten nothing since early morning, so that we spent some time over our meal. Holmes was lost in thought, and once or twice he walked over to the window and stared earnestly out. It opened on to a squalid courtyard. In the far corner was a smithy, where a grimy lad was at work. On the side were the stables. Holmes had sat down again after one of these excursions, when he suddenly sprang out of his chair with a loud exclamation.

'By Heaven, Watson, I believe that I've got it!' he cried. 'Yes, yes, it must be so. Watson, do you remember seeing any cow-tracks today?'

'Yes, several.'

'Where?'

'Well, everywhere. They were at the morass, and again on the path, and again near where poor Heidegger met his death.'

'Exactly. Well, now, Watson, how many cows did you see on the moor?'

'I don't remember seeing any.'

'Strange, Watson, that we should see tracks all along our line, but never a cow on the whole moor; very strange, Watson, eh?'

'Yes, it is strange.'

'Now, Watson, make an effort; throw your mind back! Can you see those tracks upon the path?'

'Yes, I can.'

'Can you recall that the tracks were sometimes like that, Watson' – he arranged a number of breadcrumbs in this fashion – : : : : : – 'and sometimes like this' – :· :· :· :· – 'and occasionally like this' – .·.·.·

'Can you remember that?'

'No, I cannot.'

'But I can. I could swear to it. However, we will go back at our leisure and verify it. What a blind beetle I have been not to draw my conclusion!'

'And what is your conclusion?'

'Only that it is a remarkable cow which walks, canters, and gallops. By George, Watson, it was no brain of a country publican that thought out such a blind as that! The coast seems to be clear, save for that lad in the smithy. Let us slip out and see what we can see.'

There were two rough-haired, unkempt horses in the tumbledown stable. Holmes raised the hind leg of one of them and laughed loud.

'Old shoes, but newly shod – old shoes, but new nails. This case deserves to be a classic. Let us go across to the smithy.'

The lad continued his work without regarding us. I saw Holmes's eye darting to right and left among the litter of iron and wood, which was scattered about the floor. Suddenly, however, we heard a step behind us, and there was the landlord, his heavy eyebrows drawn down over his savage eyes, his swarthy features convulsed with passion.

He held a short metal-headed stick in his hand, and he advanced in so menacing a fashion that I was right glad to feel the revolver in my pocket.

'You infernal spies!' the man cried. 'What are you doing there?'

‘Why, Mr Reuben Hayes,’ said Holmes coolly, ‘one might think that you were afraid of our finding something out.’

The man mastered himself with a violent effort, and his grim mouth loosened into a false laugh, which was more menacing than his frown.

‘You’re welcome to all you can find out in my smithy,’ said he. ‘But look here, mister, I don’t care for folk poking about my place without my leave, so the sooner you pay your score and get out of this the better I shall be pleased.’

‘All right, Mr Hayes – no harm meant,’ said Holmes. ‘We have been having a look at your horses; but I think I’ll walk after all. It’s not far, I believe.’

‘Not more than two miles to the Hall gates. That’s the road to the left.’ He watched us with sullen eyes until we had left his premises.

We did not go very far along the road, for Holmes stopped the instant that the curve hid us from the landlord’s view.

‘We were warm, as the children say, at that inn,’ said he. ‘I seem to grow colder every step that I take away from it. No, no; I can’t possibly leave it.’

‘I am convinced,’ said I, ‘that this Reuben Hayes knows all about it. A more self-evident villain I never saw.’

‘Oh! he impressed you in that way, did he? There are the horses, there is the smithy. Yes, it is an interesting place, this Fighting Cock. I think we shall have another look at it in an unobtrusive way.’

A long, sloping hillside, dotted with grey limestone boulders, stretched behind us. We had turned off the road, and were making our way up the hill, when, looking in the direction of Holdernesse Hall, I saw a cyclist coming swiftly along.

'Get down, Watson!' cried Holmes, with a heavy hand upon my shoulder. We had hardly sunk from view when the man flew past us on the road. Amid a rolling cloud of dust I caught a glimpse of a pale, agitated face – a face with horror in every lineament, the mouth open, the eyes staring wildly in front. It was like some strange caricature of the dapper James Wilder whom we had seen the night before.

'The duke's secretary!' cried Holmes. 'Come, Watson, let us see what he does.'

We scrambled from rock to rock until in a few moments we had made our way to a point from which we could see the front door of the inn. Wilder's bicycle was leaning against the wall beside it. No one was moving about the house, nor could we catch a glimpse of any faces at the windows. Slowly the twilight crept down as the sun sank behind the high towers of Holdernesse Hall. Then in the gloom we saw the two side-lamps of a trap light up in the stable-yard of the inn, and shortly afterwards heard the rattle of hoofs, as it wheeled out into the road and tore off at a furious pace in the direction of Chesterfield.

'What do you make of that, Watson?' Holmes whispered.

'It looks like a flight.'

'A single man in a dog-cart, so far as I could see. Well, it certainly was not Mr James Wilder, for there he is at the door.'

A red square of light had sprung out of the darkness. In the middle of it was the black figure of the secretary, his head advanced, peering out into the night. It was evident that he was expecting someone. Then at last there were steps in the road, a second figure was visible for an instant against the light, the door shut, and all was black once more. Five minutes later a lamp was lit in a room upon the first floor.

'It seems to be a curious class of custom that is done by the Fighting Cock,' said Holmes.

'The bar is on the other side.'

'Quite so. These are what one may call the private guests. Now, what in the world is Mr James Wilder doing in that den at this hour of night, and who is the companion who comes to meet him there? Come, Watson, we must really take a risk and try to investigate this a little more closely.'

Together we stole down to the road and crept across to the door of the inn. The bicycle still leaned against the wall. Holmes struck a match and held it to the back wheel, and I heard him chuckle as the light fell upon a patched Dunlop tyre. Up above us was the lighted window.

'I must have a peep through that, Watson. If you bend your back and support yourself upon the wall, I think that I can manage.'

An instant later his feet were on my shoulders. But he was hardly up before he was down again.

'Come, my friend,' said he, 'our day's work has been quite long enough. I think that we have gathered all that we can. It's a long walk to the school, and the sooner we get started the better.'

He hardly opened his lips during that weary trudge across the moor, nor would he enter the school when he reached it, but went on to Mackleton Station, whence he could send some telegrams. Late at night I heard him consoling Dr Huxtable, prostrated by the tragedy of his master's death, and later still he entered my room as alert and vigorous as he had been when he started in the morning. 'All goes well, my friend,' said he. 'I promise that before tomorrow evening we shall have reached the solution of the mystery.'

At eleven o'clock next morning my friend and I were walking up the famous yew avenue of Holdernesse Hall. We were ushered through the magnificent Elizabethan doorway and into his Grace's study. There we found Mr James Wilder, demure and courtly, but with some trace of that wild terror of the night before still lurking in his furtive eyes and in his twitching features.

'You have come to see his Grace? I am sorry; but the fact is that the duke is far from well. He has been very much upset by the tragic news. We received a telegram from Dr Huxtable yesterday afternoon, which told us of your discovery.'

'I must see the duke, Mr Wilder.'

'But he is in his room.'

'Then I must go to his room.'

'I believe he is in his bed.'

'I will see him there.'

Holmes's cold and inexorable manner showed the secretary that it was useless to argue with him.

'Very good, Mr Holmes; I will tell him that you are here.'

After half an hour's delay the great nobleman appeared. His face was more cadaverous than ever, his shoulders had rounded, and he seemed to me to be an altogether older man than he had been the morning before. He greeted us with a stately courtesy, and seated himself at his desk, his red beard streaming down on to the table.

'Well, Mr Holmes?' said he.

But my friend's eyes were fixed upon the secretary, who stood by his master's chair.

'I think, your Grace, that I could speak more freely in Mr Wilder's absence.'

The man turned a shade paler and cast a malignant glance at Holmes.

'If your Grace wishes –'

'Yes, yes; you had better go. Now, Mr Holmes, what have you to say?'

My friend waited until the door had closed behind the retreating secretary.

'The fact is, your Grace,' said he, 'that my colleague, Dr

Watson, and myself had an assurance from Dr Huxtable that a reward had been offered in this case. I should like to have this confirmed from your own lips.'

'Certainly, Mr Holmes.'

'It amounted, if I am correctly informed, to five thousand pounds to anyone who will tell you where your son is?'

'Exactly.'

'And another thousand to the man who will name the person or persons who keep him in custody?'

'Exactly.'

'Under the latter heading is included, no doubt, not only those who may have taken him away, but also those who conspire to keep him in his present position?'

'Yes, yes,' cried the duke impatiently. 'If you do your work well, Mr Sherlock Holmes, you will have no reason to complain of niggardly treatment.'

My friend rubbed his thin hands together with an appearance of avidity which was a surprise to me, who knew his frugal tastes.

'I fancy that I see your Grace's cheque-book upon the table,' said he. 'I should be glad if you would make me out a cheque for six thousand pounds. It would be as well, perhaps, for you to cross it. The Capital and Counties Bank, Oxford Street branch, are my agents.'

His Grace sat very stern and upright in his chair, and looked stonily at my friend.

'Is this a joke, Mr Holmes? It is hardly a subject for pleasantry.'

'Not at all, your Grace. I was never more earnest in my life.'

'What do you mean, then?'

'I mean that I have earned the reward, I know where your son is, and I know some, at least, of those who are holding him.'

The duke's beard had turned more aggressively red than ever against his ghastly white face.

'Where is he?' he gasped.

'He is, or was last night, at the Fighting Cock Inn, about two miles from your park gate.'

The duke fell back in his chair.

'And whom do you accuse?'

Sherlock Holmes's answer was an astounding one. He stepped swiftly forward and touched the duke upon the shoulder.

'I accuse *you*,' said he. 'And now, your Grace, I'll trouble you for that cheque.'

Never shall I forget the duke's appearance as he sprang up and clawed with his hands like one who is sinking into an abyss. Then, with an extraordinary effort of aristocratic self-command, he sat down and sank his face in his hands. It was some minutes before he spoke.

'How much do you know? he asked at last, without raising his head.

'I saw you together last night.'

'Does anyone else besides your friend know?'

'I have spoken to no one.'

The duke took a pen in his quivering fingers and opened his cheque-book.

'I shall be as good as my word, Mr Holmes. I am about to write your cheque, however unwelcome the information which you have gained may be to me. When the offer was first made I little thought the turn which events would take. But you and your friend are men of discretion, Mr Holmes?'

'I hardly understand your Grace.'

'I must put it plainly, Mr Holmes. If only you two know of the incident, there is no reason why it should go any farther. I think twelve thousand pounds is the sum that I owe you, is it not?'

But Holmes smiled, and shook his head.

'I fear, your Grace, that matters can hardly be arranged so easily. There is the death of this schoolmaster to be accounted for.'

'But James knew nothing of that. You cannot hold him responsible for that. It was the work of this brutal ruffian whom he had the misfortune to employ.'

'I must take the view, your Grace, that when a man embarks upon a crime he is morally guilty of any other crime which may spring from it.'

'Morally, Mr Holmes. No doubt you are right. But surely not in the eyes of the law. A man cannot be condemned for a murder at which he was not present, and which he loathes and abhors as much as you do. The instant that he heard of it he made a complete confession to me, so filled was he with horror and remorse. He lost not an hour in breaking entirely with the murderer. Oh, Mr Holmes, you must save him – you must save him! I tell you that you must save him!' The duke had dropped the last attempt at self-command, and was pacing the room with a convulsed face and with his clenched hands raving in the air. At last he mastered himself and sat down once more at his desk. 'I appreciate your conduct in coming here before you spoke to anyone else,' said he. 'At least we may take counsel how far we can minimize this hideous scandal.'

'Exactly,' said Holmes. 'I think, your Grace, that this can only be done by absolute and complete frankness between us. I am disposed to help your Grace to the best of my ability; but in order to do so I must understand to the last detail how the matter stands. I realize that your words applied to Mr James Wilder, and that he is not the murderer.'

'No; the murderer has escaped.'

Sherlock Holmes smiled demurely.

'Your Grace can hardly have heard of any small reputation which I possess, or you would not imagine that it is so easy to escape me. Mr Reuben Hayes was arrested at Chesterfield on my information at eleven o'clock last night. I had a telegram from the head of the local police before I left the school this morning.'

The duke leaned back in his chair and stared with amazement at my friend.

'You seem to have powers that are hardly human,' said he. 'So Reuben Hayes is taken? I am right glad to hear it, if it will not react upon the fate of James.'

'Your secretary?'

'No, sir; my son.'

It was Holmes's turn to look astonished.

'I confess that this is entirely new to me, your Grace, I must beg of you to be more explicit.'

'I will conceal nothing from you. I agree with you that complete frankness, however painful it may be to me, is the best policy in this desperate situation to which James's folly and jealousy have reduced us. When I was a young man, Mr Holmes, I loved with such a love as comes only once in a lifetime. I offered the lady marriage, but she refused it on the grounds that such a match might mar my career. Had she lived, I would certainly have never married anyone else. She died, and left this one child, whom for her sake I have cherished and cared for. I could not acknowledge the paternity to the world; but I gave him the best of educations, and since he came to manhood I have kept him near my person. He surprised my secret, and has presumed ever since upon the claim which he has upon me and upon his power of provoking a scandal, which would be abhorrent to me. His presence had something to do with the unhappy issue of my marriage. Above all, he hated my young legitimate heir from the first with a persistent hatred. You may well ask me why, under these circumstances, I still kept James under my roof. I answer that it was because I could see his mother's face in his, and that for her dear sake there was no end to my long suffering. All her pretty ways, too – there was not one of them which he could not suggest and bring back to my memory. I *could* not send him away. But I feared so lest he should do Arthur – that is, Lord Saltire – a mischief that I dispatched him for safety to Dr Huxtable's school.

'James came into contact with this fellow Hayes because the man was a tenant of mine, and James acted as agent. The fellow was a rascal from the beginning; but in some extraordinary way James became intimate with him. He had always a taste for low company. When James determined to kidnap Lord Saltire it was of this man's service that he availed himself. You remember that I wrote to Arthur upon that last day. Well, James opened the letter and inserted a note asking Arthur to meet him in a little wood called the Ragged Shaw which is near to the school. He used the duchess's name, and in that way got the boy to come. That evening James cycled over – I am telling you what he has himself confessed to me – and he told Arthur, whom he met in the wood, that his mother longed to see him, that she was awaiting him on the moor, and that if he would come back into the wood at midnight he would find a man with a horse, who would take him to her. Poor Arthur fell into the trap. He came to the appointment and found this fellow Hayes with a led pony. Arthur mounted, and they set off together. It appears – though this James only heard yesterday – that they were pursued, that Hayes struck the pursuer with his stick, and that the man died of his injuries. Hayes brought Arthur to his public-house, the Fighting Cock, where he was confined in an upper room, under the care of Mrs Hayes, who is a kindly woman, but entirely under the control of her brutal husband.

'Well, Mr Holmes, that was the state of affairs when I first saw you two days ago. I had no more idea of the truth than you. You will ask me what was James's motive in doing such a deed. I answer that there was a great deal which was unreasoning and fanatical in the hatred which he bore my heir. In his view he himself should have been heir of all my estates, and he deeply resented those social laws which made it impossible. At the same time, he had a definite motive also. He was eager that I should break the entail, and he was of opinion that it lay in my power to do so. He intended to make a bargain with me – to restore Arthur if I would break the entail, and so make it possible for the estate to be left to him by will. He knew well that I should never willingly invoke the aid of the police against him. I say that he would have proposed such a bargain to me, but he did not actually do so, for events moved too quickly for him, and he had not time to put his plans into practice.

'What brought all his wicked scheme to wreck was your discovery of this man Heidegger's dead body. James was seized with horror at the news. It came to us yesterday as we sat together in this study. Dr Huxtable had sent a telegram. James was so overwhelmed with grief and agitation that my suspicions, which had never been entirely absent, rose instantly to a certainty, and I taxed him with the deed. He made a complete voluntary confession. Then he implored me to keep his secret for three days longer, so as to give his wretched accomplice a chance of saving his guilty life. I yielded – as I have always yielded – to his prayers, and instantly James hurried off to the Fighting Cock to warn Hayes and give him the means of flight. I could not go there by daylight without provoking comment, but as soon as night fell I hurried off to see my dear Arthur. I found him safe and well, but horrified beyond expression by the dreadful deed he had witnessed. In deference to my promise, and much against my will, I consented to leave him there for three days under the charge of Mrs Hayes, since it was evident that it was impossible to inform the police where he was without telling them also who was the murderer, and I could not see how that murderer could be punished without ruin to my unfortunate James. You asked for frankness, Mr Holmes, and I have taken you at your word, for I have now told you everything without an attempt at circumlocution or concealment. Do you in your turn be as frank with me.'

'I will,' said Holmes. 'In the first place, your Grace, I am bound to tell you that you have placed yourself in a most serious position in the eyes of the law. You have condoned a felony, and you have aided the escape of a murderer; for I cannot doubt that any money which was taken by James Wilder to aid his accomplice in his flight came from your Grace's purse.'

The duke bowed his assent.

'This is indeed a most serious matter. Even more culpable in my opinion, your Grace, is your attitude towards your younger son. You leave him in this den for three days.'

'Under solemn promises –'

'What are promises to such people as these? You have no guarantee that he will not be spirited away again. To humour your guilty elder son you have exposed your innocent younger son to imminent and unnecessary danger. It was a most unjustifiable action.'

The proud lord of Holdernesse was not accustomed to be so rated in his own ducal hall. The blood flushed into his high forehead, but his conscience held him dumb.

'I will help you, but on one condition only. It is that you ring for the footman and let me give such orders as I like.'

Without a word the duke pressed the electric button. A servant entered.

'You will be glad to hear,' said Holmes, 'that your young master is found. It is the duke's desire that the carriage shall go at once to the Fighting Cock Inn to bring Lord Saltire home.'

'Now,' said Holmes, when the rejoicing lackey had disappeared, 'having secured the future we can afford to be more lenient with the past. I am not in an official position, and there is no reason, so long as the ends of justice are served, why I should disclose all that I know. As to Hayes I say nothing. The gallows awaits him, and I would do nothing to save him from it. What he will divulge I cannot tell, but I have no doubt that your Grace could make him understand that it is to his interest to be silent. From the police point of view he will have kidnapped the boy for the purpose of ransom. If they do not themselves find it out I see no reason why I should prompt them to take a broader view. I would warn your Grace, however, that the continued presence of Mr James Wilder in your household can only lead to misfortune.'

'I understand that, Mr Holmes, and it is already settled that he shall leave me for ever and go to seek his fortune in Australia.'

'In that case, your Grace, since you have yourself stated that any unhappiness in your married life was caused by his presence, I would suggest that you make such amends as you can to the duchess, and that you try to resume those relations which have been so unhappily interrupted.'

'That also I have arranged, Mr Holmes. I wrote to the duchess this morning.'

'In that case,' said Holmes, rising, 'I think that my friend and I can congratulate ourselves upon several most happy results from our little visit to the North. There is one other small point upon which I desire some light. This fellow Hayes had shod his horses with shoes which counterfeited the tracks of cows. Was it from Mr Wilder that he learned so extraordinary a device?'

The duke stood in thought for a moment, with a look of intense surprise on his face. Then he opened a door and showed us into a large room furnished as a museum. He led the way to a glass case in a corner, and pointed to the inscription.

'These shoes,' it ran, 'were dug up in the moat of Holdernesse Hall. They are for the use of horses; but they are shaped below with a cloven foot of iron, so as to throw pursuers off the track. They are supposed to have belonged to some of the marauding Barons of Holdernesse in the Middle Ages.'

Holmes opened the case, and, moistening his finger, he passed it along the shoe. A thin film of recent mud was left upon his skin.

'Thank you,' said he, as he replaced the glass. 'It is the second most interesting object that I have seen in the North.'

'And the first?'

Holmes folded up his cheque, and placed it carefully in his notebook. 'I am a poor man,' said he, as he patted it affectionately, and thrust it into the depths of his inner pocket.

The Beryl Coronet

'Holmes,' said I, as I stood one morning in our bow-window looking down the street, 'here is a madman coming along. It seems rather sad that his relatives should allow him to come out alone.'

My friend rose lazily from his armchair, and stood with his hands in the pockets of his dressing-gown, looking over my shoulder. It was a bright, crisp February morning, and the snow of the day before still lay deep upon the ground, shimmering brightly in the wintry sun. Down the centre of Baker Street it had been ploughed into a brown crumbly band by the traffic, but at either side and on the heaped-up edges of the footpaths it still lay as white as when it fell. The grey pavement had been cleaned and scraped, but was still dangerously slippery, so that there were fewer passengers than usual. Indeed, from the direction of the Metropolitan station no one was coming save the single gentleman whose eccentric conduct had drawn my attention.

He was a man of about fifty, tall, portly, and imposing, with a massive, strongly marked face and a commanding figure. He was dressed in a sombre yet rich style, in black frock-coat, shining hat, neat brown gaiters, and well-cut pearl-grey trousers. Yet his actions were in absurd contrast to the dignity of his dress and features, for he was running hard, with occasional little springs, such as a weary man gives who is little accustomed to set any tax upon his legs. As he ran he jerked his hands up and down, waggled his head, and writhed his face into the most extraordinary contortions.

'What on earth can be the matter with him?' I asked. 'He is looking up at the numbers of the houses.'

'I believe that he is coming here,' said Holmes, rubbing his hands.

'Here?'

'Yes; I rather think he is coming to consult me professionally. I think that I recognize the symptoms. Ha! did I not tell you?' As he spoke, the man, puffing and blowing, rushed at our door, and pulled at our bell until the whole house resounded with the clanging.

A few moments later he was in our room, still puffing, still gesticulating, but with so fixed a look of grief and despair in his eyes that our smiles were turned in an instant to horror and pity. For a while he could not get his words out, but swayed his body and plucked at his hair like one who has been driven to the extreme limits of his reason. Then, suddenly springing to his feet, he beat his head against the wall with such force that we both rushed upon him, and tore him away to the centre of the room. Sherlock Holmes pushed him down into the easy chair, and, sitting beside him, patted his hand, and chatted with him in the easy, soothing tones which he knew so well how to employ.

'You have come to me to tell me your story, have you not?' said he. 'You are fatigued with your haste. Pray wait until you have recovered yourself, and then I shall be most happy to look into any little problem which you may submit to me.'

The man sat for a minute or more with a heaving chest, fighting against his emotion. Then he passed his handkerchief over his brow, set his lips tight, and turned his face towards us.

'No doubt you think me mad?' said he.

'I see that you have had some great trouble,' responded Holmes.

'God knows I have! – a trouble which is enough to unseat my reason, so sudden and so terrible is it. Public disgrace I might have faced, although I am a man whose character has never yet borne a stain. Private affliction also is the lot of every man; but the two coming together, and in so frightful a form, have been enough to shake my very soul. Besides, it is not I alone. The very nobles in the land may suffer, unless some way be found out of this horrible affair.'

'Pray compose yourself, sir,' said Holmes, 'and let me have a clear account of who you are, and what it is that has befallen you.'

'My name,' answered our visitor, 'is probably familiar to your ears. I am Alexander Holder, of the banking firm of Holder & Stevenson, of Threadneedle Street.'

The name was indeed well known to us, as belonging to the senior partner in the second largest private banking concern in the City of London. What could have happened, then, to bring one of the foremost citizens of London to this most pitiable pass? We waited, all curiosity, until with another effort he braced himself to tell his story.

'I feel that time is of value,' said he, 'that is why I hastened here when the police inspector suggested that I should secure your co-operation. I came to Baker Street by the Underground, and hurried from there on foot, for the cabs go slowly through this snow. That is why I was so out of breath, for I am a man who takes very little exercise. I feel better now, and I will put the facts before you as shortly and yet as clearly as I can.

'It is, of course, well known to you, that in a successful banking business as much depends upon our being able to find remunerative investments for our funds, as upon our increasing our connection and the number of our depositors. One of our most lucrative means of laying out money is in the shape of loans, where the security is unimpeachable. We have done a good deal in this direction during the last few years, and there are many noble families to whom we have advanced large sums upon the security of their pictures, libraries, or plate.

'Yesterday morning I was seated in my office at the bank, when a card was brought in to me by one of the clerks. I started when I saw the name, for it was that of none other than – well, perhaps even to you I had better say no more than it was a name which is a household word all over the earth – one of the highest, noblest, most exalted names in England. I was overwhelmed by the honour, and attempted, when he entered, to say so, but he plunged at once into business with the air of a man who wishes to hurry quickly through a disagreeable task.

'"Mr Holder," said he, "I have been informed that you are in the habit of advancing money."

'"The firm do so when the security is good," I answered.

'"It is absolutely essential to me," said he, "that I should have fifty thousand pounds at once. I could of course borrow so trifling a sum ten times over from my friends, but I much prefer to make it a matter of business, and to carry out that business myself. In my position you can readily understand that it is unwise to place oneself under obligations."

'"For how long, may I ask, do you want this sum?" I asked.

'"Next Monday I have a large sum due to me, and I shall then most certainly repay what you advance, with whatever interest you think it right to charge. But it is very essential to me that the money should be paid at once."

'"I should be happy to advance it without further parley

from my own private purse," said I, "were it not that the strain would be rather more than it could bear. If, on the other hand, I am to do it in the name of the firm, then in justice to my partner I must insist that, even in your case, every business-like precaution should be taken."

'"I should much prefer to have it so," said he, raising up a square, black morocco case which he had laid beside his chair. "You have doubtless heard of the beryl coronet?"

'"One of the most precious public possessions of the Empire," said I.

'"Precisely." He opened the case, and there, embedded in soft, flesh-coloured velvet, lay the magnificent piece of jewellery which he had named. "There are thirty-nine enormous beryls," said he, "and the price of the gold chasing is incalculable. The lowest estimate would put the worth of the coronet at double the sum which I have asked. I am prepared to leave it with you as my security."

'I took the precious case into my hands and looked in some perplexity from it to my illustrious client.

'"You doubt its value?" he asked.

'"Not at all. I only doubt –"

'"The propriety of my leaving it. You may set your mind at rest about that. I should not dream of doing so were it not absolutely certain that I should be able in four days to reclaim it. It is a pure matter of form. Is the security sufficient?"

'"Ample."

'"You understand, Mr Holder, that I am giving you a strong proof of the confidence which I have in you, founded upon all that I have heard of you. I rely upon you not only to be discreet and to refrain from all gossip upon the matter, but, above all, to preserve this coronet with every possible precaution, because I need not say that a great public scandal would be caused if any harm were to befall it. Any injury to it would be almost as serious as its complete loss, for there are no beryls in the world to match these, and it would be impossible to replace them. I leave it with you, however, with every confidence, and I shall call for it in person on Monday morning."

'Seeing that my client was anxious to leave, I said no more; but, calling for my cashier, I ordered him to pay over fifty thousand pound notes. When I was alone once more, however, with the precious case lying upon the table in front of me, I could not but think with some misgivings of the immense responsibility which it entailed upon me. There could be no doubt that, as it was a national possession, a horrible scandal would ensue if any misfortune should occur to it. I already regretted having ever consented to take charge of it. However, it was too late to alter the matter now, so I locked it up in my private safe, and turned once more to my work.

'When evening came, I felt that it would be an imprudence to leave so precious a thing in the office behind me. Bankers' safes had been forced before now, and why should not mine be? If so, how terrible would be the position in which I should find myself! I determined, therefore, that for the next few days I would always carry the case backwards and forwards with me, so that it might never be really out of my reach. With this intention, I called a cab, and drove out to my house at Streatham, carrying the jewel with me. I did not breathe freely until I had taken it upstairs, and locked it in the bureau of my dressing-room.

'And now a word as to my household, Mr Holmes, for I wish you to thoroughly understand the situation. My groom and my page sleep out of the house, and may be set aside altogether. I have three maidservants who have been with me a number of years, and whose absolute reliability is quite above suspicion. Another, Lucy Parr, the second waiting-maid, has only been in my service a few months. She came with excellent character, however, and has always given me satisfaction. She is a very pretty girl, and has attracted admirers who have occasionally hung about the place. That is the only drawback which we have found to her, but we believe her to be a thoroughly good girl in every way.

'So much for the servants. My family itself is so small that it will not take me long to describe it. I am a widower, and have an only son, Arthur. He has been a disappointment to me, Mr Holmes, a grievous disappointment. I have no doubt that I am myself to blame. People tell me that I have spoiled him. Very likely I have. When my dear wife died I felt that he was all I had to love. I could not bear to see the smile fade even for a moment from his face. I have never denied him a wish. Perhaps it would have been better for both of us had I been sterner, but I meant it for the best.

'It was naturally my intention that he should succeed me in my business, but he was not of a business turn. He was wild, wayward, and, to speak the truth, I could not trust him in the handling of large sums of money. When he was young he became a member of an aristocratic club, and there, having charming manners, he was soon the intimate of a number of men with long purses and expensive habits. He learned to play heavily at cards and to squander money on the turf, until he had again and again to come to me and implore me to give him an advance upon his allowance, that he might settle his debts of honour. He tried more than once to break away from the dangerous company which he was keeping, but each time the influence of his friend Sir George Burnwell was enough to draw him back again.

'And, indeed, I could not wonder that such a man as Sir George Burnwell should gain an influence over him, for he has frequently brought him to my house, and I have found myself that I could hardly resist the fascination of his manner. He is older than Arthur, a man of the world to his fingertips, one who has been everywhere, seen everything, a brilliant talker, and a man of great personal beauty. Yet when I think of him in cold blood, far away from the glamour of his presence, I am convinced from his cynical speech, and the look which I have caught in his eyes, that he is one who should be deeply distrusted. So I think, and so, too, thinks my little Mary, who has a woman's quick insight into character.

'And now there is only she to be described. She is my niece; but when my brother died five years ago and left her alone in the world I adopted her and have looked upon her ever since as my daughter. She is a sunbeam in my house – sweet, loving, beautiful, a wonderful manager and house-keeper, yet as tender and quiet and gentle as a woman could be. She is my right hand. I do not know what I could do without her. In only one matter has she ever gone against my wishes. Twice my boy has asked her to marry him, for he loves her devotedly, but each time she has refused him. I think that if anyone could have drawn him into the right path it would have been she, and that his marriage might have changed his whole life; but now, alas! it is too late – for ever too late!

'Now, Mr Holmes, you know the people who live under my roof, and I shall continue with my miserable story.

'When we were taking coffee in the drawing-room that night, after dinner, I told Arthur and Mary my experience, and of the precious treasure which we had under our roof, suppressing only the name of my client. Lucy Parr, who had brought in the coffee, had, I am sure, left the room; but I cannot swear that the door was closed. Mary and Arthur were much interested, and wished to see the famous coronet, but I thought it better not to disturb it.

'"Where have you put it?" asked Arthur.

'"In my own bureau."

'"Well, I hope to goodness the house won't be burgled during the night," said he.

'"It is locked up," I answered.

'"Oh, any old key will fit that bureau. When I was a youngster I have opened it myself with the key of the box-room cupboard."

'He often had a wild way of talking, so that I thought little of what he said. He followed me to my room, however, that night with a very grave face.

'"Look here, Dad," said he, with his eyes cast down. "Can you let me have two hundred pounds?"

'"No, I cannot!" I answered sharply. "I have been far too generous with you in money matters."

'"You have been very kind," said he; "but I must have this money, or else I can never show my face inside the club again."

'"And a very good thing, too!" I cried.

'"Yes, but you would not have me leave it a dishonoured man," said he. "I could not bear the disgrace. I must raise the money in some way, and if you will not let me have it, then I must try other means."

'I was very angry, for this was the third demand during the month. "You shall not have a farthing from me," I cried, on which he bowed and left the room without another word.

'When he was gone I unlocked my bureau, made sure

that my treasure was safe, and locked it again. Then I started to go round the house to see that all was secure – a duty which I usually leave to Mary, but which I thought it well to perform myself that night. As I came down the stairs I saw Mary herself at the side-window of the hall, which she closed and fastened as I approached.

'"Tell me, Dad," said she, looking, I thought, a little disturbed, "did you give Lucy, the maid, leave to go out tonight?"

'"Certainly not."

'"She came in just now by the back door. I have no doubt that she has only been to the side gate to see someone but I think that it is hardly safe, and should be stopped."

'"You must speak to her in the morning, or I will, if you prefer it. Are you sure that everything is fastened?"

'"Quite sure, Dad."

'"Then, goodnight." I kissed her, and went to my bedroom, where I was soon asleep.

'I am endeavouring to tell you everything, Mr Holmes, which may have any bearing upon the case, but I beg that you will question me upon any point which I do not make clear.'

'On the contrary, your statement is singularly lucid.'

'I come to a part of my story now in which I should wish to be particularly so. I am not a very heavy sleeper, and the anxiety in my mind tended, no doubt, to make me even less so than usual. About two in the morning, then, I was awakened by some sound in the house. It had ceased ere I was wide awake, but it had left an impression behind it as though a window had gently closed somewhere. I lay listening with all my ears. Suddenly, to my horror, there was a distinct sound of footsteps moving softly in the next room. I slipped out of bed, all palpitating with fear, and peeped round the corner of my dressing-room door.

'"Arthur!" I screamed, "you villain! you thief! How dare you touch that coronet?"

'The gas was half up, as I had left it, and my unhappy boy, dressed only in his shirt and trousers, was standing beside the light, holding the coronet in his hands. He appeared to be wrenching at it, or bending it with all his strength. At my cry he dropped it from his grasp, and turned as pale as death. I snatched it up and examined it. One of the gold corners, with three of the beryls in it, was missing.

'"You blackguard!" I shouted, beside myself with rage. "You have destroyed it! You have dishonoured me for ever! Where are the jewels you have stolen?"

'"Stolen!" he cried.

'"Yes, you thief!" I roared, shaking him by the shoulder.

'"There are none missing. There cannot be any missing," said he.

'"There are three missing. And you know where they are. Must I call you a liar as well as a thief? Did I not see you trying to tear off another piece?"

'"You have called me names enough," said he; "I will not

stand it any longer. I shall not say another word about this business since you have chosen to insult me. I will leave your house in the morning, and make my own way in the world."

'"You shall leave it in the hands of the police!" I cried, half mad with grief and rage. "I shall have this matter probed to the bottom."

'"You shall learn nothing from me," said he, with a passion such as I should not have thought was in his nature. "If you choose to call the police, let them find what they can."

'By this time the whole house was astir, for I had raised my voice in my anger. Mary was the first to rush into my room, and at the sight of the coronet and of Arthur's face, she read the whole story, and, with a scream, fell down senseless on the ground. I sent the housemaid for the police, and put the investigation into their hands at once. When the inspector and a constable entered the house, Arthur, who had stood sullenly with his arms folded, asked me whether it was my intention to charge him with theft. I answered that it had ceased to be a private matter, but had become a public one, since the ruined coronet was national property. I was determined that the law should have its way in everything.

'"At least," said he, "you will not have me arrested at once. It would be to your advantage as well as mine if I might leave the house for five minutes."

'"That you may get away, or perhaps that you may conceal what you have stolen," said I. And then realizing the dreadful position in which I was placed, I implored him to remember that not only my honour, but that of one who was far greater than I, was at stake; and that he threatened to raise a scandal which would convulse the nation. He might avert it all if he would but tell me what he had done with the three missing stones.

'"You may as well face the matter," said I; "you have been caught in the act, and no confession could make your guilt more heinous. If you make such reparation as is in your power, by telling us where the beryls are, all shall be forgiven and forgotten."

'"Keep your forgiveness for those who ask for it," he answered, turning away from me with a sneer. I saw that he was too hardened for any words of mine to influence him. There was but one way for it. I called in the inspector, and gave him into custody. A search was made at once, not only of his person, but of his room, and of every portion of the house where he could possibly have concealed the gems; but no trace of them could be found, nor would the wretched boy open his mouth for all our persuasions and our threats. This morning he was removed to a cell, and I, after going through all the police formalities, have hurried round to you, to implore you to use your skill in unravelling the matter. The police have openly confessed that they can at present make nothing of it. You may go to any expense which you think necessary. I have already offered a reward of a thousand pounds. My God, what shall I do! I have lost my honour, my gems, and my son in one night. Oh, what shall I do!'

He put a hand on either side of his head, and rocked himself to and fro, droning to himself like a child whose grief has got beyond words.

Sherlock Holmes sat silent for some minutes, with his brows knitted and his eyes fixed upon the fire.

'Do you receive much company?' he asked.

'None, save my partner with his family, and an occasional friend of Arthur's. Sir George Burnwell has been several times lately. No one else, I think.'

'Do you go out much in society?'

'Arthur does. Mary and I stay at home. We neither of us care for it.'

'That is unusual in a young girl.'

'She is of a quiet nature. Besides, she is not so very young. She is four-and-twenty.'

'This matter, from what you say, seems to have been a shock to her also.'

'Terrible! She is even more affected than I.'

'You have neither of you any doubt as to your son's guilt?'

'How can we have, when I saw him with my own eyes with the coronet in his hands?'

'I hardly consider that a conclusive proof. Was the remainder of the coronet at all injured?'

'Yes, it was twisted.'

'Do you not think, then, that he might have been trying to straighten it?'

'God bless you! You are doing what you can for him and for me. But it is too heavy a task. What was he doing there at all? If his purpose were innocent, why did he not say so?'

'Precisely. And if he were guilty, why did he not invent a lie? His silence appears to me to cut both ways. There are several singular points about the case. What did the police think of the noise which awoke you from your sleep?'

'They considered that it might be caused by Arthur's closing his bedroom door.'

'A likely story! As if a man bent on felony would slam the door so as to awake a household. What did they say, then, of the disappearance of these gems?'

'They are still sounding the planking and probing the furniture in the hope of finding them.'

'Have they thought of looking outside the house?'

'Yes, they have shown extraordinary energy. The whole garden has already been minutely examined.'

'Now, my dear sir,' said Holmes, 'is it not obvious to you now that this matter really strikes much deeper than either you or the police were at first inclined to think? It appeared to you to be a simple case; to me it seems exceedingly complex. Consider what is involved by your theory. You suppose that your son came down from his bed, went, at great risk, to your dressing-room, opened your bureau, took out your coronet, broke off by main force a small portion of it, went off to some other place, concealed three gems out of the thirty-nine, with such skill that nobody can find them, and then returned with the other thirty-six into the room in which he exposed himself to the greatest danger of being discovered. I ask you now, is such a theory tenable?'

'But what other is there?' cried the banker with a gesture of despair. 'If his motives were innocent, why does he not explain them?'

'It is our task to find out,' replied Holmes, 'so now, if you please, Mr Holder, we will set off for Streatham together and devote an hour to glancing a little more closely into details.'

My friend insisted upon my accompanying them in their expedition, which I was eager enough to do, for my curiosity and sympathy were deeply stirred by the story to which we had listened. I confess that the guilt of the banker's son appeared to me to be as obvious as it did to his unhappy father, but still I had such faith in Holmes's judgement that I felt that there must be some grounds for hope as long as he was dissatisfied with the accepted explanation. He hardly spoke a word the whole way out to the southern suburb, but sat with his chin upon his breast, and his hat drawn over his eyes, sunk in the deepest thought. Our client appeared to have taken fresh heart at the little glimpse of hope which had been presented to him, and he even broke into a desultory chat with me over his business affairs. A short railway journey, and a shorter walk, brought us to Fairbank, the modest residence of the great financier.

Fairbank was a good-sized square house of white stone, standing back a little from the road. A double carriage sweep, with a snow-clad lawn, stretched down in front to the two large iron gates which closed the entrance. On the right side was a small wooden thicket which led into a narrow path between two neat hedges stretching from the road to the kitchen door, and forming the tradesmen's entrance. On the left ran a lane which led to the stables, and was not itself within the grounds at all, being a public, though little used, thoroughfare. Holmes left us standing at the door, and walked slowly all round the house, across the front, down the tradesmen's path, and so round by the garden behind into the stable lane. So long was he that Mr Holder and I went into the dining-room, and waited by the fire until he should return. We were sitting there in silence when the door opened, and a young lady came in. She was rather above the middle height, slim, with dark hair and eyes, which seemed the darker against the absolute pallor of her skin. I do not think that I have ever seen such deadly paleness in a woman's face. Her lips, too, were bloodless, but her eyes were flushed with crying. As she swept silently into the room she impressed me with a greater sense of her grief than the banker had done in the morning, and it was the more striking in her as she was evidently a woman of striking character, with immense capacity for self-restraint.

Disregarding my presence, she went straight to her uncle, and passed her hand over his head with a sweet womanly caress.

'You have given orders that Arthur should be liberated, have you not, Dad?' she asked.

'No, no, my girl, the matter must be probed to the bottom.'

'But I am so sure that he is innocent. You know what women's instincts are. I know that he had done no harm, and that you will be sorry for having acted so harshly.'

'Why is he silent, then, if he is innocent?'

'Who knows? Perhaps because he was so angry that you should suspect him.'

'How could I help suspecting him, when I actually saw him with the coronet in his hand?'

'Oh, but he had only picked it up to look at it. Oh, do, do take my word for it that he is innocent. Let the matter drop, and say no more. It is so dreadful to think of our dear Arthur in prison!'

'I shall never let it drop until the gems are found – never, Mary! Your affection for Arthur blinds you as to the awful consequences to me. Far from hushing the thing up, I have brought a gentleman down from London to inquire more deeply into it.'

'This gentleman?' she asked, facing round to me.

'No, his friend. He wished us to leave him alone. He is round in the stable lane now.'

'The stable lane?' She raised her dark eyebrows. 'What can he hope to find there? Ah, this, I suppose, is he. I trust, sir, that you will succeed in proving, what I feel sure is the truth, that my cousin Arthur is innocent of this crime.'

'I fully share your opinion, and, I trust with you, that we may prove it,' returned Holmes, going back to the mat to knock the snow from his shoes. 'I believe I have the honour of addressing Miss Mary Holder. Might I ask you a question or two?'

'Pray do, sir, if it may help, to clear this horrible affair up.'

'You heard nothing yourself last night?'

'Nothing, until my uncle here began to speak loudly. I heard that, and I came down.'

'You shut up the windows and doors the night before. Did you fasten all the windows?'

'Yes.'

'Were they all fastened this morning?'

'Yes.'

'You have a maid who has a sweetheart? I think that you remarked to your uncle last night that she had been out to see him?'

'Yes, and she was the girl who waited in the drawing-room, and who may have heard uncle's remarks about the coronet.'

'I see. You infer that she may have gone out to tell her sweetheart, and that the two may have planned the robbery.'

'But what is the good of all these vague theories,' cried the banker impatiently, 'when I have told you that I saw Arthur with the coronet in his hands?'

'Wait a little, Mr Holder. We must come back to that. About this girl, Miss Holder. You saw her return by the kitchen door, I presume?'

'Yes; when I went to see if the door was fastened for the night I met her slipping in. I saw the man, too, in the gloom.'

'Do you know him?'

'Oh, yes; he is the greengrocer who brings our vegetables round. His name is Francis Prosper.'

'He stood,' said Holmes, 'to the left of the door – that is to say, farther up the path than is necessary to reach the door?'

'Yes, he did.'

'And he is a man with a wooden leg?'

Something like fear sprang up in the young lady's expressive black eyes. 'Why, you are like a magician,' said she. 'How do you know that?' She smiled, but there was no answering smile in Holmes's thin, eager face.

'I should be very glad now to go upstairs,' said he. 'I shall probably wish to go over the outside of the house again. Perhaps I had better take a look at the lower windows before I go up.'

He walked swiftly round from one to the other, pausing only at the large one which looked from the hall on to the stable lane. This he opened, and made a very careful examination of the sill with his powerful magnifying lens. 'Now we shall go upstairs,' said he, at last.

The banker's dressing-room was a plainly furnished little chamber with a grey carpet, a large bureau, and a long mirror. Holmes went to the bureau first, and looked hard at the lock.

'Which key was used to open it?' he asked.

'That which my son himself indicated – that of the cupboard of the lumber-room.'

'Have you it here?'

'That is it on the dressing-table.'

Sherlock Holmes took it up and opened the bureau.

'It is a noiseless lock,' said he. 'It is no wonder that it did not wake you. This case, I presume, contains the coronet. We must have a look at it.' He opened the case, and, taking out the diadem, he laid it upon the table. It was a magnificent specimen of the jeweller's art, and the thirty-six stones were the finest that I have ever seen. At one side of the coronet was a crooked cracked edge, where a corner holding three gems had been torn away.

'Now, Mr Holder,' said Holmes; 'here is the corner which corresponds to that which has been so unfortunately lost. Might I beg that you will break it off.'

The banker recoiled in horror. 'I should not dream of trying,' said he.

'Then I will.' Holmes suddenly bent his strength upon it, but without result. 'I feel it give a little,' said he; 'but, though

I am exceptionally strong in the fingers, it would take me all my time to break it. An ordinary man could not do it. Now, what do you think would happen if I did break it, Mr Holder? There would be a noise like a pistol shot. Do you tell me that all this happened within a few yards of your bed, and that you heard nothing of it?'

'I do not know what to think. It is all dark to me.'

'But perhaps it may grow lighter as we go. What do you think, Miss Holder?'

'I confess that I still share my uncle's perplexity.'

'Your son had no shoes or slippers on when you saw him?'

'He had nothing on save only his trousers and shirt.'

'Thank you. We have certainly been favoured with extraordinary luck during this inquiry, and it will be entirely our own fault if we do not succeed in clearing the matter up. With your permission, Mr Holder, I shall now continue my investigations outside.'

He went alone, at his own request, for he explained that any unnecessary footmarks might make his task more difficult. For an hour or more he was at work, returning at last with his feet heavy with snow and his features as inscrutable as ever.

'I think that I have seen now all that there is to see, Mr Holder,' said he; 'I can serve you best by returning to my rooms.'

'But the gems, Mr Holmes. Where are they?'

'I cannot tell.'

The banker wrung his hands. 'I shall never see them again!' he cried. 'And my son? You give me hopes?'

'My opinion is in no way altered.'

'Then for God's sake what was this dark business which was acted in my house last night?'

'If you can call upon me at my Baker Street rooms tomorrow morning between nine and ten I shall be happy to do what I can to make it clearer. I understand that you give me *carte blanche* to act for you, provided only that I get back the gems, and that you place no limit on the sum I may draw.'

'I would give my fortune to have them back.'

'Very good. I shall look into the matter between this and then. Goodbye; it is just possible that I may have to come over here again before evening.'

It was obvious to me that my companion's mind was now made up about the case, although what his conclusions were was more than I could even dimly imagine. Several times during our homeward journey I endeavoured to sound him upon that point, but he always glided away to some other topic, until at last I gave it over in despair. It was not yet three when we found ourselves in our room once more. He hurried to his chamber, and was down again in a few minutes dressed as a common loafer. With his collar turned up, his shiny seedy coat, his red cravat, and his worn boots, he was a perfect sample of the class.

'I think that this should do,' said he, glancing into the glass above the fireplace. 'I only wish that you could come with me, Watson, but I fear that it won't do. I may be on the trail in this matter, or I may be following a will-o'-the-wisp, but I shall soon know which it is. I hope that I may be back in a few hours.' He cut a slice of beef from the joint upon the sideboard, sandwiched it between two rounds of bread, and, thrusting this rude meal into his pocket, he started off upon his expedition.

I had just finished my tea when he returned, evidently in excellent spirits, swinging an old elastic-sided boot in his hand. He chucked it down into a corner and helped himself to a cup of tea.

'I only looked in as I passed,' said he. 'I am going right on.'

'Where to?'

'Oh, to the other side of the West End. It may be some time before I get back. Don't wait up for me in case I should be late.'

'How are you getting on?'

'Oh, so-so. Nothing to complain of. I have been out to Streatham since I saw you last, but I did not call at the house. It is a very sweet little problem, and I would not have missed it for a good deal. However, I must not sit gossiping here, but must get these disreputable clothes off and return to my highly respectable self.'

I could see by his manner that he had stronger reasons

for satisfaction than his words alone would imply. His eyes twinkled, and there was even a touch of colour upon his sallow cheeks. He hastened upstairs, and a few minutes later I heard the slam of the hall door, which told me that he was off once more upon his congenial hunt.

I waited until midnight, but there was no sign of his return, so I retired to my room. It was no uncommon thing for him to be away for days and nights on end when he was hot upon a scent, so that his lateness caused me no surprise. I do not know at what hour he came in, but when I came down to breakfast in the morning, there he was with a cup of coffee in one hand and the paper in the other, as fresh and trim as possible.

'You will excuse my beginning without you, Watson,' said he; 'but you remember that our client has rather an early appointment this morning.'

'Why, it is after nine now,' I answered. 'I should not be surprised if that were he. I thought I heard a ring.'

It was, indeed, our friend the financier. I was shocked by the change which had come over him, for his face, which was naturally of a broad and massive mould, was now pinched and fallen in, while his hair seemed to be at least a shade whiter. He entered with a weariness and lethargy which was even more painful than his violence of the morning before, and he dropped heavily into the armchair which I pushed forward for him.

'I do not know what I have done to be so severely tried,'

said he. 'Only two days ago I was a happy and prosperous man, without a care in the world. Now I am left to a lonely and dishonoured age. One sorrow comes close upon the heels of another. My niece Mary has deserted me.'

'Deserted you?'

'Yes. Her bed this morning had not been slept in, her room was empty, and a note lay for me upon the hall table. I had said to her last night, in sorrow and not in anger, that if she had married my boy all might have been well with him. Perhaps it was thoughtless of me to say so. It is to that remark that she refers in this note:

> My Dearest Uncle – I feel that I have brought this trouble upon you, and that if I had acted differently this terrible misfortune might never have occurred. I cannot, with this thought in my mind, ever again be happy under your roof, and I feel that I must leave you for ever. Do not worry about my future, for that is provided for; and, above all, do not search for me, for it will be fruitless labour, and an ill service to me. In life or in death, I am ever your loving
>
> MARY

'What could she mean by that note, Mr Holmes? Do you think it points to suicide?'

'No, no, nothing of the kind. It is perhaps the best possible solution. I trust, Mr Holder, that you are nearing the end of your troubles.'

'Ha! You say so! You have heard something, Mr Holmes: you have learned something! Where are the gems?'

'You would not think a thousand pounds apiece an excessive sum for them?'

'I would pay ten.'

'That would be unnecessary. Three thousand will cover the matter. And there is a little reward, I fancy. Have you your cheque-book? Here is a pen. Better make it out for four thousand pounds.'

With a dazed face the banker made out the required cheque. Holmes walked over to his desk, took out a little triangular piece of gold with three gems in it, and threw it down upon the table.

With a shriek of joy our client clutched it up.

'You have it?' he gasped. 'I am saved! I am saved!'

The reaction of joy was as passionate as his grief had been, and he hugged his recovered gems to his bosom.

'There is one other thing you owe, Mr Holder,' said Sherlock Holmes, rather sternly.

'Owe!' He caught up a pen. 'Name the sum, and I will pay it.'

'No, the debt is not to me. You owe a very humble apology to that noble lad, your son, who has carried himself in this matter as I should be proud to see my own son do, should I ever chance to have one.'

'Then it was not Arthur who took them?'

'I told you yesterday, and I repeat today, that it was not.'

'You are sure of it! Then let us hurry to him at once, to let him know that the truth is known.'

'He knows it already. When I had cleared it all up I had an interview with him, and finding that he would not tell me the story, I told it to him, on which he had to confess that I was right, and to add the very few details which were not yet quite clear to me. Your news of this morning, however, may open his lips.'

'For Heaven's sake tell me, then, what is this extraordinary mystery!'

'I will do so, and I will show you the steps by which I reached it. And let me say to you, first, what it is hardest for me to say and for you to hear. There has been an understanding between Sir George Burnwell and your niece, Mary. They have now fled together.'

'My Mary? Impossible!'

'It is, unfortunately, more than possible; it is certain. Neither you nor your son knew the true character of this man when you admitted him into your family circle. He is one of the most dangerous men in England – a ruined gambler, an absolutely desperate villain; a man without heart or conscience. Your niece knew nothing of such men. When he breathed his vows to her, as he had done to a hundred before her, she flattered herself that she alone had touched his heart. The devil knows best what he said, but at last she became his tool, and was in the habit of seeing him nearly every evening.'

'I cannot, and I will not, believe it!' cried the banker with an ashen face.

'I will tell you, then, what occurred in your house that night. Your niece, when you had, as she thought, gone to your room, slipped down and talked to her lover through the window which leads into the stable lane. His footmarks had pressed right through the snow, so long had he stood there. She told him of the coronet. His wicked lust for gold kindled at the news, and he bent her to his will. I have no doubt that she loved you, but there are women in whom the love of a lover extinguishes all other loves, and I think that she must have been one. She had hardly listened to his instructions when she saw you coming downstairs, on which she closed the window rapidly, and told you about one of the servants' escapade with her wooden-legged lover, which was all perfectly true.

'Your boy, Arthur, went to bed after his interview with you, but he slept badly on account of his uneasiness about his club debts. In the middle of the night he heard a soft tread pass his door, so he rose, and looking out, was surprised to see his cousin walking very stealthily along the passage, until she disappeared into your dressing-room. Petrified with astonishment the lad slipped on some clothes, and waited there in the dark to see what would come of this strange affair. Presently she emerged from the room again, and in the light of the passage lamp your son saw that she carried the precious coronet in her hands. She passed down the stairs, and he, thrilling with horror, ran along and slipped behind the curtain near your door, whence he could see what passed in the hall beneath. He saw her stealthily open the window, hand out the coronet to someone in the gloom, and then closing it once more hurry back to her room, passing quite close to where he stood hid behind the curtain.

'As long as she was on the scene he could not take any action without a horrible exposure of the woman whom he loved. But the instant she was gone he realized how crushing a misfortune this would be for you, and how all-important it was to set it right. He rushed down, just as he was, in his bare feet, opened the window, sprang out into the snow, and ran down the lane, where he could see a dark figure in the moonlight. Sir George Burnwell tried to get away, but Arthur caught him, and there was a struggle between them, your lad tugging at one side of the coronet, and his opponent at the other. In the scuffle, your son struck Sir George, and cut him over the eye. Then something suddenly snapped, and your son, finding that he had the coronet in his hands, rushed back, closed the window, ascending to your room, and had just observed that the coronet had been twisted in the struggle and was endeavouring to straighten it, when you appeared upon the scene.'

'Is it possible?' gasped the banker.

'You then roused his anger by calling him names at a moment when he felt that he had deserved your warmest thanks. He could not explain the true state of affairs without betraying the one who certainly deserved little enough consideration at his hands. He took the more chivalrous view, however, and preserved her secret.'

'And that was why she shrieked and fainted when she saw the coronet,' cried Mr Holder. 'Oh, my God! What a blind fool I have been. And his asking to be allowed to go out for five minutes! The dear fellow wanted to see if the missing piece were at the scene of the struggle. How cruelly I have misjudged him!'

'When I arrived at the house,' continued Holmes, 'I at once went very carefully round it to observe if there were any traces in the snow which might help me. I knew that none had fallen since the evening before, and also that there had been a strong frost to preserve impressions. I passed along the tradesmen's path, but found it all trampled down and indistinguishable. Just beyond it, however, at the far side of the kitchen door, a woman had stood and talked with a man, whose round impression on one side showed that he had a wooden leg. I could even tell that they had been disturbed, for the woman had run back swiftly to the door, as was shown by the deep toe and light heelmarks, while Wooden-leg had waited a little, and then had gone away. I thought at the time that this might be the maid and her sweetheart, of whom you had already spoken to me, and inquiry showed it was so. I passed round the garden without seeing anything more than random tracks, which I took to be the police; but when I got into the stable lane a very long and complex story was written in the snow in front of me.

'There was a double line of tracks of a booted man, and a second double line which I saw with delight belonged to a man with naked feet. I was at once convinced from what you had told me that the latter was your son. The first had walked both ways, but the other had run swiftly, and, as his tread was marked in places over the depression of the boot, it was obvious that he had passed after the other. I followed them up, and found that they led to the hall window, where Boots had worn all the snow away while waiting. Then I walked to the other end, which was a hundred yards or more down the lane. I saw where Boots had faced round, where the snow was cut up, as though there had been a struggle, and, finally, where a few drops of blood had fallen, to show me that I was not mistaken. Boots had then run down the lane, and another little smudge of blood showed that it was he who had been hurt. When he came to the high-road at the other end, I found that the pavement had been cleared, so there was an end to that clue.

'On entering the house, however, I examined, as you remember, the sill and framework of the hall window with my lens, and I could at once see that someone had passed out. I could distinguish the outline of an instep where the wet foot had been placed in coming in. I was then beginning to be able to form an opinion as to what had occurred. A man had waited outside the window, someone had brought him the gems; the deed had been overseen by your son, he had pursued the thief, had struggled with him, they had each tugged at the coronet, their united strength causing injuries which neither alone could have effected. He had returned with the prize, but had left a fragment in the grasp of his opponent. So far I was clear. The question now was, who was the man, and who was it brought him the coronet?

'It is an old maxim of mine that when you have excluded the impossible, whatever remains, however improbable, must be the truth. Now, I knew that it was not you who had brought it down, so there only remained your niece and the maids. But if it were the maids, why should your son allow himself to be accused in their place? There could be no possible reason. As he loved his cousin, however, there was an excellent explanation why he should retain her secret – the more so as the secret was a disgraceful one. When I remembered that you had seen her at that window, and how she had fainted on seeing the coronet again, my conjecture became a certainty.

'And who could it be who was her confederate? A lover evidently, for who else could outweigh the love and gratitude which she must feel to you? I knew that you went out little, and that your circle of friends was a very limited one. But among them was Sir George Burnwell. I had heard of him before as being a man of evil reputation among women. It must have been he who wore those boots, and retained the missing gems. Even though he knew that Arthur had discovered him, he might still flatter himself that he was safe, for the lad could not say a word without compromising his own family.

'Well, your own good sense will suggest what measures I took next. I went in the shape of a loafer to Sir George's house, managed to pick up an acquaintance with his valet, learned that his master had cut his head the night before, and finally, at the expense of six shillings, made all sure by buying a pair of his cast-off shoes. With those I journeyed down to Streatham, and saw that they exactly fitted the tracks.'

'I saw an ill-dressed vagabond in the lane yesterday evening,' said Mr Holder.

'Precisely. It was I. I found that I had my man, so I came home and changed my clothes. It was a delicate part which I had to play then, for I saw that a prosecution must be avoided to avert scandal, and I knew that so astute a villain would see that our hands were tied in the matter. I went and saw him. At first, of course, he denied everything. But when I gave him every particular that had occurred, he tried to bluster, and took down a life-preserver from the wall. I knew my man, however, and I clapped a pistol to his head before he could strike. Then he became a little more reasonable. I told him that we would give him a price for the stones he held – a thousand pounds apiece. That brought out the first signs of grief he had shown. "Why, dash it all!" said he, "I've let them go at six hundred for the three!" I soon managed to get the address of the receiver who had them, on promising him that there would be no prosecution. Off I set to him, and after much chaffering I got our stones at a thousand apiece. Then I looked in upon your son, told him that all was right, and eventually got to my bed about two o'clock after what I may call a really hard day's work.'

'A day which has saved England from a great public scandal,' said the banker, rising. 'Sir, I cannot find words to thank you. But you shall not find me ungrateful for what you have done. Your skill has indeed exceeded all that I have ever heard of it. And now I must fly to my dear boy to apologize to him for the wrong which I have done him. As to what you tell me of poor Mary, it goes to my heart. Not even your skill can inform me where she is now.'

'I think that we may safely say,' returned Holmes, 'that she is wherever Sir George Burnwell is. It is equally certain, too, that whatever her sins are, they will soon receive a more than sufficient punishment.'

The Engineer's Thumb

Of all the problems which have been submitted to my friend Mr Sherlock Holmes for solution during the years of our intimacy, there were only two which I was the means of introducing to his notice, that of Mr Hatherley's thumb and that of Colonel Warburton's madness. Of these the latter may have afforded a finer field for an acute and original observer, but the other was so strange in its inception and so dramatic in its details, that it may be the more worthy of being placed upon record, even if it gave my friend fewer openings for those deductive methods of reasoning by which he achieved such remarkable results. The story has, I believe, been told more than once in the newspapers, but, like all such narratives, its effect is much less striking when set forth *en bloc* in a single half-column of print than when the facts slowly evolve before your own eyes and the mystery clears gradually away as each new discovery furnishes a step which leads on to the complete truth. At the time the circumstances made a deep impression upon me, and the lapse of two years has hardly served to weaken the effect.

It was in the summer of '89, not long after my marriage, that the events occurred which I am now about to summarize. I had returned to civil practice, and had finally abandoned Holmes in his Baker Street rooms, although I continually visited him, and occasionally even persuaded him to forgo his Bohemian habits so far as to come and visit us. My practice had steadily increased, and as I happened to live at no very great distance from Paddington Station, I got a few patients from among the officials. One of these whom I had cured of a painful and lingering disease was never weary of advertising my virtues, and of endeavouring to send me on every sufferer over whom he might have any influence.

One morning, at a little before seven o'clock, I was awakened by the maid tapping at the door, to announce that two men had come from Paddington, and were waiting in the consulting room. I dressed hurriedly, for I knew by experience that railway cases were seldom trivial, and hastened downstairs. As I descended, my old ally, the guard, came out of the room, and closed the door tightly behind him.

'I've got him here,' he whispered, jerking his thumb over his shoulder; 'he's all right.'

'What is it, then?' I asked, for his manner suggested that it was some strange creature which he had caged up in my room.

'It's a new patient,' he whispered. 'I thought I'd bring him round myself; then he couldn't slip away. There he is, all safe and sound. I must go now, Doctor, I have my dooties, just the same as you.' And off he went, this trusty tout, without even giving me time to thank him.

I entered my consulting room, and found a gentleman seated by the table. He was quietly dressed in a suit of heather tweed, with a soft cloth cap, which he had laid down upon my books. Round one of his hands he had a handkerchief wrapped, which was mottled all over with blood-stains. He was young, not more than five-and-twenty, I should say, with a strong masculine face; but he was exceedingly pale, and gave me the impression of a man who was suffering from some strong agitation, which it took all his strength of mind to control.

'I am sorry to knock you up so early, Doctor,' said he. 'But I have had a very serious accident during the night. I came in by train this morning, and on inquiring at Paddington as to where I might find a doctor, a worthy fellow very kindly escorted me here. I gave the maid a card, but I see that she has left it upon the side table.'

I took it up and glanced at it. 'Mr Victor Hatherley, hydraulic engineer, 16a Victoria Street (3rd floor).' That was the name, style, and abode of my morning visitor. 'I regret that I have kept you waiting,' said I, sitting down in my library chair. 'You are fresh from a night journey, I understand, which is in itself a monotonous occupation.'

'Oh, my night could not be called monotonous,' said he, and laughed. He laughed very heartily, with a high ringing note, leaning back in his chair, and shaking his sides. All my medical instincts rose up against that laugh.

'Stop it!' I cried. 'Pull yourself together!' And I poured some water from a carafe.

It was useless, however. He was off in one of those hysterical outbursts which come upon a strong nature when some great crisis is over and gone. Presently he came to himself once more, very weary and blushing hotly.

'I have been making a fool of myself,' he gasped.

'Not at all. Drink this!' I dashed some brandy into the water, and the colour began to come back to his bloodless cheeks.

'That's better!' said he. 'And now, Doctor, perhaps you would kindly attend to my thumb, or rather to the place where my thumb used to be.'

He unwound the handkerchief and held out his hand. It gave even my hardened nerves a shudder to look at it.

'Good heavens!' I cried, 'this is a terrible injury. It must have bled considerably.'

'Yes, it did. I fainted when it was done; and I think that I must have been senseless for a long time. When I came to, I found that it was still bleeding, so I tied one end of my handkerchief very tightly round the wrist, and braced it up with a twig.'

'Excellent! You should have been a surgeon.'

'It is a question of hydraulics, you see, and came within my own province.'

'This has been done,' said I, examining the wound, 'by a very heavy and sharp instrument.'

'A thing like a cleaver,' said he.

'An accident, I presume?'

'By no means.'

'What, a murderous attack!'

'Very murderous indeed.'

'You horrify me.'

I sponged the wound, cleaned it, dressed it; and, finally, covered it over with cotton wadding and carbolized bandages. He lay back without wincing, though he bit his lip from time to time.

'How is that?' I asked, when I had finished.

'Capital! Between your brandy and your bandage, I feel a new man. I was very weak, but I have had a good deal to go through.'

'Perhaps you had better not speak of the matter. It is evidently trying to your nerves.'

'Oh, no; not now. I shall have to tell my tale to the police; but, between ourselves, if it were not for the convincing evidence of this wound of mine, I should be surprised if they believed my statement, for it is a very extraordinary one, and I have not much in the way of proof with which to back it up. And, even if they believe me, the clues which I can give them are so vague that it is a question whether justice will be done.'

'Ha!' cried I, 'if it is anything in the nature of a problem which you desire to see solved, I should strongly recommend you to come to my friend Mr Sherlock Holmes before you go to the official police.'

'Oh, I have heard of that fellow,' answered my visitor, 'and I should be very glad if he would take the matter up, though of course I must use the official police as well. Would you give me an introduction to him?'

'I'll do better. I'll take you round to him myself.'

'I should be immensely obliged to you.'

'We'll call a cab and go together. We shall just be in time to have a little breakfast with him. Do you feel equal to it?'

'Yes. I shall not feel easy until I have told my story.'

'Then my servant will call a cab, and I shall be with you in an instant.' I rushed upstairs, explained the matter shortly to my wife, and in five minutes was inside a hansom, driving with my new acquaintance to Baker Street.

Sherlock Holmes was, as I expected, lounging about his sitting-room in his dressing-gown, reading the agony column of *The Times*, and smoking his before-breakfast pipe, which was composed of all the plugs and dottles left from his smokes of the day before, all carefully dried and collected on the corner of the mantelpiece. He received us in his quietly genial fashion, ordered fresh rashers and eggs, and joined us in a hearty meal. When it was concluded he settled our new acquaintance upon the sofa, placed a pillow beneath his head, and laid a glass of brandy and water within his reach.

'It is easy to see that your experience has been no common one, Mr Hatherley,' said he. 'Pray lie down there and make yourself absolutely at home. Tell us what you can, but stop when you are tired, and keep up your strength with a little stimulant.'

'Thank you,' said my patient, 'but I have felt another man since the doctor bandaged me, and I think that your breakfast has completed the cure. I shall take up as little of your valuable time as possible, so I shall start at once upon my peculiar experiences.'

Holmes sat in his big armchair, with the weary, heavy-lidded expression which veiled his keen and eager nature, while I sat opposite to him, and we listened in silence to the strange story which our visitor detailed to us.

'You must know,' said he, 'that I am an orphan and a bachelor, residing alone in lodgings in London. By profession I am a hydraulic engineer, and have had considerable experience of my work during the seven years that I was apprenticed to Venner & Matheson, the well-known firm of Greenwich. Two years ago, having served my time, and having also come into a fair sum of money through my poor father's death, I determined to start in business for myself, and took professional chambers in Victoria Street.

'I suppose that everyone finds his first independent start in business a dreary experience. To me it has been exceptionally so. During two years I have had three consultations and one small job, and that is absolutely all that my profession has brought me. My gross takings amount to twenty-seven pounds ten. Every day, from nine in the morning until four in the afternoon, I waited in my little den, until at last my heart began to sink, and I came to believe that I should never have any practice at all.

'Yesterday, however, just as I was thinking of leaving the office, my clerk entered to say there was a gentleman waiting who wished to see me upon business. He brought up a card, too, with the name of "Colonel Lysander Stark" engraved upon it. Close at his heels came the colonel himself, a man rather over the middle size but of an exceeding thinness. I do not think that I have ever seen so thin a man. His whole face sharpened away into nose and chin, and the skin of his cheeks was drawn quite tense over his outstanding bones. Yet this emaciation seemed to be his natural habit, and due to no disease, for his eye was bright, his step brisk, and his bearing assured. He was plainly but neatly dressed, and his age, I should judge, would be nearer forty than thirty.

'"Mr Hatherley?" said he, with something of a German accent. "You have been recommended to me, Mr Hatherley, as being a man who is not only proficient in his profession, but is also discreet and capable of preserving a secret."

'I bowed, feeling as flattered as any young man would at such an address. "May I ask who it was who gave me so good a character?" I asked.

'"Well, perhaps it is better that I should not tell you just at this moment. I have it from the same source that you are both an orphan and a bachelor, and are residing alone in London."

'"That is quite correct," I answered, "but you will excuse me if I say that I cannot see how all this bears upon my professional qualifications. I understood that it was on a professional matter that you wished to speak to me?"

'"Undoubtedly so. But you will find that all I say is really to the point. I have a professional commission for you, but absolute secrecy is quite essential – *absolute* secrecy, you understand, and of course we may expect that more from a man who is alone than from one who lives in the bosom of his family."

'"If I promise to keep a secret," said I, "you may absolutely depend upon my doing so."

'He looked very hard at me as I spoke, and it seemed to me that I had never seen so suspicious and questioning an eye.

'"You do promise, then?" said he at last.

'"Yes, I promise."

'"Absolute and complete silence, before, during, and after? No reference to the matter at all, either in word or writing?"

'"I have already given you my word."

'"Very good." He suddenly sprang up, and darting like lightning across the room he flung open the door. The passage outside was empty.

'"That's all right," said he, coming back. "I know that

clerks are sometimes curious as to their masters' affairs. Now we can talk in safety." He drew up his chair very close to mine, and began to stare at me again with the same questioning, and thoughtful look.

'A feeling of repulsion and of something akin to fear had begun to rise within me at the strange antics of this fleshless man. Even my dread of losing a client could not restrain me from showing my impatience.

'"I beg that you will state your business, sir," said I; "my time is of value." Heaven forgive me for that last sentence, but the words came to my lips.

'"How would fifty guineas for a night's work suit you?" he asked.

'"Most admirably."

'"I say a night's work, but an hour's would be nearer the mark. I simply want your opinion about a hydraulic stamping machine which has got out of gear. If you show us what is wrong we shall soon set it right ourselves. What do you think of such a commission as that?"

'"The work appears to be light, and the pay munificent."

'"Precisely so. We shall want you to come tonight by the last train."

'"Where to?"

'"To Eyford, in Berkshire. It is a little place near the borders of Oxfordshire, and within seven miles of Reading. There is a train from Paddington which would bring you in there at about 11.15."

'"Very good."

'"I shall come down in a carriage to meet you."

'"There is a drive, then?"

'"Yes, our little place is quite out in the country. It is a good seven miles from Eyford station."

'"Then we can hardly get there before midnight. I suppose there would be no chance of a train back. I should be compelled to stop the night."

'"Yes, we could easily give you a shakedown."

'"That is very awkward. Could I not come at some more convenient hour?"

'"We have judged it best that you should come late. It is to recompense you for any inconvenience that we are paying you, a young and unknown man, a fee which would buy an opinion from the very heads of your profession. Still, of course, if you would like to draw out of the business, there is plenty of time to do so."

'I thought of the fifty guineas, and of how very useful they would be to me. "Not at all," said I; "I shall be very happy to accommodate myself to your wishes. I should like, however, to understand a little more clearly what it is that you wish me to do."

'"Quite so. It is very natural that the pledge of secrecy which we have exacted from you should have aroused your curiosity. I have no wish to commit you to anything without your having it all laid before you. I suppose that we are absolutely safe from eavesdroppers?"

'"Entirely."

'"Then the matter stands thus. You are probably aware that fuller's earth is a valuable product, and that it is only found in one or two places in England?"

'"I have heard so."

'"Some little time ago I bought a small place – a very small place – within ten miles of Reading. I was fortunate enough to discover that there was a deposit of fuller's earth in one of my fields. On examining it, however, I found that this deposit was a comparatively small one, and that it formed a link between two very much larger ones upon the right and the left – both of them, however, in the grounds of my neighbours. These good people were absolutely ignorant that their land contained that which was quite as valuable as a gold mine. Naturally, it was to my interest to buy their land before they discovered its true value; but, unfortunately, I had no capital by which I could do this. I took a few of my friends into the secret, however, and they suggested that we should quietly and secretly work our own little deposit, and that in this way we should earn the money which would enable us to buy the neighbouring fields. This we have now been doing for some time, and in order to help us in our operations we erected a hydraulic press. This press, as I have already explained, has got out of order, and we wish your advice upon the subject. We guard our secret very jealously, however, and if it once became known that we had hydraulic engineers coming to our little house, it would soon rouse inquiry, and then, if the facts came out, it would be goodbye to any chance of getting these fields and carrying out our plans. That is why I have made you promise me that you will not tell a human being that you are going to Eyford tonight. I hope that I make it all plain?"

'"I quite follow you," said I. "The only point which I could not quite understand, was what use you could make of a hydraulic press in excavating fuller's earth, which, as I understand, is dug out like gravel from a pit."

'"Ah!" said he carelessly, "we have our own process. We compress the earth into bricks, so as to remove them without revealing what they are. But that is a mere detail. I have taken you fully into my confidence now, Mr Hatherley, and I have shown you how I trust you." He rose as he spoke. "I shall expect you, then, at Eyford, at 11.15."

'"I shall certainly be there."

'"And not a word to a soul." He looked at me with a last long, questioning gaze, and then, pressing my hand in a cold, dank grasp, he hurried from the room.

'Well, when I came to think it all over in cool blood I was very much astonished, as you may both think, at this sudden commission which had been entrusted to me. On the one hand, of course, I was glad, for the fee was at least tenfold what I should have asked had I set a price upon my own services, and it was possible that this order might lead to other ones. On the other hand, the face and manner of my patron had made an unpleasant impression upon me, and I could not think that his explanation of the fuller's earth was sufficient to explain the necessity for my coming at midnight, and his extreme anxiety lest I should tell anyone of my errand. However, I threw all my fears to the winds, ate a hearty supper, drove to Paddington, and started off, having obeyed to the letter the injunction as to holding my tongue.

'At Reading I had to change not only my carriage but my station. However, I was in time for the last train to Eyford, and I reached the little dim-lit station after eleven o'clock. I was the only passenger who got out there, and there was no one upon the platform save a single sleepy porter with a lantern. As I passed out through the wicket-gate, however, I found my acquaintance of the morning waiting in the shadow upon the other side. Without a word he grasped my arm and hurried me into a carriage, the door of which was standing open. He drew up the windows on either side, tapped on the woodwork, and away we went as hard as the horse could go.'

'One horse?' interjected Holmes.

'Yes, only one.'

'Did you observe the colour?'

'Yes, I saw it by the sidelights when I was stepping into the carriage. It was a chestnut.'

'Tired-looking or fresh?'

'Oh, fresh and glossy.'

'Thank you. I am sorry to have interrupted you. Pray continue your most interesting statement.'

'Away we went then, and we drove for at least an hour. Colonel Lysander Stark had said that it was only seven miles, but I should think, from the rate that we seemed to go, and the time we took, that it must have been nearer twelve. He sat at my side in silence all the time, and I was aware, more than once when I glanced in his direction, that he was looking at me with great intensity. The country roads seemed to be not very good in that part of the world, for we lurched and jolted terribly. I tried to look out of the windows to see something of where we were, but they were made of frosted glass, and I could make out nothing save an occasional blur of a passing light. Now and then I hazarded some remark to break the monotony of the journey, but the colonel answered only in monosyllables, and the conversation soon flagged. At last, however, the bumping of the road was exchanged for the crisp smoothness of a gravel drive and the carriage came to a stand. Colonel Lysander Stark sprang out, and, as I followed after him, pulled me swiftly into a porch which gaped in front of us. We stepped, as it were, right out of the carriage and into the hall, so that I failed to catch the most fleeting glance of the front of the house. The instant that I had crossed the threshold the door slammed heavily behind us, and I heard faintly the rattle of the wheels as the carriage drove away.

‘It was pitch dark inside the house, and the colonel fumbled about looking for matches, and muttering under his breath. Suddenly a door opened at the other end of the passage, and a long, golden bar of light shot out in our direction. It grew broader, and a woman appeared with a lamp in her hand, which she held above her head, pushing her face forward and peering at us. I could see that she was pretty, and from the gloss with which the light shone upon her dark dress I knew that it was a rich material. She spoke a few words in a foreign tongue in a tone as though asking a question, and when my companion answered in a gruff monosyllable she gave such a start that the lamp nearly fell from her hand. Colonel Stark went up to her, whispered something in her ear, and then, pushing her back into the room from whence she had come, he walked towards me again with the lamp in his hand.

‘“Perhaps you will have the kindness to wait in this room for a few minutes,” said he, throwing open another door. It was a quiet little plainly furnished room, with a round table in the centre, on which several German books were scattered. Colonel Stark laid down the lamp on the top of a harmonium beside the door. “I shall not keep you waiting an instant,” said he, and vanished into the darkness.

‘I glanced at the books upon the table, and in spite of my ignorance of German, I could see that two of them were treatises on science, the others being volumes of poetry. Then I walked across to the window, hoping that I might catch some glimpse of the countryside, but an oak shutter, heavily barred, was folded across it. It was a wonderfully silent house. There was an old clock ticking loudly somewhere in the passage, but otherwise everything was deadly still. A vague feeling of uneasiness began to steal over me. Who were these German people, and what were they doing, living in this strange, out-of-the-way place? And where was the place? I was ten miles or so from Eyford, that was all I knew, but whether north, south, east, or west, I had no idea. For that matter, Reading, and possibly other large towns, were within that radius, so the place might not be so secluded after all. Yet it was quite certain from the absolute stillness that we were in the country. I paced up and down the room humming a tune under my breath to keep up my spirits, and feeling that I was thoroughly earning my fifty-guinea fee.

'Suddenly, without any preliminary sound in the midst of the utter stillness, the door of my room swung slowly open. The woman was standing in the aperture, the darkness of the hall behind her, the yellow light from my lamp beating upon her eager and beautiful face. I could see at a glance that she was sick with fear, and the sight sent a chill to my own heart. She held up one shaking finger to warn me to be silent, and she shot a few whispered words of broken English at me, her eyes glancing back, like those of a frightened horse, into the gloom behind her.

'"I would go," said she, trying hard, as it seemed to me,

to speak calmly; "I would go. I should not stay here. There is no good for you to do."

'"But, madam," said I, "I have not yet done what I came for. I cannot possibly leave until I have seen the machine."

'"It is not worth your while to wait," she went on. "You can pass through the door; no one hinders." And then, seeing that I smiled and shook my head, she suddenly threw aside her constraint, and made a step forward, with her hands wrung together. "For the love of Heaven!" she whispered, "get away from here before it is too late!"

'But I am somewhat headstrong by nature, and the more ready to engage in an affair when there is some obstacle in the way. I thought of my fifty-guinea fee, of my wearisome journey, and of the unpleasant night which seemed to be before me. Was it all to go for nothing? Why should I slink away without having carried out my commission, and without the payment which was my due? This woman might, for all I knew, be a monomaniac. With a stout bearing, therefore, though her manner had shaken me more than I cared to confess, I still shook my head, and declared my intention of remaining where I was. She was about to renew her entreaties when a door slammed overhead, and the sound of several footsteps was heard upon the stairs. She listened for an instant, threw up her hands with a despairing gesture, and vanished as suddenly and noiselessly as she had come.

'The newcomers were Colonel Lysander Stark, and a

short thick man with a chinchilla beard growing out of the creases of his double chin, who was introduced to me as Mr Ferguson.

'"This is my secretary and manager," said the colonel. "By the way, I was under the impression that I left this door shut just now. I fear that you have felt the draught."

'"On the contrary," said I, "I opened the door myself, because I felt the room to be a little close."

'He shot one of his suspicious glances at me. "Perhaps we had better proceed to business, then," said he. "Mr Ferguson and I will take you up to see the machine."

'"I had better put my hat on, I suppose."

'"Oh no, it is in the house."

'"What, do you dig fuller's earth in the house?"

'"No, no. This is only where we compress it. But never mind that! All we wish you to do is to examine the machine and to let us know what is wrong with it."

'We went upstairs together, the colonel first with the lamp, the fat manager and I behind him. It was a labyrinth of an old house, with corridors, passages, narrow winding staircases, and little low doors, the thresholds of which were hollowed out by the generations who had crossed them. There were no carpets, and no signs of any furniture above the ground floor, while the plaster was peeling off the walls, and the damp was breaking through in green, unhealthy blotches. I tried to put on as unconcerned an air as possible, but I had not forgotten the warnings of the lady, even though I disregarded them, and I kept a keen eye upon my two companions. Ferguson appeared to be a morose and silent man, but I could see from the little that he said that he was at least a fellow-countryman.

'Colonel Lysander Stark stopped at last before a low door, which he unlocked. Within was a small square room, in which the three of us could hardly get at one time. Ferguson remained outside, and the colonel ushered me in.

'"We are now," said he, "actually within the hydraulic press, and it would be a particularly unpleasant thing for us if anyone were to turn it on. The ceiling of this small chamber is really the end of the descending piston, and it comes down with the force of many tons upon this metal floor. There are small lateral columns of water outside which receive the force, and which transmit and multiply it in the manner which is familiar to you. The machine goes readily enough, but there is some stiffness in the working of it and it has lost a little of its force. Perhaps you will have the goodness to look it over, and to show us how we can set it right."

'I took the lamp from him, and I examined the machine very thoroughly. It was indeed a gigantic one, and capable of exercising enormous pressure. When I passed outside, however, and pressed down the levers which controlled it, I knew at once by the whishing sound that there was a slight leakage, which allowed a regurgitation of water through one of the side-cylinders. An examination showed that one of the india-rubber bands which was round the head of a driving-rod had shrunk so as not quite to fill the socket along which it worked. This was clearly the cause of the loss of power, and I pointed it out to my companions, who followed my remarks very carefully, and asked several practical questions as to how they should proceed to set it right. When I had made it clear to them, I returned to the main chamber of the machine, and took a good look at it to satisfy my own curiosity. It was obvious at a glance that the story of the fuller's earth was the merest fabrication, for it would be absurd to suppose that so powerful an engine could be designed for so inadequate a purpose. The walls were of wood, but the floor consisted of a large iron trough, and when I came to examine it I could see a crust of metallic deposit all over it. I had stooped and was scraping at this to see exactly what it was, when I heard a muttered exclamation in German, and saw the cadaverous face of the colonel looking down at me.

'"What are you doing there?" he asked.

'I felt angry at having been tricked by so elaborate a story as that which he had told me. "I was admiring your fuller's earth," said I; "I think that I should be better able to advise you as to your machine if I knew what the exact purpose was for which it was used."

'The instant that I uttered the words I regretted the rashness of my speech. His face set hard, and a baleful light sprang up in his grey eyes.

'"Very well," said he, "you shall know all about the machine." He took a step backward, slammed the little door, and turned the key in the lock. I rushed towards it and pulled at the handle, but it was quite secure, and did not give in the least to my kicks and shoves. "Hallo!" I yelled. "Hallo! Colonel! Let me out!"

'And then suddenly in the silence I heard a sound which sent my heart into my mouth. It was the clank of the levers, and the swish of the leaking cylinder. He had set the engine at work. The lamp still stood upon the floor where I had placed it when examining the trough. By its light I saw that the black ceiling was coming down upon me, slowly, jerkily, but, as none knew better than myself, with a force which must within a minute grind me to a shapeless pulp. I threw myself, screaming, against the door, and dragged with my nails at the lock. I implored the colonel to let me out, but the remorseless clanking of the levers drowned my cries. The ceiling was only a foot or two above my head, and with my hand upraised I could feel its hard rough surface. Then it flashed through my mind that the pain of my death would depend very much upon the position in which I met it. If I lay on my face the weight would come upon my spine, and I shuddered to think of that dreadful snap. Easier the other way, perhaps, and yet had I the nerve to lie and look up at that deadly black shadow wavering down upon me? Already I was unable to stand erect, when my eye caught something which brought a gush of hope back to my heart.

‘I have said that though floor and ceiling were of iron, the walls were of wood. As I gave a last hurried glance around, I saw a thin line of yellow light between two of the boards, which broadened and broadened as a small panel was pushed backwards. For an instant I could hardly believe that here was indeed a door which led away from death. The next I threw myself through, and lay half fainting upon the other side. The panel had closed again behind me, but the crash of the lamp, and a few moments afterwards the clang of the two slabs of metal, told me how narrow had been my escape.

‘I was recalled to myself by a frantic plucking at my wrist, and I found myself lying upon the stone floor of a narrow corridor, while a woman bent over me and tugged at me with her left hand, while she held a candle in her right. It was the same good friend whose warning I had so foolishly rejected.

‘“Come! Come!” she cried breathlessly. “They will be here in a moment. They will see that you are not there. Oh, do not waste the so precious time, but come!”

‘This time, at least, I did not scorn her advice. I staggered to my feet, and ran with her along the corridor and down a winding stair. The latter led to another broad passage, and, just as we reached it, we heard the sound of running feet and the shouting of two voices – one answering the other – from the floor on which we were, and from the one beneath. My guide stopped, and looked about her like one who is at her wits' end. Then she threw open a door which led into a bedroom, through the window of which the moon was shining brightly.

'"It is your only chance," said she. "It is high, but it may be that you can jump it."

'As she spoke a light sprang into view at the further end of the passage, and I saw the lean figure of Colonel Lysander Stark rushing forward with a lantern in one hand, and a weapon like a butcher's cleaver in the other. I rushed across the bedroom, flung open the window, and looked out. How quiet and sweet and wholesome the garden looked in the moonlight, and it could not be more than thirty feet down. I clambered out upon the sill, but hesitated to jump, until I should have heard what passed between my saviour and the ruffian who pursued me. If she were ill-used, then at risk I was determined to go back to her assistance. The thought had hardly flashed through my mind before he was at the door, pushing his way past her; but she threw her arms round him, and tried to hold him back.

'"Fritz! Fritz!" she cried in English, "remember your promise after the last time. You said it should not be again. He will be silent! Oh, he will be silent!"

'"You are mad, Elise!" he shouted, struggling to break away from her. "You will be the ruin of us. He has seen too much. Let me pass, I say!" He dashed her to one side, and, rushing to the window, cut at me with his heavy weapon. I had let myself go, and was hanging with my fingers in the window slot and my hands across the sill, when his blow fell. I was conscious of a dull pain, my grip loosened, and I fell into the garden below.

'I was shaken, but not hurt by the fall; so I picked myself up and rushed off among the bushes as hard as I could run, for I understood that I was far from being out of danger yet. Suddenly, however, as I ran, a deadly dizziness and sickness came over me. I glanced down at my hand, which was throbbing painfully, and then, for the first time, saw that my thumb had been cut off, and that the blood was pouring from my wound. I endeavoured to tie my handkerchief round it, but there came a sudden buzzing in my ears, and next moment I fell in a dead faint among the rose-bushes.

'How long I remained unconscious I cannot tell. It must have been a very long time, for the moon had sunk and a bright morning was breaking when I came to myself. My clothes were all sodden with dew, and my coat-sleeve was drenched with blood from my wounded thumb. The smarting of it recalled in an instant all the particulars of my night's adventure, and I sprang to my feet with the feeling that I might hardly yet be safe from my pursuers. But, to my astonishment, when I came to look round me neither house nor garden were to be seen. I had been lying in an angle of the hedge close by the high-road, and just a little lower down was a long building, which proved, upon my approaching it, to be the very station at which I had arrived upon the previous night. Were it not for the ugly wound upon my hand, all that had passed during those dreadful hours might have been an evil dream.

'Half dazed, I went into the station, and asked about the morning train. There would be one to Reading in less than an hour. The same porter was on duty, I found, as had been there when I arrived. I inquired from him whether he had ever heard of Colonel Lysander Stark. The name was strange to him. Had he observed a carriage the night before waiting for me? No, he had not. Was there a police station anywhere near? There was one about three miles off.

'It was too far for me to go weak and ill as I was. I determined to wait until I got back to town before telling my story to the police. It was a little past six when I arrived, so I went first to have my wound dressed, and then the doctor was kind enough to bring me along here. I put the case into your hands, and shall do exactly what you advise.'

We both sat in silence for some little time after listening to this extraordinary narrative. Then Sherlock Holmes pulled down from the shelf one of the ponderous commonplace books in which he placed his cuttings.

'Here is an advertisement which will interest you,' said he. 'It appeared in all the papers about a year ago. Listen to this – "Lost on the 9th inst., Mr Jeremiah Hayling, aged 26, a hydraulic engineer. Left his lodgings at ten o'clock at night, and has not been heard of since. Was dressed in," etc. etc.

Ha! That represents the last time that the colonel needed to have his machine overhauled, I fancy.'

'Good heavens!' cried my patient. 'Then that explains what the girl said.'

'Undoubtedly. It is quite clear that the colonel was a cool and desperate man, who was absolutely determined that nothing should stand in the way of his little game, like those out-and-out pirates who will leave no survivor from a captured ship. Well, every moment now is precious, so, if you feel equal to it, we shall go down to Scotland Yard at once as a preliminary to starting for Eyford.'

Some three hours or so afterwards we were all in the train together, bound from Reading to the little Berkshire village. There were Sherlock Holmes, the hydraulic engineer, Inspector Bradstreet of Scotland Yard, a plain-clothes man, and myself. Bradstreet had spread an ordnance map of the county out upon the seat, and was busy with his compasses drawing a circle with Eyford for its centre.

'There you are,' said he. 'That circle is drawn at a radius of ten miles from the village. The place we want must be somewhere near that line. You said ten miles, I think, sir?'

'It was an hour's good drive.'

'And you think that they brought you back all that way when you were unconscious?'

'They must have done so. I have a confused memory, too, of having been lifted and conveyed somewhere.'

'What I cannot understand,' said I, 'is why they should

have spared you when they found you lying fainting in the garden. Perhaps the villain was softened by the woman's entreaties.'

'I hardly think that likely. I never saw a more inexorable face in my life.'

'Oh, we shall soon clear up all that,' said Bradstreet. 'Well, I have drawn my circle, and I only wish I knew at what point upon it the folk that we are in search of are to be found.'

'I think I could lay my finger on it,' said Holmes quietly.

'Really, now!' cried the inspector, 'you have formed your opinion! Come now, we shall see who agrees with you. I say south, for the country is more deserted there.'

'And I say east,' said my patient.

'I am for west,' remarked the plain-clothes man. 'There are several quiet little villages up there.'

'And I am for north,' said I; 'because there are no hills there, and our friend says that he did not notice the carriage go up any.'

'Come,' said the inspector, laughing; 'it's a very pretty diversity of opinion. We have boxed the compass among us. Who do you give your casting vote to?'

'You are all wrong.'

'But we can't *all* be.'

'Oh, yes, you can. This is my point,' he placed his finger on the centre of the circle. 'This is where we shall find them.'

'But the twelve-mile drive?' gasped Hatherley.

'Six out and six back. Nothing simpler. You say yourself that the horse was fresh and glossy when you got in. How could it be that, if it had gone twelve miles over heavy roads?'

'Indeed it is a likely ruse enough,' observed Bradstreet thoughtfully. 'Of course there can be no doubt as to the nature of this gang.'

'None at all,' said Holmes. 'They are coiners on a large scale, and have used the machine to form the amalgam which has taken the place of silver.'

'We have known for some time that a clever gang was at work,' said the inspector. 'They have been turning out half-crowns by the thousand. We even traced them as far as Reading, but could get no further; for they had covered their traces in a way that showed that they were very old hands. But now, thanks to this lucky chance, I think that we have got them right enough.'

But the inspector was mistaken, for those criminals were not destined to fall into the hands of justice. As we rolled into Eyford station we saw a gigantic column of smoke which streamed up from behind a small clump of trees in the neighbourhood, and hung like an immense ostrich feather over the landscape.

'A house on fire?' asked Bradstreet, as the train steamed off again on its way.

'Yes, sir,' said the stationmaster.

'When did it break out?'

‘I hear that it was during the night, sir, but it has got worse, and the whole place is in a blaze.’

‘Whose house is it?’

‘Dr Becher’s.’

‘Tell me,’ broke in the engineer, ‘is Dr Becher a German, very thin, with a long sharp nose?’

The stationmaster laughed heartily. ‘No, sir, Dr Becher is an Englishman, and there isn’t a man in the parish who has a better lined waistcoat. But he has a gentleman staying with him, a patient as I understand, who is a foreigner, and he looks as if a little good Berkshire beef would do him no harm.’

The stationmaster had not finished his speech before we were all hastening in the direction of the fire. The road topped a low hill, and there was a great widespread white-washed building in front of us, spouting fire at every chink and window, while in the garden in front three fire-engines were vainly striving to keep the flames under.

‘That’s it!’ cried Hatherley, in intense excitement. ‘There is the gravel drive, and there are the rose-bushes where I lay. That second window is the one that I jumped from.’

‘Well, at least,’ said Holmes, ‘you have had your revenge upon them. There can be no doubt that it was your oil lamp which, when it was crushed in the press, set fire to the wooden walls, though no doubt they were too excited in the chase after you to observe it at the time. Now keep your eyes open in this crowd for your friends of last night, though

I very much fear that they are a good hundred miles off by now.'

And Holmes's fears came to be realized, for from that day to this no word has ever been heard either of the beautiful woman, the sinister German, or the morose Englishman. Early that morning a peasant had met a cart, containing several people and some very bulky boxes, driving rapidly in the direction of Reading, but there all traces of the fugitives disappeared, and even Holmes's ingenuity failed to discover the least clue to their whereabouts.

The firemen had been much perturbed at the strange arrangements which they found within, and still more so by discovering a newly severed human thumb upon a window-sill of the second floor. About sunset, however, their efforts were at last successful, and they subdued the flames, but not before the roof had fallen in, and the whole place reduced to such absolute ruin that, save some twisted cylinders and iron piping, not a trace remained of the machinery which had cost our unfortunate acquaintance so dearly. Large masses of nickel and of tin were discovered stored in an outhouse, but no coins were to be found, which may have explained the presence of those bulky boxes which have been already referred to.

How our hydraulic engineer had been conveyed from the garden to the spot where he recovered his senses might have remained for ever a mystery were it not for the soft mould which told us a very plain tale. He had evidently been carried down by two persons, one of whom had remarkably small feet, and the other unusually large ones. On the whole, it was most probable that the silent Englishman, being less bold or less murderous than his companion, had assisted the woman to bear the unconscious man out of the way of danger.

'Well,' said our engineer ruefully, as we took our seats to return to London, 'it has been a pretty business for me! I have lost my thumb, and I have lost a fifty-guinea fee, and what have I gained!'

'Experience,' said Holmes, laughing. 'Indirectly it may be of value, you know; you have only to put it into words to gain the reputation of being excellent company for the remainder of your existence.'

The Red-Headed League

I had called upon my friend, Mr Sherlock Holmes, one day in the autumn of last year, and found him in deep conversation with a very stout, florid-faced, elderly gentleman, with fiery red hair. With an apology for my intrusion, I was about to withdraw, when Holmes pulled me abruptly into the room, and closed the door behind me.

'You could not possibly have come at a better time, my dear Watson,' he said cordially.

'I was afraid that you were engaged.'

'So I am. Very much so.'

'Then I can wait in the next room.'

'Not at all. This gentleman, Mr Wilson, has been my partner and helper in many of my most successful cases, and I have no doubt that he will be of the utmost use to me in yours also.'

The stout gentleman half rose from his chair, and gave a bob of greeting, with a quick little questioning glance from his small, fat-encircled eyes.

'Try the settee,' said Holmes, relapsing into his armchair,

and putting his fingertips together, as was his custom when in judicial moods. 'I know, my dear Watson, that you share my love of all that is bizarre and outside the conventions and humdrum routine of everyday life. You have shown your relish for it by the enthusiasm which has prompted you to chronicle, and, if you will excuse my saying so, somewhat to embellish so many of my own little adventures.'

'Your cases have indeed been of the greatest interest to me,' I observed.

'You will remember that I remarked the other day, just before we went into the very simple problem presented by Miss Mary Sutherland, that for strange effects and extraordinary combinations we must go to life itself, which is always far more daring than any effort of the imagination.'

'A proposition which I took the liberty of doubting.'

'You did, Doctor, but none the less you must come round to my view, for otherwise I shall keep piling fact upon fact on you, until your reason breaks down under them and acknowledges me to be right. Now, Mr Jabez Wilson here has been good enough to call upon me this morning, and to begin a narrative which promises to be one of the most singular which I have listened to for some time. You have heard me remark that the strangest and most unique things are very often connected not with the larger but with the smaller crimes, and occasionally, indeed, where there is room for doubt whether any positive crime has been committed. As far as I have heard, it is impossible for me to say whether the present case is an instance of crime or not, but the course of events is certainly among the most singular that I have ever listened to. Perhaps, Mr Wilson, you would have the great kindness to recommence your narrative. I ask you not merely because my friend Dr Watson has not heard the opening part, but also because the peculiar nature of the story makes me anxious to have every possible detail from your lips. As a rule, when I have heard some slight indication of the course of events I am able to guide myself by the thousands of other similar cases which occur to my memory. In the present instance I am forced to admit that the facts are, to the best of my belief, unique.'

The portly client puffed out his chest with an appearance of some little pride, and pulled a dirty and wrinkled newspaper from the inside pocket of his greatcoat. As he glanced down the advertisement column, with his head thrust forward, and the paper flattened out upon his knee, I took a good look at the man, and endeavoured after the fashion of my companion to read the indications which might be presented by his dress or appearance.

I did not gain very much, however, by my inspection. Our visitor bore every mark of being an average commonplace British tradesman, obese, pompous, and slow. He wore rather baggy grey shepherds' check trousers, a not over-clean black frock-coat, unbuttoned in the front, and a drab waistcoat with a heavy brassy Albert chain, and a square pierced bit of metal dangling down as an ornament. A frayed top-hat, and a faded brown overcoat with a wrinkled velvet collar lay upon a chair beside him. Altogether, look as I would, there was nothing remarkable about the man save his blazing red head, and the expression of extreme chagrin and discontent upon his features.

Sherlock Holmes's quick eye took in my occupation and he shook his head with a smile as he noticed my questioning glances. 'Beyond the obvious facts that he has at some time done manual labour, that he takes snuff, that he is a Freemason, that he has been in China, and that he has done a considerable amount of writing lately, I can deduce nothing else.'

Mr Jabez Wilson started up in his chair, with his forefinger upon the paper, but his eyes upon my companion.

'How, in the name of good fortune, did you know that, Mr Holmes?' he asked. 'How did you know, for example, that I did manual labour? It's as true as gospel, and I began as a ship's carpenter.'

'Your hands, my dear sir. Your right hand is quite a size larger than your left. You have worked with it, and the muscles are more developed.'

'Well, the snuff, then, and the Freemasonry?'

'I won't insult your intelligence by telling you how I read that, especially as, rather against the strict rules of your order, you use an arc and compass breastpin.'

'Ah, of course, I forgot that. But the writing?'

'What else can be indicated by that right cuff so very shiny for five inches, and the left one with the smooth patch near the elbow where you rest it upon the desk.'

'Well, but China?'

'The fish which you have tattooed immediately above your right wrist could only have been done in China. I have made a small study of tattoo marks, and have even contributed to the literature of the subject. That trick of staining the fishes' scales of a delicate pink is quite peculiar to China. When, in addition, I see a Chinese coin hanging from your watch-chain, the matter becomes even more simple.'

Mr Jabez Wilson laughed heavily. 'Well, I never!' said he. 'I thought at first you had done something clever, but I see that there was nothing in it after all.'

'I begin to think, Watson,' said Holmes, 'that I make a mistake in explaining. "Omne ignotum pro magnifico," you know, and my poor little reputation, such as it is, will suffer shipwreck if I am so candid. Can you not find the advertisement, Mr Wilson?'

'Yes, I have got it now,' he answered, with his thick, red finger planted halfway down the column. 'Here it is. This is what began it all. You must read it for yourself, sir.'

I took the paper from him and read as follows:

> To the Red-Headed League – On account of the bequest of the late Ezekiah Hopkins of Lebanon, Penn., USA, there is now another vacancy open which

> entitles a member of the League to a salary of four pounds a week for purely nominal services. All red-headed men who are sound in body and mind, and above the age of twenty-one years, are eligible. Apply in person on Monday, at eleven o'clock, to Duncan Ross, at the offices of the League, 7 Pope's Court, Fleet Street.

'What on earth does this mean?' I ejaculated, after I had twice read over the extraordinary announcement.

Holmes chuckled, and wriggled in his chair, as was his habit when in high spirits. 'It is a little off the beaten track, isn't it?' said he. 'And now, Mr Wilson, off you go at scratch, and tell us all about yourself, your household, and the effect which this advertisement had upon your fortunes. You will first make a note, Doctor, of the paper and the date.'

'It is *The Morning Chronicle*, of 27 April 1890. Just two months ago.'

'Very good. Now, Mr Wilson?'

'Well, it is just as I have been telling you, Mr Sherlock Holmes,' said Jabez Wilson, mopping his forehead, 'I have a small pawnbroker's business at Coburg Square, near the City. It's not a very large affair, and of late years it has not done more than just give me a living. I used to be able to keep two assistants, but now I only keep one; and I would have a job to pay him, but that he is willing to come for half wages, so as to learn the business.'

'What is the name of this obliging youth?' asked Sherlock Holmes.

'His name is Vincent Spaulding, and he's not such a youth either. It's hard to say his age. I should not wish a smarter assistant, Mr Holmes; and I know very well that he could better himself, and even twice what I am able to give him. But after all, if he is satisfied, why should I put ideas in his head?'

'Why, indeed? You seem most fortunate in having an employee who comes under the full market price. It is not a common experience among employers in this age. I don't know that your assistant is not as remarkable as your advertisement.'

'Oh, he has his faults, too,' said Mr Wilson. 'Never was such a fellow for photography. Snapping away with a camera when he ought to be improving his mind, and then diving down into the cellar like a rabbit into its hole to develop his pictures. That is his main fault; but on the whole, he's a good worker. There's no vice in him.'

'He is still with you, I presume?'

'Yes, sir. He and a girl of fourteen, who does a bit of simple cooking, and keeps the place clean – that's all I have in the house, for I am a widower, and never had any family. We live very quietly, sir, the three of us; and we keep a roof over our heads, and pay our debts, if we do nothing more.

'The first thing that put us out was that advertisement. Spaulding, he came down into the office just this day eight weeks with this very paper in his hand, and he says:

'"I wish to the Lord, Mr Wilson, that I was a red-headed man."

'"Why that?" I asks.

'"Why," says he, "here's another vacancy on the League of the Red-Headed Men. It's worth quite a little fortune to any man who gets it, and I understand that there are more vacancies than there are men, so that the trustees are at their wits' end what to do with the money. If my hair would only change colour, here's a nice little crib all ready for me to step into."

'"Why, what is it, then!" I asked. You see, Mr Holmes, I am a very stay-at-home man, and, as my business came to me instead of my having to go to it, I was often weeks on end without putting my foot over the door-mat. In that way I didn't know much of what was going on outside, and I was always glad of a bit of news.

'"Have you never heard of the League of the Red-Headed Men?" he asked, with his eyes open.

'"Never."

'"Why, I wonder at that, for you are eligible yourself for one of the vacancies."

'"And what are they worth?" I asked.

'"Oh, merely a couple of hundred a year, but the work is slight, and it need not interfere much with one's other occupations."

'Well, you can easily think that that made me prick up my ears, for the business has not been over good for some years, and an extra couple of hundred would have been very handy.

'"Tell me all about it," said I.

'"Well," said he, showing me the advertisement, "you can see for yourself that the League has a vacancy, and there is the address where you should apply for particulars. As far as I can make out, the League was founded by an American millionaire, Ezekiah Hopkins, who was very peculiar in his ways. He was himself red-headed, and he had a great sympathy for all red-headed men; so, when he died, it was found that he had left his enormous fortune in the hands of trustees, with instructions to apply the interest to the providing of easy berths to men whose hair is of that colour. From all I hear it is splendid pay, and very little to do."

'"But," said I, "there would be millions of red-headed men who would apply."

'"Not so many as you might think," he answered. "You see it is really confined to Londoners, and to grown men. This American had started from London when he was young, and he wanted to do the old town a good turn. Then, again, I have heard it is no use your applying if you hair is light red, or dark red, or anything but real, bright, blazing, fiery red. Now, if you cared to apply, Mr Wilson, you would just walk in; but perhaps it would hardly be worth your while to put yourself out of the way for the sake of a few hundred pounds."

'Now, it is a fact, gentlemen, as you may see for yourselves, that my hair is of a very full and rich tint, so that it seemed to me that, if there was to be any competition in the matter, I stood as good a chance as any man that I had ever met. Vincent Spaulding seemed to know so much about it that I thought he might prove useful, so I just ordered him to put up the shutters for the day, and to come right away with me. He was very willing to have a holiday, so we shut the business up, and started off for the address that was given us in the advertisement.

'I never hope to see such a sight as that again, Mr Holmes. From north, south, east, and west every man who had a shade of red in his hair had tramped into the City to answer the advertisement. Fleet Street was choked with red-headed folk, and Pope's Court looked like a coster's orange barrow. I should not have thought there were so many in the whole country as were brought together by that single advertisement. Every shade of colour they were – straw, lemon, orange, brick, Irish setter, liver, clay; but, as Spaulding said, there were not many who had the real vivid flame-coloured tint. When I saw how many were waiting I would have given it up in despair; but Spaulding would not hear of it. How he did it I could not imagine, but he pushed and pulled and butted until he got me through the crowd, and right up to the steps which led to the office. There was a double stream upon the stair, some going up in hope, and some coming back dejected; but we wedged in as well as we could, and soon found ourselves in the office.'

'Your experience has been a most entertaining one,' remarked Holmes, as his client paused and refreshed his memory with a huge pinch of snuff. 'Pray continue your very interesting statement.'

'There was nothing in the office but a couple of wooden chairs and a deal table, behind which sat a small man, with a head that was even redder than mine. He said a few words to each candidate as he came up, and then he always managed to find some fault in them which would disqualify them. Getting a vacancy did not seem to be such a very easy matter after all. However, when our turn came, the little man was more favourable to me than to any of the others, and he closed the door as we entered, so that he might have a private word with us.

'"This is Mr Jabez Wilson," said my assistant, "and he is willing to fill a vacancy in the League."

'"And he is admirably suited for it," the other answered. "He has every requirement. I cannot recall when I have seen anything so fine." He took a step backwards, cocked his head on one side, and gazed at my hair until I felt quite bashful. Then suddenly he plunged forward, wrung my hand, and congratulated me warmly on my success.

'"It would be injustice to hesitate," said he. "You will, however, I am sure, excuse me for taking an obvious precaution." With that he seized my hair in both his hands, and tugged until I yelled with the pain. "There is water in your eyes," said he, as he released me. "I perceive that all is as it should be. But we have to be careful, for we have twice been deceived by wigs and once by paint. I could tell you tales of cobbler's wax which would disgust you with human nature." He stepped over to the window, and shouted through it at the top of his voice that the vacancy was filled. A groan of disappointment came up from below, and the folk all trooped away in different directions, until there was not a red head to be seen except my own and that of the manager.

'"My name," said he, "is Mr Duncan Ross, and I am myself one of the pensioners upon the fund left by our noble benefactor. Are you a married man, Mr Wilson? Have you a family?"

'I answered that I had not.

'His face fell immediately.

'"Dear me!" he said gravely, "that is very serious indeed! I am sorry to hear you say that. The fund was, of course, for the propagation and spread of the red heads as well as for their maintenance. It is exceedingly unfortunate that you should be a bachelor."

'My face lengthened at this, Mr Holmes, for I thought that I was not to have the vacancy after all; but after thinking it over for a few minutes, he said that it would be all right.

'"In the case of another," said he, "the objection might be fatal, but we must stretch a point in favour of a man with such a head of hair as yours. When shall you be able to enter upon your new duties?"

'"Well, it is a little awkward, for I have a business already," said I.

'"Oh, never mind about that, Mr Wilson!" said Vincent Spaulding. "I shall be able to look after that for you."

'"What would be the hours?" I asked.

'"Ten to two."

'Now a pawnbroker's business is mostly done of an evening, Mr Holmes, especially Thursday and Friday evening, which is just before pay-day; so it would suit me very well to earn a little in the mornings. Besides, I knew that my assistant was a good man, and that he would see to anything that turned up.

'"That would suit me very well," said I. "And the pay?"

'"Is four pounds a week."

'"And the work?"

'"Is purely nominal."

'"What do you call purely nominal?"

'"Well, you have to be in the office, or at least in the building, the whole time. If you leave, you forfeit your whole position for ever. The will is very clear upon that point. You don't comply with the conditions if you budge from the office during that time."

'"It's only four hours a day, and I should not think of leaving," said I.

'"No excuse will avail," said Mr Duncan Ross, "neither sickness, nor business, nor anything else. There you must stay, or you lose your billet."

'"And the work?"

'"Is to copy out the *Encyclopedia Britannica*. There is the first volume of it in that press. You must find your own ink, pens, and blotting-paper, but we provide this table and chair. Will you be ready tomorrow?"

'"Certainly," I answered.

'"Then goodbye, Mr Jabez Wilson, and let me congratulate you once more on the important position which you have been fortunate enough to gain." He bowed me out of the room, and I went home with my assistant, hardly knowing what to say or do, I was so pleased at my own good fortune.

'Well, I thought over the matter all day, and by evening I was in low spirits again; for I had quite persuaded myself that the whole affair must be some great hoax or fraud, though what its object might be I could not imagine. It seemed altogether past belief that anyone could make such a will, or that they would pay a sum for doing anything so simple as copying out the *Encyclopedia Britannica*. Vincent Spaulding did what he could to cheer me up, but by bedtime I had reasoned myself out of the whole thing. However, in the morning I determined to have a look at it anyhow, so I bought a penny bottle of ink, and with a quill pen, and seven sheets of foolscap paper, I started off for Pope's Court.

'Well, to my surprise and delight everything was as right as possible. The table was set out ready for me, and Mr Duncan Ross was there to see that I got fairly to work. He started me off upon the letter A, and then he left me; but he would drop in from time to time to see that all was right with me. At two o'clock he bade me good day, complimented me upon the amount that I had written, and locked the door of the office after me.

'This went on day after day, Mr Holmes, and on Saturday the manager came in and planked down four golden sovereigns for my week's work. It was the same next week, and the same the week after. Every morning I was there at ten, and every afternoon I left at two. By degrees Mr Duncan Ross took to coming in only once of a morning, and then, after a time, he did not come in at all. Still, of course, I never dared to leave the room for an instant, for I was not sure when he might come, and the billet was such a good one, and suited me so well, that I would not risk the loss of it.

'Eight weeks passed away like this, and I had written about Abbots, and Archery, and Armour, and Architecture, and Attica, and hoped with diligence that I might get on to the B's before very long. It cost me something in foolscap, and I had pretty nearly filled a shelf with my writings. And then suddenly the whole business came to an end.'

'To an end?'

'Yes, sir. And no later than this morning. I went to my work as usual at ten o'clock, but the door was shut and locked, with a little square of cardboard hammered on to the middle of the panel with a tack. Here it is, and you can read for yourself.'

He held up a piece of white cardboard, about the size of a sheet of note-paper. It read in this fashion:

THE RED-HEADED LEAGUE IS DISSOLVED OCT. 9, 1890

Sherlock Holmes and I surveyed this curt announcement and the rueful face behind it, until the comical side of the affair so completely overtopped every other consideration that we both burst out into a roar of laughter.

'I cannot see that there is anything very funny,' cried our client, flushing up to the roots of his flaming head. 'If you can do nothing better than laugh at me, I can go elsewhere.'

'No, no,' cried Holmes, shoving him back into the chair from which he had half risen. 'I really wouldn't miss your case for the world. It is most refreshingly unusual. But there is, if you will excuse me saying so, something just a little funny about it. Pray what steps did you take when you found the card upon the door?'

'I was staggered, sir. I did not know what to do. Then I called at the offices round, but none of them seemed to know anything about it. Finally, I went to the landlord, who is an accountant living on the ground floor, and I asked him if he could tell me what had become of the Red-Headed League. He said that he had never heard of any such body. Then I asked him who Mr Duncan Ross was. He answered that the name was new to him.

'"Well," said I, "the gentleman at No 4."

'"What, the red-headed man?"

'"Yes."

'"Oh," said he, "his name was William Morris. He was a solicitor, and was using my room as a temporary convenience until his new premises were ready. He moved out yesterday."

'"Where could I find him?"

'"Oh, at his new offices. He did tell me the address. Yes, 17 King Edward Street, near St Paul's."

'I started off, Mr Holmes, but when I got to that address it was a manufactory of artificial knee-caps, and no one in it had ever heard of either Mr William Morris, or Mr Duncan Ross.'

'And what did you do then?' asked Holmes.

'I went home to Saxe-Coburg Square, and I took the advice of my assistant. But he could not help me in any way. He could only say that if I waited I should hear by post. But that was not quite good enough, Mr Holmes. I did not wish to lose such a place without a struggle, so, as I had heard that you were good enough to give advice to poor folk who were in need of it, I came right away to you.'

'And you did very wisely,' said Holmes. 'Your case is an exceedingly remarkable one, and I shall be happy to look into it. From what you have told me I think that it is possible that graver issues hang from it than might at first sight appear.'

'Grave enough!' said Mr Jabez Wilson. 'Why, I have lost four pounds a week.'

'As far as you are personally concerned,' remarked Holmes, 'I do not see that you have any grievance against this extraordinary league. On the contrary, you are, as I understand, richer by some thirty pounds, to say nothing of the minute knowledge which you have gained on every subject which comes under the letter A. You have lost nothing by them.'

'No, sir. But I want to find out about them, and who they are, and what their object was in playing this prank – if it was a prank – upon me. It was a pretty expensive joke for them, for it cost them two-and-thirty pounds.'

'We shall endeavour to clear up these points for you. And, first, one or two questions, Mr Wilson. This assistant of yours who first called your attention to the advertisement – how long had he been with you?'

'About a month then.'

'How did he come?'

'In answer to an advertisement.'

'Was he the only applicant?'

'No, I had a dozen.'

'Why did you pick him?'

'Because he was handy, and would come cheap.'

'At half wages, in fact.'

'Yes.'

'What is he like, this Vincent Spaulding?'

'Small, stout-built, very quick in his ways, no hair on his face, though he's not short of thirty. Has a white splash of acid upon his forehead.'

Holmes sat up in his chair in considerable excitement.

'I thought as much,' said he. 'Have you ever observed that his ears are pierced for ear-rings?'

'Yes, sir. He told me that a gypsy had done it for him when he was a lad.'

'Hum!' said Holmes, sinking back deep in thought. 'He is still with you?'

'Oh, yes, sir, I have only just left him.'

'And has your business been attended to in your absence?'

'Nothing to complain of, sir. There's never very much to do of a morning.'

'That will do, Mr Wilson. I shall be happy to give you an opinion upon the subject in the course of a day or two. Today is Saturday, and I hope that by Monday we may come to a conclusion.'

'Well, Watson,' said Holmes, when our visitor had left us, 'what do you make of it all?'

'I make nothing of it,' I answered, frankly. 'It is a most mysterious business.'

'As a rule,' said Holmes, 'the more bizarre a thing is the less mysterious it proves to be. It is your commonplace, featureless crimes which are really puzzling, just as a commonplace face is the most difficult to identify. But I must be prompt over this matter.'

'What are you going to do, then?' I asked.

'To smoke,' he answered. 'It is quite a three-pipe problem, and I beg that you won't speak to me for fifty minutes.' He curled himself up in his chair, with his thin knees drawn up to his hawk-like nose, and there he sat with his eyes closed and his black clay pipe thrusting out like the bill of some strange bird. I had come to the conclusion that he had dropped asleep, and indeed was nodding myself, when he suddenly sprang out of his chair with the gesture of a man who had made up his mind, and put his pipe down upon the mantelpiece.

'Sarasate plays at the St James's Hall this afternoon,' he remarked. 'What do you think, Watson? Could your patients spare you for a few hours?'

'I have nothing to do today. My practice is never very absorbing.'

'Then put on your hat, and come. I am going through the City first, and we can have some lunch on the way. I observe that there is a good deal of German music on the programme which is rather more to my taste than Italian or French. It is introspective, and I want to introspect. Come along!'

We travelled by the Underground as far as Aldersgate; and a short walk took us to Saxe-Coburg Square, the scene of the singular story which he had listened to in the morning. It was a pokey, little, shabby-genteel place, where four lines of dingy two-storied brick houses looked out into a small railed-in enclosure, where a lawn of weedy grass and a few clumps of faded laurel bushes made a hard fight against a smoke-laden and uncongenial atmosphere. Three gilt balls and a brown board with JABEZ WILSON in white letters upon a corner house, announced the place where our red-headed client carried on his business. Sherlock Holmes stopped in front of it with his head on one side and looked it all over, with his eyes shining brightly between puckered lids. Then he walked slowly up the street and then down again to the corner, still looking at the houses. Finally he returned to the pawnbroker's, and, having thumped vigorously upon the pavement with his stick two or three times, he went up to the door and knocked. It was instantly opened by a bright-looking, clean-shaven young fellow, who asked him to step in.

'Thank you,' said Holmes, 'I only wished to ask you how you would go from here to the Strand.'

'Third right, fourth left,' answered the assistant promptly, closing the door.

'Smart fellow, that,' observed Holmes as we walked away. 'He is, in my judgement, the fourth smartest man in London, and for daring I am not sure that he has not a claim to be third. I have known something of him before.'

'Evidently,' said I, 'Mr Wilson's assistant counts for a good deal in this mystery of the Red-Headed League. I am sure that you inquired your way merely in order that you might see him.'

'Not him.'

'What then?'

'The knees of his trousers.'

'And what did you see?'

'What I expected to see.'

'Why did you beat the pavement?'

'My dear Doctor, this is a time for observation, not for talk. We are spies in an enemy's country. We know something of Saxe-Coburg Square. Let us now explore the paths which lie behind it.'

The road in which we found ourselves as we turned round the corner from the retired Saxe-Coburg Square presented as great a contrast to it as the front of a picture does to the back. It was one of the main arteries which convey the traffic of the City to the north and west. The roadway was blocked with the immense stream of commerce flowing in a double tide inwards and outwards, while the footpaths were black with the hurrying swarm of pedestrians. It was difficult to realize as we looked at the line of fine shops and stately business premises that they really abutted on the other side upon the faded and stagnant square which we had just quitted.

'Let me see,' said Holmes, standing at the corner, and glancing along the line, 'I should like just to remember the order of the houses here. It is a hobby of mine to have an exact knowledge of London. There is Mortimer's, the tobacconist, the little newspaper shop, the Coburg branch of the City and Suburban Bank, the Vegetarian Restaurant, and McFarlane's carriage-building depot. That carries us right on to the other block. And now, Doctor, we've done our work, so it's time we had some play. A sandwich and a cup of coffee, and then off to violin land, where all is sweetness and delicacy and harmony, and there are no red-headed clients to vex us with their conundrums.'

My friend was an enthusiastic musician, being himself not only a very capable performer, but a composer of no ordinary merit. All the afternoon he sat in the stalls wrapped in the most perfect happiness, gently waving his long thin fingers in time to the music, while his gently smiling face and his languid, dreamy eyes were as unlike those of Holmes the sleuth-hound, Holmes the relentless, keen-witted, ready-handed criminal agent, as it was possible to conceive. In his singular character the dual nature alternately asserted itself and his extreme exactness and astuteness represented, as I have often thought, the reaction against the poetic and contemplative mood which occasionally predominated in him. The swing of his nature took him from extreme languor to devouring energy; and, as I knew well, he was never so truly formidable as when, for days on end, he had been lounging in his armchair amid his improvisations and his black-letter editions. Then it was that the lust of the chase would suddenly come upon him, and that his brilliant reasoning power would rise to the level of intuition, until those who were unacquainted with his methods would look askance at him as on a man whose knowledge was not that of other mortals. When I saw him that afternoon so enwrapped in the music at St James's Hall I felt that an evil time might be coming upon those whom he had set himself to hunt down.

'You want to go home, no doubt, Doctor,' he remarked, as we emerged.

'Yes, it would be as well.'

'And I have some business to do which will take some hours. This business at Coburg Square is serious.'

'Why serious?'

'A considerable crime is in contemplation. I have every reason to believe that we shall be in time to stop it. But today being Saturday rather complicates matters. I shall want your help tonight.'

'At what time?'

'Ten will be early enough.'

'I shall be at Baker Street at ten.'

'Very well. And I say, Doctor! there may be some little danger, so kindly put your army revolver in your pocket.' He waved his hand, turned on his heel, and disappeared in an instant among the crowd.

I trust that I am not more dense than my neighbours, but I was always oppressed with a sense of my own stupidity in my dealings with Sherlock Holmes. Here I had heard what he had heard, I had seen what he had seen, and yet from his words it was evident that he saw clearly not only what had happened, but what was about to happen, while to me the whole business was still confused and grotesque.

As I drove home to my house in Kensington I thought over it all, from the extraordinary story of the red-headed copier of the *Encyclopedia* down to the visit to Saxe-Coburg Square, and the ominous words with which he had parted from me. What was this nocturnal expedition, and why should I go armed? Where were we going, and what were we to do? I had the hint from Holmes that this smooth-faced pawnbroker's assistant was a formidable man – a man who might play a deep game. I tried to puzzle it out, but gave it up in despair, and set the matter aside until night should bring an explanation.

It was a quarter past nine when I started from home and made my way across the park, and so through Oxford Street to Baker Street. Two hansoms were standing at the door, and, as I entered the passage, I heard the sound of voices from above. On entering his room, I found Holmes in animated conversation with two men, one of whom I recognized as Peter Jones, the official police agent; while the other was a long, thin, sad-faced man, with a very shiny hat and oppressively respectable frock-coat.

'Ha! our party is complete, said Holmes, buttoning up his pea-jacket, and taking his heavy hunting-crop from the rack. 'Watson, I think you know Mr Jones, of Scotland Yard? Let me introduce you to Mr Merryweather, who is to be our companion in tonight's adventure.'

'We're hunting in couples again, Doctor, you see,' said Jones in his consequential way. 'Our friend here is a wonderful man for starting a chase. All he wants is an old dog to help him to do the running down.'

'I hope a wild goose may not prove to be the end of our chase,' observed Mr Merryweather gloomily.

'You may place considerable confidence in Mr Holmes, sir,' said the police agent loftily. 'He has his own little methods, which are, if he won't mind my saying so, just a little too theoretical and fantastic, but he has the makings of a detective in him. It is not too much to say that once or twice, as in that business of the Sholto murder and the Agra treasure, he has been more nearly correct than the official force.'

'Oh, if you say so, Mr Jones, it is all right!' said the stranger, with deference. 'Still, I confess that I miss my rubber. It is the first Saturday night for seven-and-thirty years that I have not had my rubber.'

'I think you will find,' said Sherlock Holmes, 'that you will play for a higher stake tonight than you have ever done yet, and that the play will be more exciting. For you, Mr Merryweather, the stake will be some thirty thousand pounds; and for you, Jones, it will be the man upon whom you wish to lay your hands.'

'John Clay, the murderer, thief, smasher, and forger. He's a young man, Mr Merryweather, but he is at the head of his profession and I would rather have my bracelets on him than on any criminal in London. He's a remarkable man, is young John Clay. His grandfather was a Royal Duke, and he himself has been to Eton and Oxford. His brain is as cunning as his fingers, and though we meet signs of him at every turn, we never know where to find the man himself. He'll crack a crib in Scotland one week, and be raising money to build an orphanage in Cornwall the next. I've been on his track for years, and have never set eyes on him yet.'

'I hope that I may have the pleasure of introducing you tonight. I've had one or two little turns also with Mr John Clay, and I agree with you that he is at the head of his profession. It is past ten, however, and quite time that we started. If you two will take the first hansom, Watson and I will follow in the second.'

Sherlock Holmes was not very communicative during the long drive, and lay back in the cab humming the tunes which he had heard in the afternoon. We rattled through an endless labyrinth of gas-lit streets until we emerged into Farringdon Street.

'We are close there now,' my friend remarked. 'This fellow Merryweather is a bank director and personally interested in the matter. I thought it as well to have Jones with us also. He is not a bad fellow, though an absolute imbecile in his profession. He has one positive virtue. He is as brave as a bulldog, and as tenacious as a lobster if he gets his claws upon anyone. Here we are, and they are waiting for us.'

We had reached the same crowded thoroughfare in which we had found ourselves in the morning. Our cabs were dismissed, and, following the guidance of Mr Merryweather, we passed down a narrow passage, and through a side door, which he opened for us. Within there was a small corridor, which ended in a very massive iron gate. This also was opened, and led down a flight of winding stone steps, which terminated at another formidable gate. Mr Merryweather stopped to light a lantern, and then conducted us down a dark, earth-smelling passage, and so, after opening a third door, into a huge vault or cellar, which was piled all round with crates and massive boxes.

'You are not very vulnerable from above,' Holmes remarked, as he held up the lantern and gazed about him.

'Nor from below,' said Mr Merryweather, striking his stick upon the flags which lined the floor. 'Why, dear me, it sounds quite hollow!' he remarked, looking up in surprise.

'I must really ask you to be a little more quiet,' said Holmes severely. 'You have already imperilled the whole success of our expedition. Might I beg that you would have the goodness to sit down upon one of those boxes, and not to interfere?'

The solemn Mr Merryweather perched himself upon a crate, with a very injured expression upon his face, while Holmes fell upon his knees upon the floor, and, with the lantern and a magnifying lens, began to examine minutely the cracks between the stones. A few seconds sufficed to satisfy him for he sprang to his feet again, and put his glass in his pocket.

'We have at least an hour before us,' he remarked, 'for

they can hardly take any steps until the good pawnbroker is safely in bed. Then they will not lose a minute, for the sooner they do their work the longer time they will have for their escape. We are at present, Doctor – as no doubt you have divined – in the cellar of the City branch of one of the principal London banks. Mr Merryweather is the chairman of directors, and he will explain to you that there are reasons why the more daring criminals of London should take a considerable interest in this cellar at present.'

'It is our French gold,' whispered the director. 'We have had several warnings that an attempt might be made upon it.'

'Your French gold?'

'Yes. We had occasion some months ago to strengthen our resources, and borrowed, for that purpose, thirty thousand napoleons from the Bank of France. It has become known that we have never had occasion to unpack the money, and that it is still lying in our cellar. The crate upon which I sit contains two thousand napoleons packed between layers of lead foil. Our reserve of bullion is much larger at present than is usually kept in a single branch office, and the directors have had misgivings upon the subject.'

'Which were very well justified,' observed Holmes. 'And now it is time that we arranged our little plans. I expect that within an hour matters will come to a head. In the meantime, Mr Merryweather, we must put the screen over that dark lantern.'

'And sit in the dark?'

'I am afraid so. I had brought a pack of cards in my pocket, and I thought that, as we were a *partie carrée*, you might have your rubber after all. But I see that the enemy's preparations have gone so far that we cannot risk the presence of a light. And, first of all, we must choose our positions. These are daring men, and, though we shall take them at a disadvantage they may do us some harm, unless we are careful. I shall stand behind this crate, and do you conceal yourself behind those. Then, when I flash a light upon them, close in swiftly. If they fire, Watson, have no compunction about shooting them down.'

I placed my revolver, cocked, upon the top of the wooden case behind which I crouched. Holmes shot the slide across the front of his lantern, and left us in pitch darkness – such an absolute darkness as I have never before experienced. The smell of hot metal remained to assure us that the light was still there, ready to flash out at a moment's notice. To me, with my nerves worked up to a pitch of expectancy, there was something depressing and subduing in the sudden gloom, and in the cold, dank air of the vault.

'They have but one retreat,' whispered Holmes. 'That is back through the house into Saxe-Coburg Square. I hope that you have done what I asked you, Jones?'

'I have an inspector and two officers waiting at the front door.'

'Then we have stopped all the holes. And now we must be silent and wait.'

What a time it seemed! From comparing notes afterwards it was but an hour and a quarter, yet it appeared to me that the night must have almost gone, and the dawn be breaking above us. My limbs were weary and stiff, for I feared to change my position, yet my nerves were worked up to the highest pitch of tension, and my hearing was so acute that I could not only hear the gentle breathing of my companions, but I could distinguish the deeper, heavier in-breath of the bulky Jones from the thin sighing note of the bank director. From my position I could look over the case in the direction of the floor. Suddenly my eyes caught the glint of a light.

At first it was but a lurid spark upon the stone pavement. Then it lengthened out until it became a yellow line, and then, without any warning or sound, a gash seemed to open and a hand appeared, a white, almost womanly hand, which felt about in the centre of the little area of light. For a minute or more the hand, with its writhing fingers, protruded out of the floor. Then it was withdrawn as suddenly as it appeared, and all was dark again save the single lurid spark, which marked a chink between the stones.

Its disappearance, however, was but momentary. With a rending, tearing sound, one of the broad, white stones turned over upon its side and left a square gaping hole through which streamed the light of a lantern. Over the edge there peeped a clean-cut, boyish face, which looked keenly about it, and then, with a hand on either side of the aperture, drew itself shoulder high and waist high until one knee rested upon the edge. In another instant he stood at the side of the hole, and was hauling after him a companion, lithe and small like himself, with a pale face and a shock of very red hair.

'It's all clear,' he whispered. 'Have you the chisel and the bags? Great Scott! Jump, Archie, jump, and I'll swing for it!'

Sherlock Holmes had sprung out and seized the intruder by the collar. The other dived down the hole, and I heard the sound of rending cloth as Jones clutched at his skirts. The light flashed upon the barrel of a revolver, but Holmes's hunting-crop came down on the man's wrist, and the pistol clinked upon the stone floor.

'It's no use, John Clay,' said Holmes blandly; 'you have no chance at all.'

'So I see,' the other answered with the utmost coolness. 'I fancy that my pal is all right, though I see you have got his coat-tails.'

'There are three men waiting for him at the door,' said Holmes.

'Oh, indeed. You seem to have done the thing very completely. I must compliment you.'

'And I you,' Holmes answered. 'Your red-headed idea was very new and effective.'

'You'll see your pal again presently,' said Jones. 'He's

quicker at climbing down holes than I am. Just hold out while I fix the derbies.'

'I beg that you will not touch me with your filthy hands,' remarked our prisoner, as the handcuffs clattered upon his wrists. 'You may not be aware that I have royal blood in my veins. Have the goodness also when you address me always to say "sir" and "please".'

'All right,' said Jones, with a stare and a snigger. 'Well, would you please, sir, march upstairs, where we can get a cab to carry your highness to the police station.'

'That is better,' said John Clay serenely. He made a sweeping bow to the three of us, and walked quietly off in the custody of the detective.

'Really, Mr Holmes,' said Mr Merryweather, as we followed them from the cellar, 'I do not know how the bank can thank you or repay you. There is no doubt that you have detected and defeated in the most complete manner one of the most determined attempts at bank robbery that have ever come within my experience.'

'I have had one or two little scores of my own to settle with Mr John Clay,' said Holmes. 'I have been at some small expense over this matter, which I shall expect the bank to refund, but beyond that I am amply repaid by having had an experience which is in many ways unique, and by hearing the very remarkable narrative of the Red-Headed League.

*

'You see, Watson,' he explained in the early hours of the morning, as we sat over a glass of whisky-and-soda in Baker Street, 'it was perfectly obvious from the first that the only possible object of this rather fantastic business of the advertisement of the League, and the copying of the *Encyclopedia*, must be to get this not over-bright pawnbroker out of the way for a number of hours every day. It was a curious way of managing it, but really it would be difficult to suggest a better. The method was no doubt suggested to Clay's ingenious mind by the colour of his accomplice's hair. The four pounds a week was a lure which must draw him, and what was it to them, who were playing for thousands? They put in the advertisement; one rogue has the temporary office, the other rogue incites the man to apply for it, and together they manage to secure his absence every morning in the week. From the time that I heard of the assistant having come for half wages, it was obvious to me that he had some strong motive for securing the situation.'

'But how could you guess what the motive was?'

'Had there been women in the house, I should have suspected a mere vulgar intrigue. That, however, was out of the question. The man's business was a small one, and there was nothing in his house which could account for such elaborate preparations and such an expenditure as they were at. It must then be something out of the house. What could it be? I thought of the assistant's fondness for photography, and his trick of vanishing into the cellar. The cellar! There was the end of this tangled clue. Then I made inquiries as to this mysterious assistant, and found that I had to deal with one of the coolest and most daring criminals in London. He was doing something in the cellar – something which took many hours a day for months on end. What could it be, once more? I could think of nothing save that he was running a tunnel to some other building.

'So far I had got when we went to visit the scene of action. I surprised you by beating upon the pavement with my stick. I was ascertaining whether the cellar stretched out in front or behind. It was not in front. Then I rang the bell, and, as I hoped, the assistant answered it. We have had some skirmishes, but we had never set eyes on each other before. I hardly looked at his face. His knees were what I wished to see. You must yourself have remarked how worn, wrinkled and stained they were. They spoke of those hours of burrowing. The only remaining point was what they were burrowing for. I walked round the corner, saw the City and Suburban Bank abutted on our friend's premises, and felt that I had solved my problem. When you drove home after the concert I called upon Scotland Yard, and upon the chairman of the bank directors, with the result that you have seen.'

'And how could you tell that they would make their attempt tonight?' I asked.

'Well, when they closed their League offices that was a sign that they cared no longer about Mr Jabez Wilson's presence; in other words, that they had completed their tunnel. But it was essential that they should use it soon, as it might be discovered, or the bullion might be removed. Saturday would suit them better than any other day, as it would give them two days for their escape. For all these reasons I expected them to come tonight.'

'You reasoned it out beautifully,' I exclaimed in unfeigned admiration. 'It is so long a chain, and yet every link rings true.'

'It saved me from ennui,' he answered, yawning. 'Alas, I already feel it closing in upon me! My life is spent in one long effort to escape from the commonplaces of existence. These little problems help me to do so.'

'And you are a benefactor of the race,' said I.

He shrugged his shoulders. 'Well, perhaps, after all, it is of some little use,' he remarked. '"*L'homme c'est rien – l'oeuvre c'est tout*," as Gustave Flaubert wrote to George Sand.'